NAYTHORN BLACKMANE UNICORN

AND THE

GIFT OF THE WINGED HORSE

Book 3

G. D. Hanson

ISBN 13: 978-1-7340049-6-0
Library of Congress Control Number: 2018904914

This is the third part of the Blackmane Unicorns, a story that takes four other parts to tell.

Briarburr Blackmane and the Unicorn Hold

Naythorn Blackmane Unicorn and His Animal Band

Naythorn Blackmane Unicorn and the Gift of the Winged Horse

Naythorn Blackmane Unicorn and the Seventh Prince

Naythorn Blackmane Unicorn and the Ghost Wolf

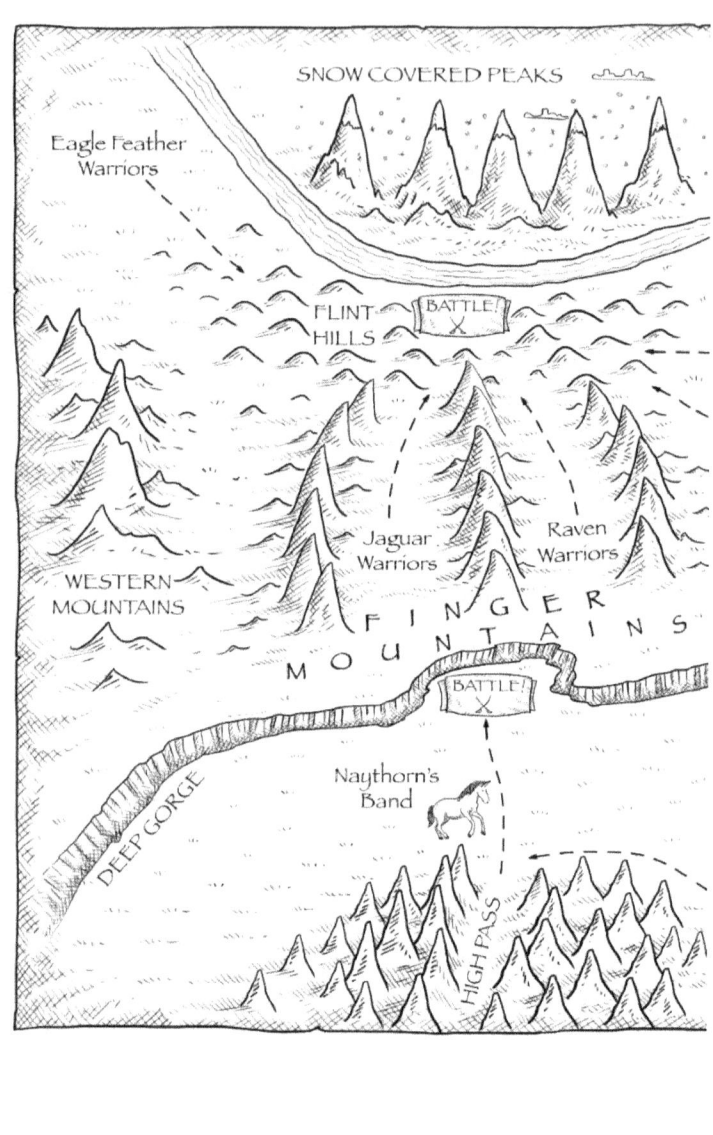

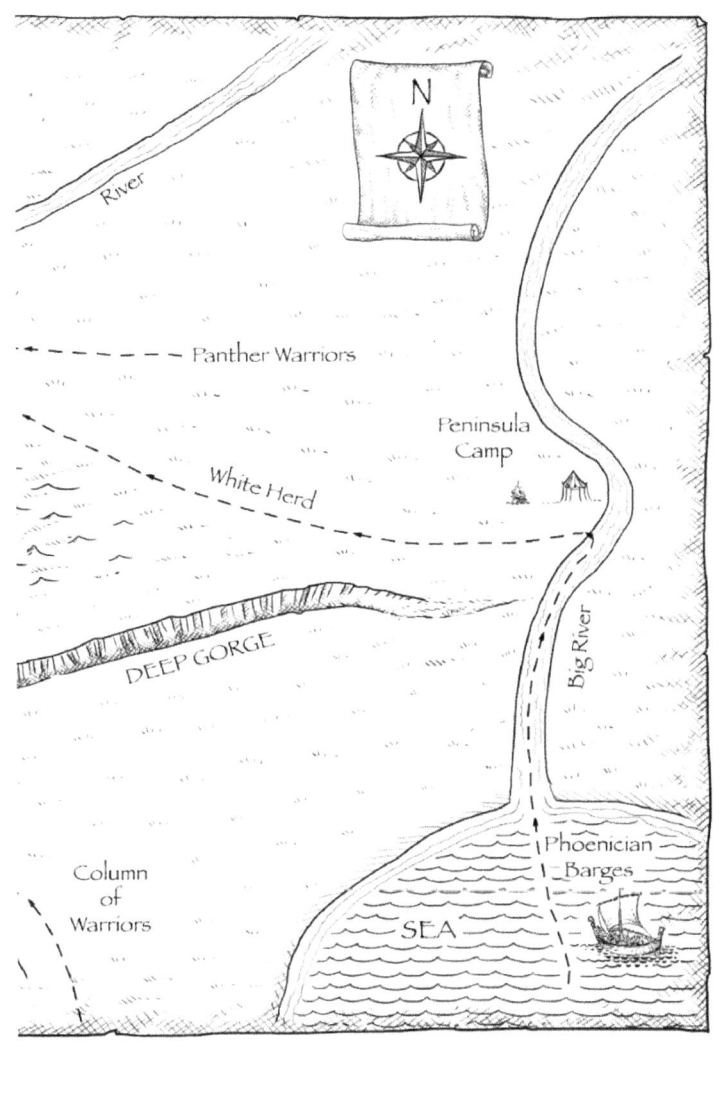

G. D. Hanson

under the shadow of thy wings

Psalms (Authorized KJV)

CHAPTER 1

WEARING BLUE GOLD ARMOR

"Hammerclaw's armor fits this ewe so well, that I have not one blister received. And it is now five days since we left behind the canyon of blue gold. How does his new armor feel on the back of my dear ram?"

"My armor feels to me strange."

"So then, Rambuncture, it needs fixing."

"No, Ewelissas... that is not it. We two mountain sheep have lived a rough and tumble life. While nestled on a bed of sharp stones, just like my ewe, I sleep soundly. My armor does not rub hair off my back. No, the problem is that my armor feels... *too well* on me. It has generous and vigorous qualities that I cannot place or understand."

"So then, I need not worry for my ram. But, since you mentioned it, my blue gold armor also has a commendable quality that is hard for me to identify."

"Would not you agree that our travel begins well, Ewelissas?" neighed the blackmaned unicorn captain joining the walk of the two mountain sheep.

"With no trouble from mean wolves, our travel has indeed started well." Two bovine bulls joined the progress of the mountain sheep and the unicorn.

"Protected by the magic of our new blue gold armor," snorted Taurington, "I say that this cattle would right now welcome combat with the monster wolf

1

Albarochk."

"The well-armored Sir Taurington could now, all by himself, defeat *twenty wolves!*" affirmed Buckmight bison.

Naythorn's band made a time of rest to sprawl bellies about on the ground.

"I might mention, Smithy, that my pessimistic mate Rambuncture finds discomfiture with his armor." At that comment Hammerclaw and Lucars, the two Phoenician blacksmiths, gathered to the sides of the ram and began to inspect his armor.

"I thought I made it clear to you that whenever, or wherever, I stand ready to adjust your armor," said a crestfallen Hammerclaw. "Since the magic blue gold is of such fine quality, the ram's problem has to be entirely due to my workmanship."

"No, Master Hammer, it is not that Ram's armor does not fit him well," clarified Ewelissas. "My mate says the magic of the blue gold armor has... *strangeness* to it."

The eyes of Hammerclaw, Lucars, Naythorn, Taurington, and Buckmight fixated on the male bighorn sheep.

"My mate has placed me in a predicament," baahed Rambuncture lowering his head. "I only told her that there is something about the armor that is for me unfathomable. The magic armor is more true to a dour and pessimistic ram than can be explained."

"I hear what you say, Rambuncture," responded knowingly the bison. "I also feel a veracity to my armor that is beyond my comprehension."

"When Naythorn's magic healed my wounds and

made feathers to grow out of my back, I felt love enter into me," neighed Rayalas shrugging her horse wings. "But the trueness of the blue gold armor fashioned by Master Hammer does indeed feel different than the magic of Naythorn's horn."

"I knew at once that the kindness I felt from the first touch of Naythorn's horn would make our captain to become from me inseparable," mrawed Taurington.

"Hmph! I just realized the difference between the touch of a unicorn horn and the feel of armor forged with blue gold," brayed the bison. "The magic of Naythorn's horn brought the gift of a new and pure kind of love, that as well permitted us to talk to each other. On the other hoof, when on my back rest the sheets of blue gold that I now carry to the Phoenician barges, I see the world more clearly... more exactly as it really is. Since we are told the power and protection of the blue gold is gained only by those who are true of heart, then the blue gold must carry within it a power of... *truth.*"

Rambuncture playfully butted the blacksmith causing him to stumble and topple over. "That for me settles it, Master Hammer! The blue gold armor you fashioned has to me brought an uncomfortable *trueness.* The wearing of your armor makes it strangely difficult for me to exaggerate my pessimistic outlook, tell lies, or even to deceive myself."

"I now understand how it is that my mountain ram has been changed for the better," offered the ewe. "We cannot receive gifts of love and truth, and not know to feel heart-peace. And I can hope that those two wondrous gifts will one day defeat the unrelenting evil carried in the breast of the monster grayback wolf."

"My heart, Ewelissas, hopes for trueness to flourish in our band," neighed Naythorn.

"Baah! But what if when a ram sees them, he does not know to recognize and value true and precious things?"

Proving Worthy

Rousing herself in middle night from a slumber made deep, Ewelissas noticed that her partner had to somewhere disappeared. She found him standing upon a stone outcrop gazing into the night.

"So my ewe looked for a rocky place and there found me."

"Who, more than you, likes bounding about in the rocks? Now tell me what on this night bothers my ram?"

"I thought I heard a wolf to howl somewhere in the distance."

"I heard no wolves. If it was not the cry of wolves, then about something else my ram is troubled."

"You know better than anyone, Ewelissas, that I am always the pessimist. Even protected by my blue gold armor I cannot help but worry that we will one day have to withstand an attack from a thousand wolves and lions." The ram bent his head low and baahed quietly, "I have lived a hardscrabble life. The high places that are safe to me have jagged stones, dangerously deep crevices, and sparse grass that is never enough to fill my stomach. In this hard life, Ewelissas, nothing was ever before given to me."

"Nor was anything before given to me."

"I confess, my dear ewe, that I feel guilty. How can I

accept the immeasurable gift of fine blue gold armor?"

"It was freely given. Perhaps it is harder for you to accept than to give a gift. Dear ram, try to be confident that the journey onward will fill with love and truth, and that those two gifts will serve to keep you and me safe."

"About our safety, I can only hope. The conflict that began with six hateful enemy wolves now grows to become a great army of wolves and lions. Albarochk commands wolves to do terrible things never before seen. How do I know that evil does not multiply faster than love, and that deceit grows not more powerful than the trueness of my blue gold armor?"

"My dear, and always pessimistic ram, consider that you have not yet seen all the magic that is to be authored by the blackmaned unicorn. And if more magic is given to you, and to me, then we must... *prove worthy.*"

CHAPTER 2

BESET BY SHARKS

A new morning found Phoenician barges off the coast of a large island. When Captain Avalcar directed the gaze of his admiral to a rocky outcrop jutting out from the beach, Zoumar detected subtle movement unlike that of water birds. The five vessels had attracted the attention of native spies.

In midafternoon Zoumar and Avalcar sighted one hundred canoes making for land. Double that number hugged the shore at the rear of the fleet. Later in the fading light of dusk the admiral, his captain, and the matriarch Elianor saw at least a thousand armed native men gathered openly on beaches.

"What do you think about so much native movement that we are openly permitted to see?" inquired the admiral of Captain Avalcar and the matriarch.

"The natives act too familiar with us," responded the captain. "They are confident that they can defeat us, or if not defeat us, weaken us gravely in battle so that we are forced to flee from this coast."

"Surely, Admiral, these natives have heard of your extraordinary victory over the death whales and their warrior confederates," added the matriarch. "If so soon after that great victory they show no fear of us, it can be expected that they will attack should we land to replenish supplies of water and food."

"Against the war canoes, Elianor, I will win battles. But as they become too many and we become too few, in the end we will lose the war."

"Yes, Admiral. There are far more of them than there are of us. Sir, since over our heads drape large sails, I think it best that you push out to sea and worry later about water and grass for my unicorns."

"I will take your counsel, Elianor, and conform to a strategy that best suits our purpose. Instead of resupplying our barges we will sail into open seas. Our duty in these waters is not to win wars, but to carry the white herd to its destination."

"Quite right, Admiral. Creation would be deeply wounded if my unicorns were to vanish from the face of the earth."

"My father used two words, that represent a profound quality of humbleness, to describe his closest companions in the army. Avalcar, Elianor, when I reflect upon your constancy on this long voyage his words, *fellow helpers,* come to my mind. You two fulfill my orders better than I myself could execute them." That said, Zoumar turned and climbed onto the rigging to study the position and progress of each vessel in his fleet of five large barges. During the next three days strong winds carried Phoenician barges in a southwesterly direction where no islands were sighted. Sailors and unicorns were put on half rations of water, food, and feed.

"It is not enough that we are become hungry and thirsty," groused Avalcar, "sharks are now found all about us. Has my admiral ever seen so many sharks?"

"There are hundreds of them, and each day their numbers increase."

"There is no reason, Admiral, that so many sharks should choose to accompany our fleet unless their purpose has to do with the unicorns we carry. Unfortunately, because of their fear of sharks our dolphin pilots have abandoned us."

"Drawn to the unicorns, the sharks frighten away the dolphins."

Hoovefort, the young lieutenant of the unicorn guards, and Elianor came to join the admiral and the first officer.

"What, Elianor, is the meaning of so many sharks come to surround this flagship?"

"The sharks push you back, Admiral," answered Hoovefort for the matriarch. "They tell you to turn around your barges and renew sail toward the island that we unicorns wanted to make the new hold of the white herd. I insisted that we not depart from that island paradise upon whose black sand beaches marched unicorns and sailors together in parade formation. Now you see that I was right."

"But Hoovefort, you know that sharks are not to unicorns friendly," responded Elianor. "Because the sharks sense that the unicorns on these barges suffer from lack of grass and water, they hope to soon devour unicorn flesh. Rather than go back, we must sail on."

"Your thinking is dangerously *wrong!*" exclaimed Hoovefort flashing forelegs at the face of Elianor. Blood oozed from a deep cut made to the cheek of the matriarch. "Your advice to the admiral will destroy the white herd!"

"How dare you strike me! I am the matriarch!"

"Bring to me the sage unicorns!"

"It is not for a guard stallion to give orders to the matriarch," insisted Avalcar. "Elianor is the leader of the unicorn herd."

"About that we shall see!" neighed Hoovefort. As sage unicorns gathered the wind died and sails hung limp.

"The sages will now listen to reason!" began Hoovefort. "Found now in a part of the sea where no islands exist, our survival is threatened by thirst and hunger. If we do not return to my black sand island we will suffer a slow and painful death, or find a quick death in the jaws of the sharks that swim everywhere about us. It was Elianor's advice to the admiral that brought us here! Since the decisions of the matriarch can no longer be trusted, it is come time for me to make myself the new leader of the unicorn herd!"

Seeing Elianor slump down her head in despair, Cabalblade charged Hoovefort. The usurper whirled and kicked rear hooves into the side of the captain of the unicorn guards, knocking him back. When Cabalblade tried to again move at Hoovefort he was restrained by the shoulders of young unicorn guard stallions.

"Turn your barges back to my island of black sand!" neighed shrilly Hoovefort to the admiral.

"Hoovefort, that is not possible to happen," neighed calmly the high escort Aneilee. "My horn magic tells me that the blackmane now searches for the unicorn herd, and that he is destined to find us. How can his hooves find to plant themselves on an island in the middle of the sea?"

"Rather than a blackmaned freak, I will have black sand!"

"*Do not,* Hoovefort, throw your life away in a rebellion against our matriarch!" neighed with emotion Aneilee. "That would be a terrible waste of the big and powerful young unicorn stallion that is admired by our entire white herd."

"It is now my turn to lead!" directed the rebel stallion to Admiral Zoumar. "Command your men to row these barges back to the island of black sand! The entire herd of unicorns wants to there establish our new hold."

"You dare not listen to Hoovefort!" exclaimed Belfloralex finding the side of the admiral. "The colossus of the sea, that still has my half horn lodged in her throat, is here with us and wants us to turn in the direction of the fixed star."

Hoovefort stretched his neck to bite the filly's rump. At that the admiral and the first officer jumped with blades drawn to protect Belfloralex.

"She *will* have her say!" exclaimed Zoumar menacing his sword at the rebel guard stallion. "The courage that Belfloralex has many times shown has *earned* her that right."

"You do know, Admiral, that by our half horns the colossus and I are still made intimate to each other? I feel her. My mind hears her thoughts. I tell you that she swims below us and knows that the sharks try to impede your vessels. She will lead us northward."

"Belfloralex cannot know that!" exclaimed Hoovefort shaking vigorously his mane. "The giant squid that twice tried to destroy this barge is our enemy!"

"I have to admit that about the monster, Hoovefort has a point," affirmed the admiral turning to the filly. "How can I trust a sea colossus that nearly destroyed my flagship? That, I *cannot* do."

"You must, admiral," responded the half horned filly, "for if you do not, we will all die of thirst."

"The leviathan only wants to herself eat unicorn flesh!" interjected Hoovefort.

"I will show the stallion that so ardently lusts for power, what knows my heart," responded Belfloralex. The filly twirled herself about once, twice, three times. Then pushed by the gust of wind she had created the filly leaped very high over the heads of unicorns, as well over the rail of the barge, and dove gracefully into the sea. As she northward swam sharks began to circle Belfloralex. Jumping after the filly the island girl Alexzana and the Phoenician lad Marsand swam to protect her. Extracting himself from the center of discordant unicorns, Captain Avalcar splashed next into the water.

"Admiral, you must rescue them or they will be by sharks destroyed!" pleaded Elianor.

"If not by the sharks, then by the sea colossus!" interjected Hoovefort. "I say good riddance to them all!"

"Turn this barge after the half horned filly!" ordered Zoumar. "I hope to once more learn that I can never disregard the counsel of Belfloralex."

The horn of Belfloralex and the swords of Marsand,

Alexzana, and Avalcar thrust at fast swimming sharks circling closer and closer. Sea water colored red with shark blood.

The water about the struggle began to boil. *The colossus was there.* As four great arms and tentacles grabbed the waists of the filly, the girl, the lad, and the captain other monstrous arms fought off relentless sharks.

"Nyeerrreehaha!" Hoovefort's laugh sounded cruel. "I was right! It serves the half horned filly right that the leviathan came after her to wreak its own revenge. Let this be a lesson for the matriarch to never again doubt my leadership!"

"Look!" exclaimed the admiral. "The giant squid swims away! The sharks disappear!"

"The leviathan takes our friends in the direction we want to travel." What the matriarch had neighed was certain. With their heads held above water, the four prisoners of the colossus were being propelled in the direction where each night in the heavens was found the fixed star.

"Row faster!" admonished the admiral. "We cannot fall behind the giant squid that leads us onward toward land!" The heads of unicorns and sailors glanced upward to see the flagship's sails suddenly bat full with south wind.

"Belfloralex not only called the colossus," neighed Elianor triumphantly, "when she twirled herself about her horn made to reawaken the wind!" The flagship barge surged ahead to soon gain the side of the giant squid.

"Tell the sea colossus that where she leads my barge follows!" shouted Zoumar. "Do not you think that it is come time for you to re-board? Oh, and one more thing. Tell her that I can never repay her for the kindness she this day showed to Phoenician barges!"

That evening a gentle and much welcomed rain slaked thirst, and wet unicorn hides and sailor shirts.

"Sir," neighed Elianor to the admiral, "it seems that I am not to die of thirst on this barge that has come to be what you called my... *room of discipline.*" When the admiral did not answer, the matriarch continued, "I never imagined that I would be purposely struck by the hooves of a young unicorn stallion. Even worse, I now know that Hoovefort has much support among the unicorns in the white herd. With him I shall have to watch my step."

"But there is now one new thing in your favor, Dame Matriarch. In that harsh and sometimes frightening place that I refer to as the room of discipline, you have come to know who thwarts you."

"Not even the sage unicorns stepped in to stop the young usurper stallion. I cannot tell you, Admiral, how disappointed I am at their disloyalty. While I clearly have much to learn on my journey of obedience, I today witnessed and comprehended something very important. You, *my fellow helper,* remained loyal to the half horned filly, and to me."

CHAPTER 3

UNICORNS LANDED

The fleet of Phoenician barges, with one notable difference, again sailed through an endless expanse of water. The distinction was that at the end part of a long maritime journey the flagship of Admiral Zoumar was led on by a leviathan.

As had become their custom, when crimson-edged clouds reddened prettily the western sky at eventide, Admiral Zoumar stood with an arm gracing the withers of Elianor.

"Share with me, Dame Matriarch, your thoughts."

"I was just now thinking, Admiral, that had you harkened to the insistence of Hoovefort and turned your barges back toward the island of black sand beaches, all leadership would from me have been taken. For the remainder of my life I would have been bullied by Hoovefort.

"And that made me realize how the blackmaned misfit must have felt as he was every day bullied in Wittanor Hold. Had I known then what I now know, instead of the blackmane I would have scolded Hoovefort. As a colt Hoovefort always seemed to know exactly what to neigh to make himself look good. The smooth-neighing Hoovefort was also admired for being built big with impressively sleek lines. Admiral, I now find myself to be ashamed for not having seen through the falsity of Hoovefort's façade."

"There comes a time," replied Zoumar patting the back of the matriarch, "when every military commander learns that the smoothest and most handsome subordinates prove to be the least trustworthy. Of course there are exceptions to that rule, but in my experience they are disappointingly few. That, Elianor, is one of the reasons I trust my first officer Captain Avalcar. With what I would describe as an honest face, he has no pretenses about his looks or the smoothness of his speech. Avalcar's words are direct. His goal is to serve me and not further his own personal interests. Now, Elianor, I have a question for you. If the blackmane someday reconnects with the unicorn herd, will his desire be to... *serve you?*"

"About that I have not thought, Admiral. Although Naythorn's sire Cabalblade has long been the captain of the unicorn guards, the blackmane never bothered to gain influence from his sire's important position. I think that Naythorn knew only to be his own unicorn."

"I came to tell you that we approach our destined landing," conveyed Aneilee joining the admiral and the matriarch. "I sense that tomorrow we will sight a continent. *Nyerrrhahrrarr!* And just imagine that we are there led by the fearsome colossus of the sea!"

The admiral clapped his hands and smiled big at the two unicorn leaders. "The crimson tone of this sunset tells me that no storm winds are tomorrow in the offing. I cannot imagine to have sailed so far with five hundred nervous and hungry unicorns pacing my decks, while not suffering even one storm gale."

"As we have many times assured the admiral," answered Elianor, "the magic of the white herd can be so great as to even hold sway over the winds."

"Only a short time ago Belfloralex demonstrated that to me, and to my crew."

Aneilee turned to leave. She stopped, looked back at Elianor and Zoumar, and neighed, "If you happened to have just now been talking about the blackmane, I can assure you that he will come to reunite with the unicorn herd. And here is something more. Upon Naythorn refinding the white herd my life, and as well the life of Elianor, will become even more interesting and challenging."

"Hmph! How did she know that we were talking about Naythorn?" inquired the admiral as he watched the high escort step hooves away.

"The magical gift of the high escort... is prescience."

The Waited Coast

Favorable winds carried northward five Phoenician barges to a wide land dissected by a mighty river. Sped on by a determined south wind, the five barges navigated seven days northward the impressive river. Anchors were dropped before a prominent peninsula gracing the sunset side of the wide channel.

Both the unicorn high escort and the matriarch comprehended that this was the place they had long needed to find in order to complete the first part of their journey. However, while the unicorns had crossed the ocean to land on a promontory extending into an immense river, they were not yet grazing peacefully in a safe and secure hold offering protection from all who would mean them harm. Along with the entire white herd, the two leaders had high hopes that the remaining part of their journey in quest for a new hold would be less difficult, and far less dangerous.

The triangular jut of land provided fresh water, plentiful grass, roots, and game for sailors to hunt. Mariners and unicorns ate, rested, and felt thankful for achieving safe harbor at the end of long sea passage. The silence of their landed safe haven, with no tall waves constantly washing, was pleasant to the ears of both horned horses and sailors. Not one native drum, not even a small one, could be heard above or below the camp shared by unicorns and sailors.

With the delivery of the unicorn herd to the new land, half of Zoumar's orders had been fulfilled. The other half of his charge, to secure the blue gold, remained to be accomplished. Zoumar mused about which of his two orders was the more important. At first, he decided his priority was to secure the magic blue gold destined to protect and make strong the Phoenician army. But upon considering more the question, his conscience averred. The admiral admitted to himself that the safety and survival of unicorn flesh and magic had to him become paramount. While he had fulfilled his obligation to the unicorn herd, the admiral did not welcome the thought of departing with the blue gold while the white herd remained unsettled. He wished he could have done more for the matriarch and the high escort.

Zoumar had hoped against hope that along the lower

reaches of the wide river Hammerclaw and Lucars would have been found waiting to greet the arrival of the fleet laden with magic horses. Unfortunately the blacksmith and his apprentice remained to be found, and the sooner found the better.

When he was summoned to Zoumar, Captain Avalcar surmised that he would not long share the rest become so welcomed by sailors.

Search Party and Windage

"I need you, Avalcar, to lead westward a party of men to find the blacksmith I before sent to mine and bring back the blue gold. Since the old unicorn that remained behind in Wittanor Hold knew the location of the blue gold, surely Hammerclaw has by now found and dug the precious ore that we require. Once found, the attraction of the magic blue gold to the white herd can be counted on to lead Hammerclaw here to us."

"I shall, Admiral, do whatever is required to find Hammerclaw and Lucars."

"You are to lead a small squad that is not easily noticed. Select ten men that you trust, whose obedience and loyalty cannot be questioned, and search out the blacksmith and his apprentice. Your scouts will find them burdened heavily by five stone weight of blue gold, traveling slowly eastward. Here on this hill I will await you. Be returned to me in thirty days."

"Aye, Sir, I have my orders."

"One thing more, Captain. You decide if it be wise to take with you a unicorn. If so, it must be a unicorn that is brave, swift, and strong. In that regard, one of the unicorn guard stallions would serve you well."

"Aye, Sir, to speed our return I will choose a unicorn whose back can also help to freight the weight of the magic metal."

Once Avalcar had chosen the sailors he wanted to take with him as scouts, he asked Elianor to preside at a meeting with guard unicorns for the purpose of selecting a volunteer stallion to accompany the search party.

Before any guard unicorn could step forward to volunteer for duty, Belfloralex arrived and created a commotion. Shaking her head up and down with conviction, the filly reared high as she neighed, "I will go with Captain Avalcar and his men!"

"Your broken horn attests to your courage, my filly," responded Elianor, "but you are not full-grown. This mission will confront many dangers; for that a strong guard stallion will best suit the needs of the captain."

"Dame Matriarch, while guard stallions have more strength than me," persevered Belfloralex, "I am faster than any of them. My hooves can outrun and outlast the strength of stallions. Place the fastest stallion at my side, and we will both race to the bank of the river. If I arrive first, will you assent to my traveling with the captain?"

"I have to admit that does sound fair," responded Elianor. "This filly has already proven that she is very brave. Upon proving that she can run faster than a guard stallion she will make herself to be a fitting addition to the scout party."

The matriarch motioned a four-year-old stallion with a lean cut to his flanks to join himself to the side of Belfloralex.

"*Go!*" whinnied Elianor.

With long bounding strides the stallion was off. To everyone's amazement, instead of racing forward Belfloralex flashed hooves while wheeling about in circles. From the spot where Belfloralex was jumping and cutting round, Elianor and Avalcar felt a strong wind to surge. When the filly broke into a run it was as if the wind lifted her body so that her hooves barely nicked the ground. At the three quarter mark of the one league race Belfloralex overtook the fast moving stallion. Next happened something unexpected. Still floating on a carpet of wind, the filly's legs could not fully brake her pace.

As she watched the wind blow the filly outward over the river bank, Elianor held her breath. Fortunately, the diving filly managed to place her head between extended front legs. What happened next was even more amazing. The filly re-broke the surface of the river held in the tentacled grasp of the colossus, who proceeded to carry the filly to the shore.

The filly pulled herself up on the river bank and trotted lightly back to the place where the race had begun. There she was greeted by unicorn stallions with broad smiles and jumping forelegs.

"*Well done* my darling filly!" congratulated the matriarch. "For a second time the wind obeyed you!"

"When I run I talk to the wind, and the wind answers me. My heart beats to the throbbing of the wind against my sides. The only time I feel myself to be as light as a cloud, is when I dance on the wind."

"And what of your friend the colossus of the sea?"

continued Elianor.

"She waited to see how things would here go for me. She told me this was the last time she would be present to pull or push me out of the water. Since I knew she was not so far away... I am so glad that I was able to tell her *goodbye.*"

The broken-horned filly that could harness the wind, and had made a leviathan to change from enemy to friend, was the unicorn selected to accompany Avalcar on his mission.

As Avalcar's platoon commenced westward travel Belfloralex each day scouted forward, to the right, and to the left of the sailors and their officer. Negotiating their way through tall grass and thickets the sailors found bison, antelope, deer, and rabbits to be everywhere. The one thing not usual, not expected, and that did not feel right was to see so many wolves traveling singly, in two's, and in three's as they also trotted westward. The lupines showed little interest in hunting the plentiful game found on their every side. Neither Avalcar nor his men could fathom what possessed wolves to travel so purposefully.

One clear morning the scouts sighted a high and long mountain looming on the northwestern horizon. Each morning after found the mountain made closer to Avalcar's platoon.

CHAPTER 4

THE QUEST OF CABALBLADE

He had many times told himself that Naythorn's rebellious streak was the cause of his difficult relationship with his colt. Still, the captain of the unicorn guards had to admit that upon sighting his offspring in the hold of Wittanor, a black colored mane was the first thing he had always noticed. The adornment of a black mane upon the neck of any unicorn, whether young or old, was simply... *wrong*.

The departure of Belfloralex weighed on the guard captain's mind. She had volunteered to undertake a long and dangerous journey in quest of two men that she had almost certainly never even met. For Cabalblade, her example was troubling. Now with himself, he would be honest.

He began to wonder to what extent the harsh words he had so often neighed to his colt had been motivated by the sight of the unforgivable deformity that colored the topmost part of his colt's neck. Yet the stubborn blackmane was his only offspring, and for appearance's sake it did not look *proper* for the leader of the unicorn guards to have abandoned his own yearling. To make matters worse, it had been gossiped that his careless rejoinder to *go anywhere away*, had led to his colt's disobedience during the white herd's fateful last two days in Wittanor Hold.

Time had begun to drag heavily on his hooves. Cabalblade readily admitted that the long inactivity of unicorns on barges, and then in the peninsular camp set above a great river, had nearly bored him out of his mind.

A long journey into plains and mountains could provide the solution to his two problems. Travel that refound Naythorn would as well mold his body back into the fighting shape that befit a captain of the unicorn guards. His rebellious colt, hopefully grown to become a more serious and mature unicorn stallion, would be safely recommitted to the unity of the white herd. And, the guard captain might even return with scouting intelligence useful to the success of the white herd's future travel.

"I come, Matriarch Elianor, in quest of a favor. Think of it as a return gesture of thanks for the service I have long provided in command of Wittanor's company of guard stallions."

"What is in a matriarch's power shall be done for Cabalblade."

"You know that I lived for my work as captain of the guards. Insisting on perfection from all the stallions I tolerated no tardiness, no sleeping while on duty, and no marching guard in relaxed posture. I no realize that at the same time I performed faultlessly my duty to the white herd, I daily punished Naythorn for his possession of a wrongly colored mane. Now lost to me, I request leave to find and return my colt to the white herd."

"But in your castigation of Naythorn you were not

intentionally mean. You knew that the unfortunate coloration of his mane was not by his choice made."

"It was, Elianor, hard for me to not associate his stubbornness with his untoward black mane."

"Who will replace you as leader of the unicorn guards?"

"My second in command, the ambitious Hoovefort, is zealous in all matters of the unicorn guards."

"I do not like for you to leave us, Cabalblade," answered Elianor with her visage presenting serious. "It would be a terrible loss to unicorn unity should neither you, nor Naythorn, return." That neighed the matriarch tossed her head around.

"Nonetheless, our high escort believes that somehow and in some way beyond her foresight, the blackmane is destined for a great task. He is young, strong, and possesses a heart that relents not. For my part, I saw something else in your colt. Even when I nagged him hard, he was selfless. Although perhaps I gave him cause, he never toward me grew hard of heart. Captain Cabalblade, I also have come to want Naythorn returned to us." The face of the matriarch intimated a small smile on one side of her muzzle as she added, "All right. I am agreed. Go swiftly and do not fail. But if through the course of one moon you do not find your colt, I require that without him you return to me."

"I shall fulfill the duty of a sire to search for his lost colt."

"There is one last thing, Cabalblade. It may well be that Naythorn loves you more than you know... and more than he knows. When two hearts collide, struggle for acceptance and comprehension, and at last learn to cling to one another great love is born. In the quest for your colt, follow first... *your heart.*"

After deftly sparking her horn to that of the guard captain, with solemnity the two unicorn leaders bowed to each other. That accomplished, Cabalblade set his eyes on the place where the sun would that night drop down to slumber.

Cabalblade's Journey

The river Cabalblade had come to, crossed, and then followed westward deepened into a steep gorge. As Cabalblade trotted and galloped on the southern side of the gorge he hoped that along this conveniently placed river Naythorn was traveling toward him. As he traveled more westward the deepening river gorge showed promise of becoming impassable.

"Which side of this river would Naythorn take? If not far ahead of me he travels northward in the direction of the fixed star, by this gorge his way will become blocked. Would not Naythorn then have to remain on this side of the chasm?" He scrambled down to the river's edge and drank deeply. Something about this river troubled him.

"If I gallop on the northern bank of this river gorge, and Naythorn is on this southern side, then the gorge would block me from finding my colt. But on the other hoof, what if Naythorn found his path northward not blocked by the river gorge? My colt may now find himself well north of a river, that if I remain on this side, blocks me. For a long distance ahead this place looks to provide my last chance to cross the chasm." Facing a difficult choice, Cabalblade decided he needed to graze.

"What does my heart tell me?" muttered later the stallion with his belly replenished. "After all, Elianor instructed me to pay it heed. After neighing that, she even sparked my horn as if gifting me magical intuition." Cabalblade shook his head around.

"Here my heart hints to be ill at ease. My thinking wants me to remain on this southern side of this gorge, but my heart does not. I have never once given my heart priority over my head. Still..." The stallion crossed to the north bank of the river.

Once Cabalblade decided to do something, as in this case willing himself to find his wayward colt, his task became his obsession. Day after day the captain of the unicorn guard horses ran, and then ran more. At every high hill he would halt, look forward, look to his right, to his left, and as well gaze back in the direction from which he had come. Then for a second time his head turned so that his eyes penetrated every direction.

At the approach of night Cabalblade would neigh toward every far corner about him. No neigh was ever returned to him, and around him the contours of the land only deepened and heightened. About one thing the stallion was content. During the course of long travel his legs had regained strength, and the lines of his sides and hips had tautened.

After more journey westward the great rolling plain reconfigured itself into high places defined by jaggedness of rock and sheerness of climb. Always on his left, the river gorge came to descend so far downward that the flight of birds vanished into shadowy emptiness.

CHAPTER 5

RAYALAS DISAPPEARED

"After going through so much trouble to find the deposit of magic ore, unite with Naythorn and his band, and forge the blue gold into transportable sheets, I should be terribly disappointed to not *refind our barges.*"

"Never you worry about that, Master Hammer," soothed Lucars. "We have a duck, a goose, and a flying horse that can scout one hundred leagues before us. They cannot *not* find our barges."

"But because we have been too long gone I have uncomfortable dreams, more like nightmares, about our barges departing for Phoenicia before we actually reach them."

"That, Master Hammer, will not happen. Admiral Zoumar would surely be punished if he returned so far across the great sea with his cargo bay empty of blue gold. If we do not find the admiral soon, he will send scouts to find us. Besides, the magic horn of Naythorn will soon come to sense the white herd that is now freighted on our Phoenician barges. You and I need to place our trust in the blackmaned unicorn."

"I am used to relying on myself, but at that, I suppose you are right."

"Hammer, just as I have always trusted your

judgment, you must now trust Naythorn and his winged scouts to bring us to Phoenician barges."

Climb

As Naythorn and his band of animal friends escorted Hammerclaw and Lucars with their priceless forged sheets of magic blue gold, one day blended into another. On this particular day Webstir, Featherspark, and Rayalas from above led the band toward a gap into a high wall of cliffs. The opening soon came to wear the look of a deep and long river valley coursing into the heights of faraway mountains.

Leading the column, the cattle and bison had first rights to grasses best suiting their palates. At times the heads of the mountain sheep became hidden beneath a thick canopy of river bank grass. With the exercise brought by a climb reaching higher and higher, each and every animal person in the band added muscle to limbs.

"Have you noticed, Naythorn, that the legs of this wild boarling now flex strong enough to climb high mountains?"

"Roothyford's muscles have indeed become prominent. I cannot believe how fast you grow."

"Mine and the fast growing legs of Timidthy, Hamilton, and Practicia will carry four wild boarlings all the way to the top of the most far mountains."

"For my part, I think I have stopped growing."

"Naythorn, you *already* are huge enough!"

"In the midst of this beauty, which almost takes my breath away," neighed Rayalas flitting down next to Naythorn and the fast growing Roothyford, "I am thankful to be not pursued by warriors and wolves that wish to do us harm."

"The beauty of nature that here surrounds, refutes the ugliness of hatred," responded Naythorn.

"I will never give up hope for a future home in a pretty and tranquil place," interjected Roothy.

"I want to believe that in a place so beautiful as this, all new life is given the opportunity to flourish," added the filly.

Overhearing the comments, the matron wild boar turned to her girl boarling that always displayed common sense and whispered, "Practicia, have you noticed that Rayalas has added considerable girth to her belly?"

"Much of that new bulge came during the last moon. But, Mama, the filly's growing girth does not stop her from flying gracefully on the air currents that passage this high river valley."

Upon a High Pass

"Do you think that the rush of river water carved out the long valley we just traversed?" inquired the always curious Timidthy looking back at the course of the river.

"Impossible!" responded Hamilton. "For such a thing to happen, would take *forever!*"

"I am most impressed by the view northward," considered Roothyford. "From this high place the vista is breathtaking."

As they studied a panoramic view of a plateau that would take many days of hard travel to cross, the band of animal and human person friends came to stand side by side. Far beyond the wide plateau three immense mountains, set parallel to one another, shrugged northward.

Jumping front paws onto a shoulder of Naythorn, Trackler barked a spontaneous plea from the depths of dog heart, "Can we stay in this grand high place? *Raauuwrruuu!* Can we? Please?" Sheep bleated, bovines mrawed, and pigs squealed agreement to Trackler's petition.

"Captain, I know of no reason why we cannot here tonight bed down," interjected Buckmight.

"You are right bison," answered Naythorn nodding his head up and down in agreement. "We will not find a better place to spend the coming night." The unicorn's long face broke into a smile as he added, "And, having well-earned a rest, we will tomorrow know a complete day of lazing and eating to our heart's content."

Not one discordant sound was brayed, baahed, squeaked, groinked, yipped, neighed, or spoken in objection to the suggestion of a rest midst the beauty of a high place with long views toward both north and south directions. As one day led into another the rich grass, berries, fish, sparkling water, and the cool breeze of the high pass proved difficult to abandon.

On a new morning born brilliant, Rayalas complained to the sow that her belly felt bloated. The porcine matron responded that a walk might do the filly some good. When by mid-sun the winged horse failed to return to camp, Naythorn went to look for her. Not finding the filly, the blackmane wondered if she had flown to the highest place on the cliffs above the pass in order to enjoy a view even more spectacular. If so, that would not be the first time that Rayalas had gone off to explore on her own. He finally concluded that the winged filly was somewhere napping under a copse of thick leaves.

The afternoon slid smoothly into dusk and then the sky entrance of countless sparkling stars. Rayalas had never before not returned to the band by nightfall.

"Do not worry as you bed down, Captain Naythorn," groinked Hamilton loud enough for all to hear. "The worst that could have happened is that the filly went somewhere to sprout a second set of wings."

"No bird has two sets of wings," corrected Practicia. "Perhaps the filly simply wanted to escape the silly commentary and nuisancing of my brother pig."

"My sister can at least give me *some* credit for trying to cheer up our captain."

"I think it would cheer us all to talk about the nice qualities of Rayalas," groinked Roothyford. "You know *not once* has the filly been to me unkind."

"About the kindness of the winged filly, Roothy is right," agreed Hammerclaw. "When I first met her, after she had on a pyramid-crested mountain rescued Lucars from wolves, I was rude to her. But to her credit, to me she was faultless in her courtesy."

"I still cannot believe that when she batted me off the notch landing," continued Hamilton, "and then flew fast downward so that I would land on her back, the filly made me the first pig ever to fly."

"Flying with Rayalas in a V-formation is a lot of fun," hronkked the long necked Featherspark.

"It is more safe to fly with Rayalas than to fly with a

reckless goose!" interjected the duck who could not resist pestering his friend.

After every animal person present had shared sweet remembrances of the winged filly, the descent of invisible stardust made sleep to envelop, with one exception, the band. Beset by worries for the unreturned filly, the blackmaned stallion did not find sleep. What bothered him the most was that he knew that if the filly wanted to not be found, she would not be.

"Webstir, Featherspark, go look again for the filly," neighed irritably Naythorn the next afternoon.

"Be patient, Captain," soothed Mama Pig. "The duck and the goose this morning looked everywhere. Just give her time. She will soon come back to us." Naythorn reluctantly nodded consent to the request of the sow.

Not having to look for Rayalas, Webstir took it upon himself to improve the mood of the unicorn, but not even his fluttering antics could shake off or shake through the unicorn's bad mood. The blackmane finally tired of the silliness displayed by the green-head and ordered Webstir to fly off and scout for movement of wolves. To accommodate more his fractious disposition, the unicorn ordered Featherspark to follow and make sure the duck did not disappear like the winged filly had done.

Meanwhile, Rayalas continued unfound.

Flight

"*Qvaakk!* They followed us into the pass!" reported back the excited Webstir with Featherspark at his side. "The monster wolf is not far behind us!"

"*Hronkk!* The great grayback wolf leads *lots* of... at least one hundred wolves!" interrupted the duck.

Already in a terrible mood, this news made Naythorn's heart to sink, "And now, what of my Rayalas?"

"About the advancing enemy the winged filly is nowhere to be seen," answered Featherspark.

"To where can she have *gone off?* Does she scout somewhere ahead of my band?" Imagining the worst, that the winged horse was never to fly back to him, deep worry sounded in the blackmane's neighs. "It is so unlike the always responsible Rayalas to desert us, and not even neigh why."

Into the other side of the camp the two dogs made a raucus entrance. Blackler, the slightly bigger of the twin dogs, barked, "A yellow wolf, and now that I think about it he looked very familiar, found a way around us and leads many warriors toward the front of the pass where we are to next travel."

"*Yip, yripe...* the yellow wolf intends to close us shut in this place," insisted Trackler.

"But why would warriors follow a yellow wolf?" inquired Mrs. Razorthwacker.

"Mama," groinked Timidthy, "the warriors, or their medicine men, see that the giant wolf and the strangely-colored yellow wolf were by magic touched. Warrior scouts have as well noticed sun rays reflecting the magic of our blue gold armor. Following two wolves that they believe to be sacred, the warriors are drawn to our band with the purpose of stealing our armor."

"*Nyyeehhrrrr!* We will not be here trapped! This tight

pass is not a place to win a battle fought on both our front and rear sides. We move forward, *fast!*"

After stacking the sheets of blue gold on the backs of the two stalwart bovines, Hammerclaw and Lucars formed the rear guard. As Naythorn led downward toward the wide plateau, an immense blue sky spread wide before the band.

"The wings of Rayalas will float down to meet us on the plain below," encouraged Mama Pig.

"And as she glides on currents of wind, she will look very graceful," agreed Roothy.

"Upon seeing the filly to once more glide above the wild boar family, I will again wear a huge smile," brayed the panting Buckmight.

"When I next see the filly to fly, I will wear an even bigger smile than my bovine friend," mrawed the cattle.

As they scrambled down the north side of the pass Lucars admonished an out-of-breath Hammerclaw, "After a nice rest in the high pass, it does not behoove my blacksmith to fall too far behind the two bovines that carry loads meant to have been borne by you and me."

"But while it lasted... the rest was very welcomed."

The Yellow Wolf

Trotting in the lead of a column of warriors Yellowquist suddenly froze; just as quickly his feelings turned to dismay. Spilling onto the plateau that stretched before him flew two waterfowl, a running unicorn, and two fast-moving mountain sheep. They were followed by five wild boars, two dogs, two bovines, and two men. Although at that moment Yellowquist was no more than five hundred wolf paces from his blackmaned nemesis, the forward part of the battalion of warriors that followed behind him was five hundred paces to his rear. To make matters worse for the yellow wolf, his battalion of warriors could not move as fast as Naythorn's platoon.

Benefiting from the cover of rocks and trees in a fight conducted in the tight quarters of the high pass, Yellowquist's battalion would have held advantage. On the other paw, the wolf surmised that the great armored bodies of the bison, bull, and unicorn could do much damage against warriors caught in the open.

Naythorn led into the flat expanse of the welcoming plateau. With his band's escape made good, the unicorn diverted hooves to hail his old adversary.

"*Nyeerrrahah!* Did Yellowquist wake up lazy this morning? You should have had your warrior soldiers move at a double pace so that they could have blocked my escape from the high pass. For taking too much time to reach us and cut us off, your unkind cousin Albarochk will box your ears!" At that comment Naythorn thought, or imagined that he saw a frown set into the face of the diminutive wolf.

Yellowquist knew that what Naythorn had neighed was not wrong. His big grayback cousin would surely pummel him for arriving too late to spring the brilliant trap that he, the diminutive wolf, had designed.

Naythorn shot hooves back to overtake Hammer and Lucars, who both jumped onto the unicorn's back. The near ambush had been a close call, but for now the unicorn's spirit felt only relief at having escaped in the nick of time. For one more day he had kept his platoon of animal persons together. Surely by nightfall Rayalas would be again at his side, or at the latest be returned to him before the birth of the next new sun.

Naythorn gladdened to see the subtle tresses of new daylight feather softly golden. New sun revealed that during the previous night his band's lead over the column of warriors had stretched wide. Upon finding that the faraway middle mountain toward which they traveled, now stood markedly closer, every member of the blackmane's band felt hope to renew.

When Featherspark fluttered down onto the gold weighted back of Taurington, the cattle knew to draw alongside the blackmane, who promptly inquired, "You just left us. What makes the black beak so soon returned?"

"I came back to report that I just saw something," hronkked the goose while saluting with a wing. "Not so distant from the warrior column a dark spot moves toward us. I think that dark spot is *Rayalas.*"

"Go quickly, Goose! We will wait here for you to confirm that it really is her." That neighed, Naythorn and the members of his platoon stared into the distance from where they had come.

"Sir Cattle, might I remove your burden of gold sheets... just in case?" inquired Lucars.

"Right you are. Do it now." From the backs of both bovines were removed the sheets of forged gold.

It was not long before a winded Featherspark dropped down to once more crouch web feet upon the cattle's back. "It is her! It is the filly! And she... she has a foal born with... *little wings!*"

Overwhelmed by a combination of surprise and joy, for a few moments the blackmane could say nothing. After shaking his mane to gather his wits, Naythorn addressed his band.

"With me go Taurington and Buckmight to bring Rayalas and her little one back to us. The remainder of the band is to proceed ahead. Mama pig and the mountain sheep will help Lucars and Hammer to transport the gold sheets. Accompanied by our lost filly... err lost mare... and my newborn foal we will soon catch up with you."

Fleet Warriors

Upon sighting the winged horse and her offspring, Yellowquist immediately knew that Naythorn would return for them. The fact that Naythorn was now galloping back toward the yellow wolf was a lucky break from which advantage must be taken.

With a jerk of his head and paws the yellow wolf motioned the warriors trailing closest to follow after him. Accompanied by a fleet detachment of young warriors, the yellow wolf sped off to diagonally interpose himself between the filly with her foal, and Naythorn.

"He can try," muttered Yellowquist, "but the blackmane will not quickly penetrate through thirty brave warriors." A new thought brought hope, "What does the blackmane know about fighting warriors? Nothing!"

The fast galloping Naythorn, Buckmight, and Taurington soon glimpsed two moving forms, one large and colored brown, and one small and colored a lighter shade. When Naythorn and the bovines noticed the company of warriors closing to interdict the forward passage of Rayalas, they knew what must be done. The unicorn and bovines would crash horns into warriors armed with spears and swords.

Buckmight and Taurington thought on the armor that Hammerclaw had fitted to them. Spear points might dent the inter-set disks of blue gold, but could not penetrate through their armor to draw blood. Angling their progress for convergence, the warriors placed themselves in a V-wedge formation aimed at the fast moving unicorn and bovines.

Dodged expertly, the first thrown spears thudded harmlessly into dirt. Other hurled spears banged against blue gold armor. The spear that glanced against the hard skull of Taurington, bounced off. Conditioned by long established practice, the cattle shook off the searing jolt of pain that penetrated deep into his cranium.

At the last moment before confronting at close hand the three great hurling beasts, panic birthed in the hearts of the forward warriors at the point of the V. The decisions made by some of the fleet warriors to break formation and scatter right and left, saved them from bodily hurt and pain. Those remaining warriors that held firmly to their positions were by horns thrown aside, or by pounding hooves knocked down. Watching the fray unfold, Yellowquist could do little to change the fate of his contingent of fleet warriors found to be not as brave of heart as the wolf had hoped them to be.

After scattering the thirty warriors, Naythorn, Buckmight, and Taurington did not chase down their adversaries, but instead dashed on to meet up with Rayalas.

After muzzling a brief greeting to each other, the bovines, Naythorn, and Rayalas quickly began to circle around the oncoming main force of pursuing warriors. Clinging to her mare, the little foal trotted sprightly; her spindly legs were remarkably springy. The little procession paused only long enough for the foal to drink her mother's milk. Before the onset of darkness the winged horse, the bovines, and Naythorn came to reunite with the band.

Starting with Mrs. Pig, every animal person in Naythorn's platoon had to several times sniff and touch the new foal.

"This pretty foal is more than a little horse with wings," observed Ewelissas to her mate. "In exactly the right place she has a bump that will grow into a unicorn horn."

Rubbing his nose over the foal's forehead, Rambuncture felt the bump. For one of the few times in his life the lips of the dour ram split into a very wide smile as he baahed, "A foal born with wings and a horn... now that is a *real* miracle."

"Hmph! More than once my ram told me he did not have any time for little scampering hooves."

"To be sure, I did say that. But even this ram can see that with hints of black in her mane and tail, a tan coat, and black markings on her forelegs this foal is irresistible."

"Ram, that coloring identifies the foal as a bay," informed Lucars.

For having sired a most magical and beautiful foal, Naythorn felt himself become more proud and fulfilled than he had ever imagined he could be. When he thought about the little bay foal's small wings and the bump growing on her forehead, the stallion's horn tinged blue. However, it was not long before the blackmane felt something begin to weigh on his shoulders. It sank in that he was acutely responsible for the safety of the foal. What was needed to restore the strength of Rayalas, who appeared to be totally exhausted after her long run, was to find a secure place with good tasting grass.

Stepping onto a high knoll the blackmaned captain confirmed that the warriors led by Yellowquist were nowhere to be seen.

"The yellow wolf waits for reinforcements," observed the bison. "Once Albarochk and his column traverse the length of the pass, the two enemy columns will join together and as one army pursue us."

"You are surely right," neighed Naythorn nodding his head. "We *will* have to battle them again. But we must fight them in the place we want and at the time we choose. I do wish that in the fight to come we were greater in number, for they will be many more than us."

"*Mmrrraaaoo!*" snorted confidently Taurington. "Our band has the best commander. We put our trust in his great unicorn magic... and in our blue gold armor."

"I cannot *bear* the thought that we do not triumph over evil," responded Naythorn.

"Our captain used to smile with confidence. I wonder if the new sire is beginning to smile only on the inside," muttered Buckmight to Taurington.

"He of course has become very serious about the safety of his mare and foal," responded the cattle.

As the band traveled northward they glimpsed that the long mountain shouldering high up before them was sided in big ravines.

"*Groinkk!* That big mountain will surely provide us protection!" exclaimed Timidthy turning to his mama pig.

"My boarling is correct. In those ravines our band will take advantage."

"Mama," groinked Roothyford, "just as we before saw from the high pass, far to the right stands completely separate another mountain that also stretches northward, and far to the west of us looms the outline of a third unconnected mountain. In my imagination this plateau is the palm, and the three Sister Mountains are rock fingers on the hand of an enormous giant that protrudes from an arm buried deep in the earth."

"I would never have thought mountains could be like fingers," answered Mrs. Razorthwacker.

"My mama sow must nurture her imagination!"

"*Qvvaakk! Qrreekk!*"

"*Hrroonnkk! Hrraannkk!*"

The whimsy of Roothyford was interrupted by the return of Webstir and Featherspark.

"Captain, you cannot imagine what lies ahead of us, exactly against the towering..."

"Mountain!" interrupted a duck unable to remain silent. "The ground there falls incredibly deep! Because it was so far down my eyes could barely see..."

"See the river at the bottom of the..." interrupted the goose.

"The gorge," cut in Webster, "is too deep to climb down and too wide to jump..."

"Jump over!" hronkked Featherspark chugging with a wing his smaller duck friend. "The gorge presents no problem for me, the green head, and Rayalas but how do animals without wings get across a big place that goes straight down?"

Without neighing answer Naythorn raced ahead of the band to inspect for himself the newly identified barrier to the band's northward progress. At the edge of the abyss that plummeted straight down the blackmane prostrated his body, cradled his head on front legs, and crawled forward. The unicorn saw that for once Webstir and Featherspark had not even by one feather exaggerated. The unicorn was looking at a problem for which no solution presented.

Naythorn had been confident that once they were climbing skyward into the forward mountain his platoon's defensive position would become strong. Their present position had instead become precarious. If the wolf-led warriors closed on his band, retreat would be by the deep gorge blocked. The place where now rested his belly would become a trap.

With legs made tired by the rush to the gorge, the band gathered around its leader.

"In order to resume northward journey," neighed the blackmane, "I need to know where is found the closest place to ford this challenging river chasm... and I do not want to decide wrongly whether to head east or west.

But that will have to wait until the new sun again finds us. Flying through the darkness our winged scouts can miss a subtle path, like that on which the mountain sheep not long ago led us, that zig-zags downward. For now the reunited army of Albarochk and the yellow wolf remains distant. During this night we camp in safety and receive the benefit of deep sleep. And a good night's rest will replenish the strength of my dear Rayalas... who looks to be very tired."

As the unicorn watched the nervous sleep of Rayalas and the quiet sleep of her foal, in spite of the uncertainty of what would come next, he could not help but to feel hopeful.

Lament

Led by the giant wolf, the now united brigade of warriors and wolves traveled into the night. At the rear of Albarochk's army Yellowquist hobbled painfully. When the monster grayback learned that within sight of his subordinate the blackmane had escaped onto the plateau, the corporal punishment meted to the yellow wolf had been brutal. Despite his bodily hurt, the mind of the yellow wolf would not stop churning.

"I can barely open one eye only," yipped Yellowquist midst his groans. "This is my worst beating ever at the great paws of my cousin. It is a miracle that my giant cousin's dreadful blows did not make an *end of me.* Of course, my cousin has many times sworn that he would one day break my neck, or my back, or my head... or all of them at once.

"But at that I once more managed to survive, if barely, the wrath of my cousin. Perhaps the magic unicorn blood I swallowed in the fight at the secret pavilion permits my body to take such a terrible beating without my breath expiring. If that is so, it is at least something gained from the despicable Blackmane." The body of the yellow wolf collapsed down.

"Here I am looking and sounding like the most abject dog," whimpered the yellow wolf. "But... I *did* my best. It is not right to be beaten to a pulp for trying so hard. *Yripe...* the next beating will bring the end of me, forever and ever after. Not even the healing magic of Naythorn can save me from the future cuts of Albarochk's savagely sharp claws.

"But... I lived up to my part of the bargain. My plan to create a vice, a pincer movement to trap the blackmane in the high pass, was smart. Albarochk is the one that delayed an extra day before he swallowed his pride, agreed to what I had proposed, and put me in the lead of the battalion of warriors. *Yipe, yripe,* the arrogant grayback thinks that only he can lead warriors into battle..."

Raising front paws to sit upward, the wolf whimpered, "I could not be more badly... mistreated. Even if I switched sides and joined to the band of the unicorn, I would be no worse off. My mad cousin is two times a great burden. His change to pure evil betrays our shared bloodline. Twice over because he grows insanely jealous of my superior power to see things clearly, and to plan accordingly."

As his place behind his great cousin's brigade became more distant and solitary, the whimpering became tears. The deeply bruised yellow wolf was unashamedly crying.

No Way Found

The morning dawned gray and wet. With eyes that wore a notably dull sheen, Rayalas would look at no one except her little foal, who for the first time in her young life delighted in being naughty. The foal raced around her mother kicking up her heels, butting Rayalas with her delicately shaped head, and nipping at her mare's hide.

Both the green-head duck and the black-neck goose wanted to survey the flow of the river to the east. When neither would oblige to scout the course of the river to the west, Mama Pig weighed in with the threat of her considerable heft.

"If the duck does not right now stop fussing and fly west, I will thwack him. The goose goes east. And that is *that!*" Two water birds obediently flew off, one east and one west.

The master blacksmith and Lucars stood staring speechless at the profound depth of the chasm impeding their onward progress. Moving to stand next to the two Phoenicians, Taurington made what he thought to be a humorous comment, to the effect that he could jump into the chasm and count to one hundred before splashing into the river that meandered through the far off bottom. When neither man laughed, Taurington turned to better examine for himself the place where he was found. Soon the cattle also wore a frown.

Early in the afternoon the two waterfowl timed so perfectly their return from contrary directions that they both fluttered down at once. An ill-humored

Hammerclaw scolded them saying he could have made an entire gold shield in the time it took the two fowl to scout the high and low of the river course and return to the camp.

"Sir, what you say is not true," corrected Lucars with a face that faked seriousness. "Since the time Webstir and Featherspark flew off this morning you could have forged *two* blue gold shields."

Everyone had the full expectation that at least one of the bird reports would contain hopeful information, something clearly positive. But that thinking proved wrong. The duck and goose had each flown a distance of three days ground travel along the course of the river, looked everywhere, and found no place to ford the deep chasm. At their report Naythorn frowned not just with his face, but it also seemed that his entire horse body wilted.

"*This*... is terrible news," neighed the unicorn. "Even as we speak wolves and warriors are closing on us. Fly both of you together and find the location of Albarochk and his warriors... and please bring back some good news that will enlighten our next decision. Once we are certain of what to do, we will be forced to move fast."

CHAPTER 6

NAYTHORN"S BAND CORNERED

Upon their return to Naythorn's camp Webstir and Featherspark batted wings noisily. Everyone quickly gathered, this time prepared to hear the welcome news that the way was clear. Unfortunately, the intelligence brought by the waterfowl was grim. Formed in a wide front, a large army of wolves and warriors was advancing toward the band's position against the curve of the deep gorge. At the side of the wolf general walked the formidable lion captain, Lianvil.

"How bad, Captain, is this news?" brayed Buckmight.

Not answering the bison, Naythorn instead asked the duck and goose how much distance separated his band from Albarochk, and how far need they travel to escape the curve of the gorge where they were now found? On both counts the answers were exactly, *awful.* Whether along the river chasm the band was to flee either to the east or to the west, the elongated flanks of the warrior line would intercept and obstruct.

"Because the wolf general brings with him a very numerous army, and of course has good intelligence about the lay of the land, we are here stranded," neighed the blackmane with an air of resignation. "But not for one breath will we entertain the idea of surrender. One piece of good news is that the enemy numbers include only *one* lion, although at that he is particularly fearsome.

"Because our new armor will withstand the points of many arrows and spears, we can now better defend ourselves. I am also confident that from a kind hand of heaven some helpful advantage will come to us. Perhaps a torrent of rain will blind the eyes of our enemies, and so permit us to fight our way out. Looking to each other for strength, at some opportune moment we will come to find a way to advance through warrior lines. We have come too far to lose now this war." After vigorously shaking his mane Naythorn reared high to paw at the still unseen enemy. Paws set back to ground, the unicorn turned away to be alone with his thoughts.

"Some movement will be good for my limbs," observed Hammerclaw to Lucars. Off exploring, the two men soon came upon a wide stone ledge that raised above and before a brook.

"Maybe this place is not truly hopeless," offered Lucars. "If we move to position our band behind this ledge, warriors would be required to take a big step up to attack us. We need picks and shovels to here make higher a defensive wall to stand against a horde of warriors and wolves."

"*Inspiration and Man,*" answered Hammerclaw clapping together his hands. The blacksmith picked up a fallen tree trunk that was not big in diameter. "Grab with me this pole, Lucars, and help me to move boulders where we might." It was hard work, but together Hammer and Lucars levered a large boulder to the outer lip of the ledge.

Noting the activity, Buckmight and Taurington joined to the labor of the smithy and his apprentice, and with their horns began to shove rocks. When all together the two men and two bovines levered and pushed a big boulder, it was required to move. To limit the entrance of warriors into the defensive half circle, a line of large boulders was placed on the part of the ledge closest to the approaching enemy. Movement by those fighting behind the line of big rocks remained unimpeded. Stepping stones were shoved and placed so that when and where required, band members could quickly gain the height of the raised ledge and its protective boulders.

Wolves and warriors would have to jump high to surmount the boulders. So leaping, they would expose their bodies to the slashing swords of the two Phoenicians, or to the horns, sharp teeth, sharp claws, or smashing hooves of the other band members. Shielded by the boulders, the members of Naythorn's platoon were for the most part protected from the flight of spears and arrows.

"Tell me, Master Hammer, where did you before hear those words *Inspiration and Man,* for they seem to have worked. When it looked impossible, inspired hands and horns quickly accomplished a task large and improbable."

"More than once, Lucars, my father spoke those three words to me," replied the smithy sitting himself down on a just-moved boulder. "I remember a time when having stretched necks to gain grass found on the other side of a wooden fence, our cows toppled and trampled down a corral. Nightfall was upon us. We had no tools to chop down trees to make new fence rails or poles, or to dig holes for the placement of new fence posts. And it would have done no good to round up the cattle and try to secure them behind a fence that was unrepaired, and could not hold them.

"I told my sire that I was tired, thirsty, and hungry, and that the cows could on the morrow be re-found. Father asked me how many of the cows we would that night lose to thieves or predators... and about that Lucars, he was right. Come morning, more than one cow would have turned up missing.

"Somehow we found the needed wood and dug the needed post-holes to mend the fence. By the time the night had grown pitch black, the cows were again resting safe and sound inside the repaired corral." The smithy smiled as he added, "You know, Lucars, I will never forget that saying of my departed sire."

"But exactly what kind of inspiration does the saying call forth?"

"My father asked for inspiration to come down from above, from the heavens."

"I, myself, do not have much confidence in a benign heaven."

"Believe me a time shall arrive, it might be before tomorrow's fight has ended, when Lucars and I will both pray to the heavens for rescue. In spite of our protective work with these boulders, our band finds itself in a very precarious position. With our backs hard against this deep river gorge, there is no recourse for retreat. Warriors and wolves outnumber our band by perhaps twenty to one. Many arrows, spears, teeth, and claws will come to be set against and upon us.

"In battle I have never much worried about being the target of an arrow point. If a sharp point tore into my flesh... that was just how it was to be. But, Lucars, the struggle before us matters much to a mother mare. Because of the new foal this fight requires all that I can give, and all that you can give. Young man, I will not let down. I will not disappoint the fast friendships we have made with Rayalas, our captain, and the rest of his company."

"The winged horse does not eat," observed Lucars.

"Enmeshed in a place of soon battle, she is worried sick for the safety of her newborn foal."

"For her, Hammer, the little one has changed everything. Found in this dangerous place, the love of Rayalas for her foal now brings torment to the mare."

"Yes, you are right about that." The big, strapping blacksmith touched gently the shoulder of his apprentice and added, "Now, since nothing more can this day be accomplished, it is best that you and I do not pass a worrisome and fitful night."

"Having been inspired by the heavens, and my master blacksmith to do all that we could, tomorrow will take care of itself."

A Day of Battle

Wolves and warriors formed in ranks before the platoon of Naythorn. When before midday began the attack, the defense of the bouldered-ledge met with initial success.

Flanking Naythorn on each side, Buckmight and Taurington charged upward upon the rock steps, thrashed their great horns back-and-forth, and did mortal damage to succeeding waves of intrepid warriors and wolves.

Split apart, the two Phoenicians anchored both ends of the defensive line. The wild boars, mountain sheep, waterfowl, and dogs moved about fighting as if each one had twice the body heft he or she truly possessed. Armored in blue gold, band members big and small made their presence to be ruinously felt on the flesh of warriors and wolves.

Protecting her foal, Rayalas absented from the fray her accustomed winged devastation. The birth of the little filly, the flight across the plateau, and the anguish of new battle had come to deprive the winged horse of her accustomed limitless energy. With her wings protectively shrouding her foal, Rayalas seldom found occasion to look toward Naythorn. With stolen glances the blackmane glimpsed the eyes of the mare flushed red with worry. Noticing that the spirit of Rayalas had shifted inward, Blackmane wondered if the love of his heart had become terribly ill.

When about to be pushed off the defensive boulders, band members reached deep inside themselves and found some way to recover and surge back. Warriors and wolves that broke through the line were dispatched in a tumble of wild boars, dogs, and mountain sheep. The newly-forged armor served well the use that Hammer had intended. So protected, the band's defensive line somehow managed to hold.

As the western sky came to be woven into a tapestry of golden sun rays that knit into lines of gray and purple clouds, a breathless cattle bull bellowed to Naythorn, "Although this work does not stop, my bones need to rest!"

"You cannot yet rest!" neighed the blackmane. "I cannot spare you. I have no one else to bear the burden that you carry in this fight."

"How can they keep coming at us?" continued Taurington. "Just to reach us they must climb over piles of wolf and warrior bodies. How can they not pause their attack?"

As it so happened, just then the wish of Taurington came to be fulfilled. The air emptied of flying arrows and thrown spears, and the stones and boulders placed by Hammer, Lucars, and the bovines became uncrowded of violent adversaries. The warrior front parted into two halves. Through an opening corridor a huge monster wolf walked slowly toward the ledge held by the blackmane's platoon. Behind the grayback followed a small yellow wolf and a heavily muscled lion.

"We know you, Albarochk," neighed Naythorn without hesitation. "We know, as well, your clever cousin Yellowquist and the lion captain that come behind you. Let me guess what you want. As a respite from your hard work in battle there is no better reason for pause then to watch this evening a beautiful set of the sun. While you interrupt combat to admire a crimson sunset, you will as well engage us in argument with words instead of spears, arrows, teeth, and claws."

Keeping his great front limbs extended upright, the

giant wolf sat his rump down, and answered nothing. However, the diminutive yellow wolf continued to walk forward until he had mounted the ledge of rocks. Taking his time to study the members of Naythorn's company the lieutenant wolf paced, or rather hopped back-and-forth upon the large boulders. Yellowquist finally selected the highest of the boulders to seat himself. There positioned, the head of the yellow wolf raised higher than everyone present, including the giant wolf general.

"Until the red sun falls below the edge of the earth," barked Yellowquist with a voice made surprisingly pleasant to listen to, "we afford you opportunity to consider your helpless situation. Like a herd of confused deer, Captain Naythorn and his band are here penned against an abyss that falls deep behind them. Our price for this intermission from battle is your assent that we remove, with the only motive being our kindness, our valiant dead and wounded that here lie in great heaps."

"I allow for you to do that," replied Naythorn stretching high his head to the level of the small wolf.

Yellowquist turned and nodded his head toward his great-bodied cousin, whereupon Albarochk howled an order. From out of the lines of the monster wolf, warriors and wolves emerged and began to pull and drag bodies away from what had become their ledge of loss. Welcoming this break from tumultuous and seemingly unending fighting, band members relaxed and took turns drinking deeply from the little brook.

Yellowquist settled himself down onto his belly. Sensing that the wolf had something important to communicate, Mama Pig nudged Blackmane's shoulder. When Mrs. Razorthwacker rolled her squinty eyes in the direction of the yellow wolf, Naythorn caught the hint.

"It is hard for me to believe the words I am about to say to my inveterate enemy," muttered quietly Yellowquist without moving his head. "I inform you, Naythorn, that more wolves and warriors than we have this day lost, come this night to enlist to the cause of the monster wolf. Albarochk has you right where he wants you. He thinks your position entitles no escape. He is prepared for you to attempt, as you did before, to charge through his center. This time he will not be too astonished to thwart that flight." The yellow wolf jerked slightly his head as he continued, "Notice where Albarochk sits. He has told his legion that in that very spot he will devour your flesh, and become *all powerful.*"

Relaxing tensed muscles in his chest and legs, Naythorn answered nothing.

"Do you want to know why I tell the blackmane this?" continued Yellowquist. "It is because Albarochk also has me where he wants. I am helpless to prevent my enormous cousin, after he drinks all the magic flowing in your veins, from ending my paltry existence.

"I cannot fight my monster cousin. I as well cannot flee from him. Albarochk knows that I share your magic, not in my puny wolf body, but rather in my mind. You were not wrong when you once told me that Albarochk cannot trust me. The monster wolf despises me because I can think clearly, and because I am remindful of his unmagical past."

"What else say you?"

"I have a plan," answered Yellowquist. "It is the only one I can think of to save both your hide... and mine. With the help of Lianvil, I will very soon create a diversion. When I do that, with all swiftness your band must break out in two directions, both to your right and left. That will confuse Albarochk. As all the fight has been against your front, our flanking positions are poorly reinforced. The darkness can hide which of you move one way, and which of you move the other.

"In the days ahead find a place to cross over the river and somehow, somewhere, reunite with the other half of your band. As for me, I will do my utmost to follow there and find you. Naythorn, with my words and movement I am about to sow much confusion. Did you know that I can leap higher and twirl faster than any other wolf? Can you believe *that* of scrawny little me?"

"Yes, I can."

"Blackmane, you have not much time. Our dead and wounded will be soon enough cleared away permitting warriors and wolves to rush with even more strength upon your center." Yellowquist rose to leave. "One last thing... thank you for heeding my words." Before the wolf could move away from the boulder he was perched upon, he was delayed by Mama Pig who had stolen in on the conversation.

"No longer an enemy, but become a new friend of our band you must have a brand new name. Yellow hided wolf, from this ledge forward you shall be called Danseyelono, the dancing yellow wolf who is now made to be alone."

"The new name suits me. For that I thank you Mrs.

Pig."

The renaming done, Naythorn left off to conspire with his band. A strategy had formed in Naythorn's mind. When the tactics were understood and agreed to by Rayalas, a bison, a cattle, two blacksmiths, the pig family, sheep, waterfowl, and dogs the band members readied for a breakout.

It did not take long to happen. True to his word, Danseyelono began to jump about on the rocks. As he did so he barked words that astonished his enormous cousin.

"*Arrarrarrruuu!* Great Wolf General! Your monstrous body has more strength than anyone, but your dull mind is not prepared for something you have never before seen nor imagined. Flee from the grave danger of which you are unaware." Upon hearing the provocation of Danseyelono both warriors and wide-eyed wolves immediately understood that the puny yellow wolf was howling insults at the ferocious gray-backed monster.

Enraged, the wolf general howled and sprang forward. More than one young wolf private trembled in fear for what Albarochk would now do to punish the insolence of his half sized cousin. While battle against the slashing horns of Buckmight and Taurington was difficult, it was trebly worse to face the wrath of Albarochk. With muscles flexing audacious power, Albarochk began to chase after the yellow wolf.

The same as opposing wolves and warriors, Naythorn and his band stood aside while from one boulder to another Danseyelono jumped, whirled, and tumbled. It infuriated the wolf general that his small cousin could dodge faster than monstrous paws could pursue. Albarochk knew full well that it would be deeply embarrassing for wolf soldiers to observe that for all his size and strength, his jaws snapped too slow to grab hold of his insolent cousin. But, although they were sharp as knives, Albarochk's teeth failed to clamp onto a yellow dancing shadow.

"*Arrouu... grarr... graaarrkk!* Stand still you cowardly mongrel cur! I am your master!"

"You big oaf!" provoked more Danseyelono. "You are not half as smart as you think you are. Why this blackmaned unicorn has beaten you... how many times now? He first took easy bear and pig kills from you. In the pavilion palace, from out of your teeth Naythorn rescued the filly that has now grown wings. At the *Battle of Tall Trees*, when you were too slow to comprehend a tactic as old as the hills, Blackmane ran right through you.

"I gave my ferocious monster cousin a clever plan to corner Naythorn in the high mountain pass. But instead of acting fast, you wasted two days before agreeing to my brilliant strategy. The result of your delay was that the blackmane once again escaped before your advance battalion of warriors could pen him in the pass. I now inform my dull cousin that Naythorn has once again prepared a plan of escape, and you still have no idea what it is. *Arrrouhehehh!*" That barked Danseyelono tumbled about shaking his head in unbridled laughter.

While proceeded the drama authored by Danseyelono, unlike the confusion besetting the mind of his giant wolf adversary, Naythorn's thinking was calm and clear.

"We must quickly finish the plan that Danseyelono devised," instructed Naythorn his platoon. "With her foal clung to her back, Rayalas will fly across the gorge. Having before carried a man so big as Hammer, for our winged mare the weight of the foal will not prove burdensome. The rest of us will divide into two squads, one to travel upriver and the other downriver. Hammerclaw and Lucars, load quickly the blue gold sheets onto the backs of the bovines. The four of you are to run fast toward the morning sun and the waiting Phoenician barges. The rest of us will break the other way. Absent the blacksmiths that return to their homeland, somewhere on the other side of this river gorge we will all meet up again. While Hammer began to secure the forged sheets of blue gold to the armor of the bovines, Lucars set the foal on her mare's back and tied her front legs to her mare's armor.

Naythorn drew close to his mate and neighed, "Dear Rayalas, carry our precious foal quickly across the chasm, and so be delivered from danger. Have our little one to hold tight with legs pressed to your side and teeth clamped onto your mane."

Of insult Albarochk had borne enough. The grayback wolf paused his big frame at the edge of the ledge where in his rage he would crush his runt cousin. The great wolf crouched ready to spread wide his limbs so that he would surely pounce on one part or another of his yellow cousin's puny body. Unfortunately for Albarochk, that intention went unfulfilled... an insolent roaring lion sprang to land between the yellow wolf and the monster grayback. It took long moments for Albarochk to digest the treason of his own lion commander.

"Who does Lianvil think he is to threaten the great general of all wolves and lions? Have you taken leave of your senses?"

"Albarochk!" yipped Danseyelono as he shifted to lean front paws against the lion's back. "Did you not stop to ask yourself why *only one* lion is this day here with your army? Did your thick head not grasp that the lions are tired of your arrogance? The lion captain joined himself to this expedition to protect me, and mark my words, if provoked this relentless lion can and will do you great harm. Remember, Cousin, that this lion moves faster than you do. Before you can stop this powerful feline, he will slash open your belly!"

"*Rrroouuwwwuuu!* How could my runt wolf cousin turn against me?"

"That is not so difficult to understand. How can I, or the lion captain place our lives in the paws of a monster wolf that has become pure evil, and knows no loyalty except to himself?"

"I will destroy *both* my runt cousin and the arrogant lion! When you are gone no one will remember your names! But the name Albarochk will never die!"

"But today the name Danseylono will not by you be forgot!"

CHAPTER 7

A MARE'S LOVE UNREBUKABLE

"To me... you have... meant everything," neighed the winged mare looking deeply into Naythorn's eyes. With his neck Naythorn caressed Rayalas.

"Hold tight to your mare, little one," groinked Mama Pig placing front legs to the shoulder of Rayalas. "Do not forget us bovines, sheep, dogs, pigs, and water birds. Your sire, our captain, will soon find and protect you and your mare." After nodding her head the foal reached teeth to nip the serious look worn on the face of Mama Pig.

"Dear Rayalas, the wings of your *unrebukeable* love carried a blackmaned stallion to glimpse the beauty of the stars. Now be off, my darling. On your wings also flies my heart!"

With her foal clinging tightly she sprang forward, spread wide her wings, and flew upward. At her sides went the green-head duck and the white-cheek goose.

"She just... has... to make it!" exclaimed Roothyford, the most emotional member of the band.

In the light of a rising moon Naythorn, Mama Pig, Hammerclaw, and Lucars held their breaths.

"Do her wings... falter?" inquired incredulously the bison as he watched the wings of Rayalas float down beneath the rim of the gorge. The winged horse disappeared from view.

"If she does not make it to the other side, she will come to land at the bottom of the gorge," grunted Mama Pig. "But that is terribly far down."

"Her wings *will* climb back toward the other rim!" exclaimed Lucars.

"Rayalas *cannot* fail to gain the other side of the gorge," insisted Taurington.

"She... will... *make it!*" yelled Hammerclaw his voice commanding hope.

"She disappears. Her body will... crash!" baahed the ram.

Having raced to the very edge of the gorge, the dogs saw the body of the winged mare strike the rock wall twenty horse lengths below its rim. At that Trackler and Blackler howled dog lamentation.

An enormous blue and gold pulse of crystalline fragments threw away from the wall on the far side of the river gorge. Having followed Rayalas as she flew across the gorge, by bursted magic the two waterfowl were blown back to fall to the ground where stood band members crowded around Naythorn.

"That light is so marvelous!" groinked Roothyford. "It is the magic of shattered blue gold armor!"

Almost immediately a second thing happened. Points of multicolored firefly light mushroomed upward and slowly coalesced into an orb.

"The magic of her wings made to be born a brightly colored dome," groinked the matron sow.

Mesmerized, the band watched as shimmering magic lit the night fantastical. A delicate veil of deep and richly-toned colors began to float upward, and layer, and then straighten into a rainbow formed horizontal. A loving caress of rainbow reflections washed over the astonished sky-drawn faces of Naythorn and his band.

"I have never before seen a rainbow to light up the night," groinked quietly Practicia.

"This is the first time *ever...* for that to happen," responded Roothyford.

Bright satiny crystals of crimson, orange, blue, and gold interspersed into each other as the layers of rainbow light drew more skyward. The horizontal rainbow of the night melted, only to reform into wide vertical shafts that in hues of crimson, pink, purple, and lavender extended higher and higher to deeply color the night.

"Farewell, Rayalas. *Forever farewell.*" As he spoke the tough blacksmith did not care that he was seen to have tears roll down his cheeks. "The transcendence of your light shows me that you have come to know a beautiful place unknown to strife."

"We all feel terribly the loss of Rayalas and the foal," consoled Lucars patting the smithy's arm.

"No, Lucars," corrected Mama Pig. "My heart does not feel the loss of the foal." The sow would have her hope to spread to all the band members. "The rainbow of the night gives the promise that the little one lives on. She is now found on the other side of this deep chasm. Naythorn will someday greet anew the foal he sired."

At that comment Naythorn excitedly jumped hooves and swung about his head. His heart had to believe that the sow was once again, right.

"From this day on to always," grunted the sow, "the flying mare shall be remembered with the new name Rayalas Borealas. That name signifies Night Rays of the North. Her little bay foal will also have a name. She is to be called Isabaya Estraya. That can be interpreted to mean Bay Beauty of Starlight."

"At this moment of terrible loss, I cannot tell you how much I thank you for those loveliest of names," neighed Naythorn turning to the porcine matron. "Mama Pig, you give me hope that it is somehow made well for Rayalas. And that it will be made well for my foal."

With ears alerted the unicorn arched his neck and ordered, "Phoenicians and bovines, leave this place now. Carry the sheets of blue gold toward the morning sun. You that remain, follow me the opposite way."

"*Grahhff, grarrhhff,*" barked Trackler, "both ways are thinly guarded." Into gathering night disappeared eastward two men followed by two bovines with backs weighted by blue gold sheets.

Along with fast running pigs, mountain sheep, and dogs, two injured fowl fluttered and hopped after Naythorn in a westward breakout away from wolves and warriors.

"I am bruised but not busted," hronkked the black beak goose.

"Qvraakk... I am busted but not broked," responded Webstir suiting to himself the phrase of the goose.

Albarochk Undone

"For such a gigantic frame your mind is too small!" taunted the yellow wolf resting again his front paws on

Lianvil's back. "While my bites only nuisance you like the play of a wolf pup, beware the teeth of the great lion, for they bring *real pain!*" That barked, Danseylono jumped high to grab claws into the hide of the great wolf's back.

"With swords and horns they are upon us!" the yellow wolf's taunts and provocations had been interrupted by the shouts of warriors.

"Men with swords!"

"The cattle and bison crash through us!"

Shaking off his diminutive wolf cousin, Albarochk bounded toward his right flank from where the shouting had erupted.

"Follow me after them! Strike them! No one escapes me!" Moments after the breach, warriors on the great wolf's other flank started yelling.

"They escape! Over here!"

"The flight of the blackmane is unstopped!"

The battlefield descended into chaos. Unsure as to what was happening, and where, Albarochk momentarily froze.

"*Rarroouuu!* Change of orders! Leave off the right flank! Pursue the blackmane on our left flank!" Midst the confusion, at that moment worse befell Albarochk. He was of a sudden struck hard, knocked over backwards, and did not know what had hit and run through him. His eyes welled with his own blood, and he could not make his jowls to speak true-sounding wolf words.

The general pulled himself up, and after swiping at his eyes looked back to see what had torn his face and bowled him over. Rubbing away more blood to clear his vision he saw two tails melt into the darkness, one short and the other long and snapping. Upon hearing the laughter of his yellow hided cousin, Albarochk realized that the diminutive lieutenant wolf and the big lion captain had conspired to commit an act of treason most insidious. To make matters worse, after attacking the commander to whom they had sworn allegiance, they were now escaping.

More ruinous than the sharp pain that beset his jaws, the broken mouth of the monster wolf could no more howl intelligible commands. The unvoiced Albarochk could not restore order to his still formidable force of wolves and warriors.

The yellow wolf lieutenant with the talent to read his great cousin's very thoughts, and act on even an ordered whisper, had deserted. Unable to howl his anguish into the brilliantly colored night sky, the huge wolf felt himself to become incomprehensibly... alone.

Albarochk's brain began to grasp all that had just happened. Escape had simultaneously been made right, left, and center. With the help of his foul and odious wolf cousin, and the abetment of the traitor lion, the blackmane had once again outmaneuvered him. Instead of diminishing in power, somehow Naythorn's magic had grown strong enough to change the hearts of his cousin wolf and the mighty lion.

The huge wolf moved broken lips unsoundingly, "No matter this loss, on the day I devour the unicorn my power will become ten times more devastating to all who dare to challenge me."

For Albarochk's forces of wolves and warriors, the night quieted of disastrous tumult.

CHAPTER 8

CABALBLADE ASTONISHED

The allotted time to comply with the agreement he had made with the unicorn matriarch Elianor, had run out. By galloping one more day to gain one more great height, the guard captain had broken his word.

It had taken longer than he had planned to climb up and down one high mountain and then cross the succeeding valley. As his legs now clambered up a second high mountain that also flowed far northward, Cabalblade could not help but fret about his now broken promise that after the complete turn of one moon into the next he would return to the white herd... with or without Naythorn.

Upon surmounting one more great height he would attempt one last time to glimpse his blackmaned colt. The captain of the unicorn guards was confident that even from the top of a high mountain he would recognize any movement in a far valley made by Naythorn.

"How come native tribes to war so wastefully against each other?" muttered Cabalblade upon hearing clamor and conflict sounding from somewhere ahead of him.

His legs followed along a flank of the mountain toward the gorge whose far rim was the site of noisome battle. Before the captain of the unicorn guards could secure a vantage point to observe the fray, he beheld something he had never before imagined to see. Fragments of blue and gold colored light rose upward, and after was born a multicolored orb of light. The blast of light was accompanied not by the sound of thunder, but strangely by a puff of deafening silence.

Of a sudden, from the dome of light there was gently propelled outward a ball... of something. Cabalblade gasped as he saw the roundish clump kick legs upward; the floating mass possessed little hooves. It was as if the immense surging curtain of multicolored light had softly birthed a little unicorn foal. The little shape floated softly downward to land on the canyon rim below him. There immediately followed an upward burgeoning rainbow of purple, orange, and crimson light that over the rim of the river gorge pulsed and throbbed in glimmering diaphanous currents.

"How can a unicorn foal be like a comet thrown out of a curtain of light?" Through outcrops of ledges and crevices, Cabalblade's hooves scrambled downward. He came upon the little comet that had from the luminous orb dropped onto a rock shelf whose far side fell off into the deep gorge.

Cabalblade nudged to its feet a little unicorn filly that had come to miraculously possess little sprouted wings to accompany a nub of unicorn horn. When his nostrils told him the little thing before him was sired by his own Naythorn, Cabalblade felt his heart leap into his throat.

While the distant rim of the gorge once again exploded into yells and howls, Cabalblade's mind set on one idea only, the procurement of rescue and safety for the foal. Without once looking back he nudged the little filly upward toward the hiddenness that can invariably be achieved in the crannies of a big mountain.

CHAPTER 9

BLUE GOLD TOWARD BARGES

As new sunlight displaced night shadows, Hammerclaw and Lucars trotted ahead of two bovines weighted heavily by sheets of magic blue gold. Even so loaded, Buckmight and Taurington kept pace with the men. The heavily panting Hammerclaw signaled a halt.

"Instead of growing older, I find that you bovines grow stronger."

"It would appear, Master Smith, that the magic of the blue gold sheets fosters increased bison strength and stamina."

"How does Buckmight see our situation?" inquired Hammerclaw.

"Since neither warriors nor wolves are this morning seen to follow us, I say that at the conclusion of last night's battle great good fortune came to benefit us."

"Smithy," mrawed Taurington, "to where exactly do we proceed so that we rendezvous with your Phoenician commander?"

"Sir Cattle, after finding the blue gold my instruction was to carry it to the east where begins the vast ocean. Along that coast Lucars and I are to be by the admiral's barges found." After reflecting more, Hammerclaw added, "So long as it takes us in the direction of the rising sun, we shall follow the rim of this majestic river gorge. I trust that Buckmight and Taurington are in agreement?" Heads adorned with sets of impressively big horns nodded assent.

Alternatively trotting, walking, and again trotting the four member squad made steady progress until they stopped for the night. As they readied themselves to slumber, shafts of colored light spread into the western sky.

"By her glorious light Rayalas maintains a heavenly guard," observed Lucars.

"It must be that the Rayalas Borealas shines down her protective grace on another part of our band," agreed the big blacksmith.

"Refer you, Hammer, to the foal?"

"I have to believe, Buckmight, that something so precious as a unicorn foal come to be born with wings, cannot have perished."

As one day turned into the next, and then the next, the course of two Phoenicians and two bovines followed eastward the rim of the river gorge that continued deeply and impressively vertical.

Resting tired legs one night around a campfire, Lucars said to his sergeant, "Would not you say, Hammerclaw, that Naythorn and our friends must have by now crossed over this deep river chasm?" Instead of answering his apprentice the smithy motioned to redirect the question to the bovines.

"My heart would feel to know had violence stalled the magic of our blackmaned captain," replied Buckmight. "Given that assurance, I am confident that as we speak Naythorn has crossed the gorge and travels back to find the foal of Rayalas."

"It pains me to no longer count myself a member of the blackmane's band," offered quietly the youth.

Hammer Reflective

There were two reasons that as the big blacksmith traveled onward, he found himself to wear a self-satisfied smile. He liked to think that upon finding that he and Lucars had brought back the magic gold sought for transport to Phoenicia, the admiral would be effusive in his gratitude. Of course Zoumar would also be grateful for the portaging service of his bovine friends Buckmight and Taurington. The second reason the blacksmith smiled pridefully was for the workmanship of the blue gold armor he had fashioned for the bovines. Time and again the blacksmith muttered to himself, "Who else could have created such well-fitting armor for two great bulls?" The cattle and bison had more than once informed the blacksmith that their armor wore light as a feather.

Hammerclaw much liked that during the previous battle the metal's toughness had prevented many sharp and hurtful cuts to bovine hides. In fact, Hammerclaw had so closely and so many times observed his handiwork that he had memorized all the nicks and dents now found impressed into bovine armor.

"From the smiles I notice him to wear, I would say that my master thinks on something pleasant."

"Well, Lucars, I was just now imagining that once our grand adventure in this new land is done, I will be entitled to much rest swinging gently in a hammock on the barge that carries us back to Phoenicia. Truly the winds of fortune have these past days blown benignly over you and me."

"In that regard, Master Hammer, I am most pleased that during this last part of our travel toward Phoenician barges we have sighted only a few wolves, and have as well avoided all contact with warriors."

Phoenicians Reunited

Ranging far ahead of Avalcar's party, the filly saw them first. She galloped like the wind to report back. As she neighed Belfloralex whirled and jumped for joy, "I know it is them! The afternoon sun reflects on four suits of golden armor!"

"Hah ha!" chortled the captain. "The sky this day shines down a big blue smile upon us! Given the length and breadth of this vast plain, had we not followed the sweep of this great river gorge we would never have come upon Hammer and Lucars."

Sailors raced ahead each wanting to be the first to embrace the long lost Hammerclaw and Lucars, and wanting as well to be the first to see how much magic gold carried the big blacksmith and his apprentice.

"But why are they *four?*" muttered Avalcar. "Hmph! On their journey toward our barges Hammerclaw and Lucars must have enlisted two natives to provide protection."

Upon reunification with the two blacksmiths, Avalcar was absolutely amazed at the many sheets of blue gold carried on the backs of the two bulls, and was as well gladdened to hear a fierce-looking cattle and bison talk the uniform animal language.

In celebration of the long sought reunion it was unanimously decided to build a big fire. As they sat around the bonfire the Phoenician captain and his men were captivated to hear Hammerclaw, Lucars, Taurington, and Buckmight relate the adventures of the long mining expedition, including battle with Albarochk and his wolves, and their incredible escape at the conclusion of the conflict at the deep gorge.

The joy of Belfloralex was something unique to behold, for each time she moved she had to pirouette and jump up and about. The filly especially cavorted around the big bison that she immediately decided was to be her fast friend. Belfloralex teased him so much that of a sudden, in comparison to the filly, Buckmight felt himself to be very old... and very wise. The unicorn filly could be barely his age when so long past he had first adventured out on his own as a young bison bull.

"Little Belfloralex, do you suppose that losing half the weight of your horn is what makes your head to move so fast?" inquired Buckmight sporting a wide grin. "Less burden of ivory now weights down your ears."

"*Nyeerhunhunh!* I am fast because I love the rush of wind against my face. I can feel the wind delicately comb the hairs on my chin and soothe the broken edge of my half horn. You see, I am a very *sensitive* filly." She smiled at her big bison friend and added, "Do you know what? I think the power of magic is concentrated more in my half horn than in the whole and entire horn of a normal unicorn."

"Now that I have learned how your horn came to be broken, I am proud of how fast and how brave you were in the fight against the colossus of the sea."

"I once showed bravery. Fighting hard against the giant wolf, you have *many times* shown yourself to be more brave than I. You fought him as hard as did Naythorn. But, of course, the name Buckmight signifies a mighty bison."

The joyful spirit of camp reunion lasted well into the night.

Farm Acrobatics

Finding the next morning himself to be in excellent humor, Avalcar decided his men could well use a full day of rest to strengthen them for the journey back to their barges. At that news Taurington's spirit turned playful, more playful than Buckmight could ever remember to have been the mood of his bovine friend.

With the sun well past its zenith, the men cleared a wide circle of stones and brush, and commenced to play tag with Taurington. The idea was to slap Taurington on his side, rump, or back and then escape outside the circle before the cattle could push or bowl the sailor down. When Lucars joined in, the game changed.

"Sir Taurington, in my village we were half farmers, half soldiers, and half acrobats. Instead of slapping your rump, I am going to show you how as a boy I ran with the bulls. Now charge directly at me as though I were your enemy, and for goodness sake do not stop, for then it will for me end badly."

"If you promise not to complain when your rump thuds against the ground, I will charge and not stop."

The big bovine charged head down. Upon achieving the position of the youth, to Taurington's amazement

Lucars jumped up, landed a handstand on his wide back, and then flipped backwards to retouch feet first the ground. The sailors clapped and yelled approval for the acrobatic finesse of Lucar's hands and feet. For the splendid stunt Belfloralex hopped and twirled about in excitement.

When two young Phoenician sailors joined in the fun, the game became more complex. While Taurington charged at one, the second somersaulted sideways over the cattle. When the bovine closed on the object of his charge, just as Lucars had done, the young sailor leaped to tumble frontally over the cattle.

Shortly after, positioned on opposite sides of a charging cattle bull the two young men tumbled at the same time over the back of Taurington as he charged at Lucars, who again tumbled frontally. The big cattle was impressed that the young men could take advantage of his own speed to benefit their tricks. When the heavily panting Taurington called it quits, the two young sailors that had fearlessly joined Lucars in the game flopped down beside the wide-backed cattle slapping his neck and shoulders in new-found friendship.

"*Mrrawwrhaharr!* Of course you young sailors know that I was only running at... *half speed.*"

"Thank goodness you did not more accelerate!" exclaimed the youngest sailor acrobat. "For fear of your great horns, I was already running and jumping as fast and high as I could!"

Spirits in the camp remained high. Every time Avalcar looked at the stacked sheets of blue gold he told himself that he still did not know how to adequately express the great joy felt in his chest for the success of the difficult and dangerous mining mission. After so much effort and sacrifice by Hammerclaw and Lucars, surely his sailors would never permit wolves or warriors to interdict his squad's soon return to the barges.

Avalcar's Decision

"Studying your smile," observed the barge captain sitting down beside Lucars, "I find it to be less wide than the one worn by Master Hammerclaw. After long marches and hard struggles to locate, secure, and bring here the blue gold ore I would think the young smithy would be twice as proud as the much more experienced master blacksmith."

"Sir, can I speak with frankness?"

"You certainly may."

"I worry about the survival of the blackmane," said Lucars looking intently into the eyes of Avalcar. "Without the unicorn's leadership and valor, be assured that Hammer and I would now be nothing more than broken bones bleaching under a hot sun, and the blue gold would be still unfound."

"Speak on," said the captain.

"Hammer and I, along with the winged horse, Master Bison, and Sir Cattle were the backbone of very hard fights that fell to Naythorn and his band. The winged horse is no more. Now I fear that without our swords and shields to anchor his defensive line, the blackmaned unicorn and the two bovines will not long survive.

"Do not misunderstand me, Sir. To find myself right now, right here, makes me very proud. And I know that upon hearing that the blue gold was found my distinguished father will be elated for what his son, a mere soldier, helped to accomplish. For that he will be content, but my conscience does not let me to be. In my heart I feel that I should with the bovines somehow return and not abandon the unicorn captain to the terror he still confronts. I tell you, Sir, that the monster wolf has come to be pure evil. Until Albarochk has devoured every drop of unicorn blood and every morsel of unicorn flesh, the giant grayback will at nothing stop." Before answering, Avalcar reflected long.

"I comprehend what your words say, and feel deeply what your conscience informs. I credit Naythorn for great courage and leadership against insurmountable odds, and I wish I could release you to return to the side of the blackmane. After all, both you and Hammer have told me that it was Naythorn that found the blue gold. That said, my oath of allegiance to my king does not permit me to accept that Lucars, or anyone else should desert my squad of Phoenician soldiers." The captain lowered his eyes to stare at the ground.

"You must know, Lucars, that my sacred promise to the Phoenician army ties my hands. Desertion is on pain of death, including the death of the officer on duty when the soldier disappeared. Should you not return with us, I will face both the wrath of the admiral and the anger of your powerful father. If I do not bring you back, both of them will want my head." Neither soldier said more.

"Hammerclaw," queried the bison set apart from Captain Avalcar and Lucars, "am I right to guess that your apprentice wants to stay in this land with Sir Cattle and me?"

"My friend, concerning that minor detail you would be right. But if that were to happen, Avalcar would as well be charged with desertion, the penalty for which is death. By that rule our army lives... and dies."

When Taurington approached and inquired what his two friends were discussing with demeanor so serious, Hammer explained the difficult situation for Lucars, and by consequence for Avalcar.

Strangely enough the cattle set an easy smile as he mrawed, "Did you know, Buckmight, that in all of Phoenicia there are no bulls as big and strong as me? That is what I have just been informed by the men in Avalcar's platoon, and even so by Avalcar."

"Could my friend enlighten me as to how that bears on the hurting conscience of Lucars? Sir Cattle, sometimes you might want to focus hard your mind on only one issue at a time."

"*I am*, Buckmight, getting at something," answered Taurington. "Let us propose a trade to Avalcar. If I volunteer myself to take the place of Lucars, then the youth can with the bison stay behind. Just imagine the great advantages of this proposition. Where better than upon my broad back to place tomorrow a heavy load of blue gold plates? With the advantage of my brawn, the march back to the vessels will progress far faster than without my help. I can also add to this squad of sailors a new blocking and fighting presence that would come in handy if wolves and warriors were to interpose upon Avalcar.

"Once found in Phoenicia my blood would add new vigor to the cow herd. In fact, I might become the most popular sire for the cows in the king's stable. Helping the king's cows to produce strong, and might I add extra intelligent next generation progeny, would be much to my liking.

"Hammer, let us take this proposal to the Phoenician captain. I guarantee that my idea will give Avalcar pause to evaluate the enormous personal sacrifice this cattle is willing to make for the benefit not just of Lucars, but also for the entire cow herd of Phoenicia." That brayed, Taurington made very wide his smile.

Turning from the cattle, in a military sounding voice Hammer commanded Lucars to attend to him.

"Sit down, Lucars, and listen to what Taurington proposes. I believe that our loyal friend has come up with the best idea of his, ahem, long and illustrious professional life as a cattle bull."

Upon hearing Taurington's proposal, seriety encompassed the eyes and corners of the youth's face. Hammer knew that if Lucars decided to remain in the new land, he would almost assuredly never again see his father and mother. The decision to make that sacrifice would for the young man necessarily require some hard swallowing.

"Having on the scales of family, friendship, and loyalty weighed this plan and all its sacrifices, my answer is... *yes*. If accorded my commander's permission, I will exchange my place with Taurington. My allegiance has been to my sergeant and friend Master Hammerclaw. Now that my sergeant and the blue gold that he sought are both made secure, I cannot bear the thought of the blackmane's demise. I wish to never think that the noble unicorn's bones should someday be crushed in the *merciless* jaws of Albarochk." That stated, the hands of Lucars caressed in turn the shoulders of Hammer and Taurington.

"It will be a large favor, actually to me a gift, if you two help me to present this idea to Avalcar. Perhaps the weight and force of *three* voices will prevail."

Captain Avalcar needed time to weigh the arguments for and against the exchange of Taurington for Lucars, where a great cattle bull would take the place of the nimble and fleet young soldier found presently in his squad.

To further complicate matters, Avalcar had another grave issue to decide. Belfloralex insisted she would not travel back to the unicorn herd, but rather accompany those returning to the side of the blackmane. Of course Elianor would not be pleased to find that the courageous filly had abandoned the unicorn herd.

The two proposed departures would in one way or another weaken his small force. The journey to find Hammerclaw and Lucars had proceeded almost too well, and having so far traveled in a strange and dangerous land with uninterrupted good fortune tended to make Avalcar nervous. The law of averages dictated that sooner or later the return journey to Admiral Zoumar would become difficult. In order to add strength and speed to his platoon, and expand his tactical ability to counter any enemy that presented, what the captain really wanted was that Hammer, Lucars, Buckmight, Taurington, and Belfloralex should all accompany his precious cargo of magic blue gold back to the barges.

Still, Avalcar had to acknowledge that for the duty done and the sacrifices made by the two bovines, Hammer, and Lucars, his gratefulness was beyond measure. Finding them, and finding in their possession the sheets of blue gold had made his mission to be a success, and not a failure. The captain had to also admit that because the cattle's back could carry the weight of gold borne by six or seven men, Taurington's capacity to freight the metal was not to be valued slightly. As to Belfloralex, she was not exactly under his formal command but rather remained under the command of Elianor, so he might be off the hook for not insisting that the unicorn filly with him return.

The petition of Lucars presented the most difficult decision. The lad was from a distinguished family. Upon learning that his only son remained behind in the new land, his father would be furious. Then again, the preservation of the Phoenician throne was said to be linked to the preservation of the unicorn herd, and in that regard Lucars would be even more valuable to the blackmane than to the Phoenician military.

The captain began to wonder if the release of Lucars from active duty might be framed as an act of patriotism. If Lucar's absence were to be portrayed as a reassignment to help preserve the throne of Phoenicia, the family of Lucars would be praised and the prominence of their name would throughout the land be elevated. That circumstance would be to the liking of the youth's father, a man known to *not* be unwelcoming of attention and praise.

Avalcar made two difficult decisions. Lucars would

be traded for Taurington, and Belfloralex would remain behind with the apprentice blacksmith and the bison. The captain hoped to enlist the aid of Admiral Zoumar to help sell the idea behind the exchange of Lucars for Taurington. He would suggest that the admiral use his influence as the leader of the great expedition of unicorn rescue, to secure a title for the father of Lucars. As to Elianor, she could be persuaded that the filly was temporarily needed to help Naythorn until the blackmane rejoined the white herd. After all, cohesion sustained the magic of the unicorns, and the return of Naythorn would renew the unity of the white herd.

Avalcar smiled at the thought that Taurington could find a girlfriend among the cows on his own farm in Phoenicia. Pulling Avalcar's cart of wheat would be easy work for a stalwart offspring of Taurington.

Upon learning of the permission given for her and Lucars to accompany the bison back to the band of the blackmane, Belfloralex bounded about with another display of pure joy. The filly thought Lucars to be brave, sincere, kind toward others, and also one of the most attractive representatives of the race of human animal persons she would ever come to know. She would miss Hammer and Taurington, but nothing could now change the blacksmith's and cattle bull's looming departure for Phoenicia.

A Wind and a Big Cloak

With the assistance of Hammer, Taurington, and Avalcar, the bison and the youth immediately began to plan their return to the blackmane. Unfortunately the sheer walls of the deep river gorge stymied all plans.

"You cannot return all the way back to find and follow the ford that Naythorn used to cross the river gorge," insisted Hammer.

"I regret to say that on that point the smithy is exactly right," agreed the bison. "Many days would be required to so much accomplish, and then we would travel twenty days behind Blackmane." Accompanied by the captain, the four friends of Naythorn walked over to the rim of the gorge and stared down at the river below.

"I can confirm that this deep gorge extends very far eastward," cautioned Avalcar.

"It is an irony that the heights on the other side of this gorge present less difficult purchase," mused Lucars. "Upon safely reaching the river bottom we could, notwithstanding the difficulty, successfully negotiate the climb up to the plain that from the other side extends outward."

A commotion began back at the camp. Whirling and jumping, the excitable Belfloralex had created a wind that sucked cloaks and cooking utensils into a swirl of dust. Sailors jumped about trying to catch and retrieve their personals, only to be tripped by cloaks caught in the whirlwind.

"What in the name of tarnation is the filly doing to our camp?" scolded the master smith.

"Having fun!" quipped Lucars slapping his sergeant on the back. "Now that I think about it, I do wish that Belfloralex could blow me down to the river. That would solve the problem of the impossible descent. And after splashing into the current, I would relish a cool swim."

"She is certainly enjoying her fun," offered Avalcar.

"The filly has a most unusual magical ability to create wind. Well, now. There goes my cloak, my only personal possession of value, flying *high.*" The captain watched sailors chase after his burnished red cloak as it tumbled about in the revolving wind current. "Hmm, I wonder how powerful might be her wind magic. You know what, Master Bison? Let us determine if Belfloralex can float a big fellow like you right down to the river." After retrieving his cloak from the sailor that had run it down, the captain approached the snorting filly.

"It was not so long ago, Belfloralex, that I saw you whip the wind into a frenzy that propelled you into a great river. You cannot have forgotten that?"

"That was *the most fun!*"

"Is there any chance that you could make a wind push even harder than you did that day?"

"I could, Captain, if I set my mind to it. Why do you ask?"

"Could your wind magic make to move the hooves of Master Bison? It would not matter if you toppled him over. Made all muscle, Buckmight would jump right back up."

"Just you wait and see what my magic gift can do!"

Soon enough the bison walked fifty paces away and turned sideways. The filly jumped and twirled until she was moving so fast that it was hard to tell who or what was making so many bouncing revolutions. Of a sudden a strong wind gust shot toward Buckmight. Unable, in spite of the strong resistance of his hooves to withstand the force of the commanded air current, the bison toppled onto his side. But just as foreseen by the captain, in one breath the bison was back up bracing his horns into the oncoming wind gust. Needless to say the experiment with magic wind inspired an audience of Phoenician sailors to clap approval for the astonishing feat of the unicorn filly.

After Belfloralex flopped down to rest, Avalcar had another question for her, "Do you reckon that with the aid of your wind magic you could jump high over Master Bison?"

Belfloralex was quickly standing again on all fours. Without a word she twirled several times, each revolution faster than the previous. She broke to charge toward Buckmight. Some paces before reaching him she launched upward her body and soared twice as high as stood Buckmight. The great leap elicited another round of sailor *bravos* for the unicorn filly.

The captain next took off his great cloak, which was double layered to provide extra warmth on cold nights, and extended it to twice its normal size. He had Lucars help him to tie with cords each corner onto the front and back ends of Buckmight's armor.

"Belfloralex, an even bigger test now awaits you," said Avalcar cheerily. "I want you to make Master Bison, for the first time in his illustrious life, *to fly.*"

"Lucars, set yourself behind Buckmight's great neck and wrap your legs tight so that you do not fall off. When the filly makes to blow a great wind it is your job to throw upward this cloak to capture the turbulence. When the cloak billows full, press your legs to signal Buckmight to run with the advantage of the wind. Let us see if the wind helps the bison to run so fast that his hooves scarcely touch the ground."

When the cloak puffed out wide above the bison's back, Lucars gave the signal and Buckmight was off running. He was soon moving with so much speed that his body glided steps twice as long as normal for a bison bull. It seemed that his hooves were running not on the ground, but on the petals of prairie flowers. While Buckmight ran very fast, Lucars held on for dear life. The sailors that had gathered to watch the filly, burst once more into cheers. Her magic was not only amazing, it was fun and entertaining to watch.

"Praise the heavens!" exclaimed Avalcar. "Belfloralex, I believe we have discovered how Master Bison and Lucars can together clear the rocks at the bottom of the gorge and land in the middle of the rushing river. Our bison is going... *to fly.*"

"So my magic gift has found its purpose?"

"When you jumped high over the bison you showed us how high your wind can carry you. So, once Buckmight and Lucars have floated down to the river you, yourself, do not need a large billowing cloak to follow after them. All that is needed for you to splash down in the river is the swiftness and jump of your fast hooves treading upon magical wind."

It came time for Lucars, Buckmight, and Belfloralex to bid their farewells.

"You, Belfloralex, are the purest creature I have ever beheld, and along with our dear departed Rayalas, you are the *most beautiful,*" mrawed Taurington with emotion.

"Even having only a half horn?"

"Yes, even so dear filly."

When Lucars hugged Taurington's neck with his arms not quite encompassing its girth, the cattle became emotional, "You are the most valiant youth I will ever know. May the heavens reward your loyalty to the blackmane."

The cattle motioned his head toward Hammer. "And for my part I promise that I will take good care of your friend the master smithy."

As he bid farewell to Buckmight, Taurington could not restrain tears from wetting his eyes. "For claiming you, Bison, as my best friend, I was made to be a far better cattle bull. You many times gave me the strength to fight for the sake of uprightness. Because of you, I will be the best new soldier in the Phoenician army." The two bovines turned to look at the smithy and his apprentice.

"Remember, Lucars, when I spoke of my father's lesson that a miracle happens when we are woven into the cloth of inspiration?"

"I will never forget the power of Hammer's three words... *Inspiration and Man.*"

"In that regard, Lucars, through many hard and difficult days you were my sole inspiration." Hammer's long embrace of Lucars bespoke the trust and love gained through many shared adventures and hard-fought survival. The eyes of Lucars moistened. He could not speak. All he could do was one last time grab hold the strong shoulders of the blacksmith.

"Aherm, Master Bison, I dearly wish I could stay with you to help defend the blackmane and his band," said

Hammer, "but that I cannot do. My future comfort will be to know that you will never tire in defense of Naythorn, and that you will one day come to triumph over Albarochk and his vicious legion of wolves. And... take good care of my apprentice blacksmith." That said Hammer bestowed a seemingly unquitting hug to the powerful neck of Buckmight.

"I know as well that my apprentice will safeguard you, Master Bison, the same as he protected his master smithy."

Hammer turned to the filly, "And Belfloralex, I count on you to keep a close eye on both Buckmight *and* Lucars."

"For my part as a captain in the Phoenician military, I acknowledge the leadership and strength of Buckmight and Lucars that delivered the priceless magic gold to the Phoenician army. Rather than be forgotten, your courage shall be sung in the camps of soldiers. Perhaps the statues of a black bison and a noble blacksmith apprentice will one day be seen to entrance our king's palace. May a benign heaven rain blessings upon your two walks in this new land."

"This one is not so large or well-made as yours," said Lucars handing his own cloak to Avalcar. "Tell my father that to him I remain dutiful. And if you one day come upon my mother, tell her that she is every day in my heart."

One hundred paces before the steep descent of the gorge, Buckmight and Lucars prepared. Finding themselves made ready, the youth gave the signal.

Belfloralex twirled herself about even faster than

before. When a great gust of inspired wind billowed Avalcar's cloak high above Buckmight's head, the bison and his mount sped toward the chasm. The launch carried Buckmight and his rider high above the rim of the gorge. Along with Hammer and Taurington, the sailors found gathered together at the rim of the gorge witnessed the big splash into the river made by Buckmight and Lucars.

Avalcar turned and signaled to the filly that promptly began to again whirl about. Upon making another strong wind to blow, the filly was off running. Fifty paces from the rim of the gorge the filly stretched out her neck and head and gained even more speed. The sight of her enormous leap into the air left a memory that none of the bystanders would ever forget. Belfloralex glided down to the river, splashed her belly into water, and briefly cavorted in the swift current before scrambling herself to flop down on the shore.

Buckmight, Lucars, and Belfloralex found themselves set safely on the far shore of the deep river chasm. In gathering twilight, as the reddish copper colored cloak formerly worn by Avalcar dried by a fire, Lucars began to share the feelings he felt for loved ones now forever departed from his life.

"I shall truly miss my mother."

"What is her name?" inquired the unicorn filly.

"Her name is Frayta. She is the most authentic and unfalse person I have ever known. With her, everyone always knew where they stood. The quality of hardness about her was at the same time fair and kind. I shall miss her." The eyes of Lucars glazed over with tears.

"And your father, he is perhaps a general?" The filly wanted to know more.

"A great warrior, he was always busy on military matters. For that my mother made up for his absence by working very hard. Loving the trees, fields, and pastures of our farm she would not leave them to follow after my father."

To change gently the conversation the bison interjected, "I will wager that not only will Sir Cattle be the best new recruit in the Phoenician army, but that he will flirt with many beautiful cows. Although I will sorely miss him, I am happy for our cattle."

"Ha! I hope to someday find a boyfriend colt," rejoined Belfloralex.

"Errm... so Belfloralex... what will it take for a stallion to turn your head?" inquired Lucars wiping one last tear from his cheeks.

"He will surely have to be strong of heart," interjected the bison.

"Well, if that is the case," interjected Lucars, "that happens to sound like a particular blackmaned unicorn with whom I have happened to become well acquainted."

"He will have to be kind and..."

"Now that you say that, Belfloralex," continued Lucars, "that also sounds like the same unicorn that I happen to know."

"He will have to have a nice smile that lights..."

"Lucars, does what Belfloralex just said also sound like the unicorn that we both know?"

"As a matter of fact, *no*, Buckmight. That does not

sound at all like the thorny blackmane I know so well."

"Ha!" laughed the bison. "Not to me either!"

"You two are now teasing the filly that commands the wind."

CHAPTER 10

RAINSNOW'S FORD

The theatrical skullduggery of Danseyelono, no longer called Yellowquist, along with the complicity of the ferocious lion had worked brilliantly. Having sustained horrible breakage to his jaws that quitted him of voice, and having lost the brilliance of his yellow cousin's tactical execution, Albarochk had found himself roundly beset by disorder and disarray.

Taking advantage of the general confusion displayed by wolves and warriors, the horn and hooves of Naythorn had smashed through the enemy line and proceeded westward. Behind the unicorn had run wild hogs, mountain sheep, and two bruised and fluttering waterfowl bouncing feathered bottoms.

While making sure to not fall too far behind, the two dogs had stopped now and then to scratch out the tracks made by their friends moving ahead of them. On occasion the dogs created false leads to delay and impede wolf and warrior scouts. As the night of escape deepened, the howls and cries of following wolves and warriors had grown distant, and then compressed into welcomed silence.

By the time the sun had once more shrugged off its slumber, subtle images of distant high place grandeur presented to Naythorn, the wild boars, sheep, dogs, and waterfowl.

Featherspark had had enough of tumbling along at the rear of the band. After beating wings furiously for many breaths, the goose was airborne. Once his wings grabbed updraft air currents emanating from out of the river gorge, his efforts at flight progressed better. The look of big bird wings grew smaller and smaller until the goose became a far-off speck.

"Captain, it was amazing!" reported the returned Featherspark. "The most wonderful thing was that the more I flew, the better felt my wings! And after a lot of back-and-forth investigation I found a downward trail that will accommodate the laborious climbing skills of four-legged wild boars and a unicorn. You will reach the climb-down place not tomorrow, but the morning after."

An Old Acquaintance

The second night after the return of Featherspark the platoon of the blackmane had camped in a protective place above the river gorge. The next morning Featherspark had lifted off to scout the surrounding country for movement of wolves, warriors, or both. Instead of enemies, the goose sighted a big horse trotting along the edge of the gorge straight for Naythorn's band. As soon as they heard the word *horse,* Naythorn's companions knew that their captain would insist on finding out who the visitor would turn out to be.

"Naythorn, does not the gait of the approaching horse strike you as familiar?" groinked Timidthy.

"I... *know* that horse!" responded the blackmane excitedly as he broke into a run.

"To where goes your travel, big fellow?" neighed Naythorn in greeting.

"Thank goodness I found you. I search for my niece filly. For many a night Rayalas has troubled my dreams."

"It hurts me to tell you," Naythorn dropped his head, "that only a few nights past your niece Rayalas... departed from me. It happened this way. Near the conclusion of battle, in the flight to safety for herself and our little foal, her strength gave out and she failed to gain the other side of the great gorge. In a shimmering burst of colored light her spirit flew upward. She died saving our foal that is now found on the other side of this river gorge." Upon hearing that his niece was no more, the neck and shoulders of the uncle horse with a roan colored hide and golden mane, fell limp.

"I knew something terrible had taken place. But I did not want to believe that the spirit of my favorite filly niece had left me. Sadly, I could not do anything. I did not know where to go to find and help her."

"Sir Uncle Horse, know that every member of Naythorn's band loved your niece," grunted Mrs. Pig craning her thick neck up at the roan stallion. "The sweet, big-hearted, and lovely Rayalas was my special friend. You surely recall that many moons ago when her body was everywhere bleeding, Naythorn saved her life. After the evil grayback and his pack of wolves had all but killed her, it was Naythorn's blood that worked the miracle of her healing, and it was his blood that gave her wings.

"With Rayalas at our side we traveled far, and saw her to become an indescribably beautiful horse with the spirit of a bird." Mama Pig gathered herself to her full height, that although not very impressive when compared to the stature of the uncle horse, was still tall enough to matter. "Now, it is time that from me you receive an official name. That is the least that I can do for you on this day of terrible news.

"While the underlying presentation of your hide mixes brown with white, your mane and tail are distinctively golden. Perhaps the name Roanall would suit a roan colored stallion."

"That name does have a certain elegance to its sounding," responded the uncle horse.

"Hmph. But when I first saw you in the hollow mountain your coat was not so richly dappled with the white flecks of color that here and now remind me of flakes of snow and big drops of rain."

"You are correct, Mrs. Pig. My coat did not used to be so much sprinkled with white. I have wondered if that change had something to do with the touch of Naythorn's horn that happened in the hollow mountain. In fact since being horn-touched, I have found strengthened my ability to swim. There is no stallion anywhere that can swim more strongly than I. And although it is not a physical attribute, I try to be fair in life."

"Then that does it," answered Mama Pig. "Your flecks and splotches are remindful of the purity of the rain and snow that adorn your spirit and suit you well. Like newly fallen snow your heart is unsullied by falseness. The uncle horse will forever forward answer to the name of Rainsnow."

"*Nyeerrrheheh!* I do like the sounding of my new name. Mrs. Pig, I cannot thank you enough."

"It was no bother at all. Now, Rainsnow, you really must decide to with us travel. Feeling her presence, I too am certain that the foal of your niece Rayalas lives on. Naythorn has not spoken to us about our journey's next stage. He does not have to. We all know that after following a trail down the gorge, and then crossing the river, we are going to search for his foal that somewhere on the other side of the gorge yet breathes."

"Then I will pledge myself to this company, and go with Naythorn and you to find the foal of my niece filly." That neighed, the big stallion with the golden mane and dappled coat bowed low to Naythorn.

With a strange sounding mix of animal hurrahs the pigs, sheep, dogs, and waterfowl voiced their approval of the decision of the roan uncle horse to join Naythorn's platoon.

"Rainsnow is welcomed to my band of hearts that beat with trueness."

By late afternoon the band had found their way down, down, and more down until the descent of the deep gorge was at last accomplished. Where they had recently fought wolves and warriors, the chasm had been even deeper. Still, on this day it had been a very long scramble down to the river. By the time big and small animal feet, paws, and hooves tested the edge of the rushing river current, shadows in the deep canyon were lengthening.

"Naythorn, we will not find a better place to cross than right here," neighed the uncle horse after studying the rush and whirl of waters. "That must be the reason that the trail right here ended. Since the ford will not be easy, I have an idea how we might navigate this strong current with no loss to ourselves. Swimming strongly, I will position myself on the upside of the current. My body will help to shield your bodies from the pull and tug of the water.

"You, Naythorn, shall swim opposite me on the side away from the rushing water. The pigs will bite hold of our manes and hang on while together we and they paddle hard. The dogs will grab teeth to the tough tails of the pigs. One sheep needs to chomp down hard on my gold colored tail, and the other on Naythorn's white, or mostly white tail. No one can let go their hold. Although this current looks to be the trickiest I have ever navigated, until we stand on the opposite bank my legs will churn and fight."

The uncle horse turned to the sow and added, "Since you gave me the name Rainsnow, I will safely lead you through the wet storm of this river."

"Let us make Rainsnow's plan to work," instructed Naythorn his half platoon. "Clench tight your teeth and hold on for dear life's sake. When everyone is ready, I will neigh to our uncle horse to cast off."

The horse and unicorn walked into the rush of bouncing waves and stopped shoulder deep. Timidthy bit a part of the mane close to the ears of Rainsnow, and Roothyford and Hamilton locked teeth onto the middle and lower parts of the uncle horse's golden mane. Practicia grabbed in her teeth Naythorn's mane. Behind her, the mama pig clamped teeth tightly into the captain's mane.

"While it is cothy to have uth five pigths thwim together between the horthas," groinked Roothyford through chattering teeth, "the water ith bery cold."

"Thisthter, for my pwart I findth ta water ith too wrrarm," chattered the teeth of Hamilton.

"You know pwwefectly thwell, bwwothur pigth, that whatt I thaid ith cworreckk."

Trackler's teeth grabbed hold of the mama pig's tail, and Blackler clamped his teeth onto Hamilton's tail. The sheep viced teeth into horse tails.

"Since the water rushes too fast," hronkked the goose paddling energetically with the duck ahead of the horse and unicorn, "you big stallions will have to paddle very hard your legs."

Rainsnow and Naythorn made slow but steady progress... at first. Midstream, Mama Pig noticed that the blackmane had started to gulp big breaths of air, wheezing harder with each breath.

"*Nyeerraarrr!*" gasped the blackmane. "Against this strong current I cannot make headway!" As the rush of water began to pull Naythorn back, the shielding effect provided by Rainsnow's body against the turbulent current, was lost.

"With your teeth grab hold of my tail!" ordered Rainsnow.

The blackmane joined Ewelissas so that two sets of teeth became clamped into Rainsnow's tail. While the powerful turbulence pushed them down river, Rainsnow's legs kept pulling forcefully the strange raft of horse, pigs, sheep, dogs, and unicorn. At last the roan stallion's hooves crunched onto river bottom. The sturdy uncle horse guided the animal lifeline into a little cove.

From manes and tails the raft passengers unlocked jaws and pulled themselves onto welcoming sand. Naythorn was the last to beach himself. He moved slowly, head down, coughing and gasping for big breaths.

"I swallowed... too much water... the strong current nearly carried me away... I run so much better than I swim," observed Naythorn regaining his breath. "You need to be very proud of yourself, Rainsnow, for the ability to swim so vigorously. Because of your endurance no member of my band was lost to watery turbulence."

"Against such a strong current it was all I could do to make headway. But, Naythorn, the only thing that counts is that you and your friends now find yourselves across the river."

"*Qvaackhekhek!*" nuisanced Webstir jumping webbed feet onto the belly of a sprawled Hamilton. "That was fun!"

"That river provided exactly the refreshing my poor snout had been wanting," responded Hamilton. "It is so nice to top off the evening with an *easy* swim."

"Webstir can for now have his fun with us," neighed a recovered Naythorn. "As for me I am going to practice my swimming stroke, and next time just like the duck I'll bob gently across the waves."

The following morning the mountain sheep took the lead upward out of the river gorge. To not slip backward big and small animal hooves and paws dug into soil and sand, and gripped against rock. But because they were moving on dry land, and were not caught in an unrelenting and scary rush of water, no member of the band complained.

Despite Naythorn's half band taking their time to climb upward, well before the sun had set they found themselves standing on the waited north rim of the gorge. A big valley extended before them. To their left rose a craggy and impressively long mountain that stretched its jagged backbone northward. Across the valley to their right another high mountain thrust northward.

"I wonder if snow has fallen in these mountains. I have never before galloped through snow."

"Nor have I, Rainsnow," answered Naythorn.

"What think the horse and unicorn concerning tomorrow's travel?" inquired Timidthy. "Am I the only one that thinks something does not feel right, that something about this place feels wrong?"

"We need yet this evening that our two waterfowl perform a scout," replied Naythorn. "After yesterday's bath in the river, neither the duck nor goose seems the least bit tired today." Hearing that, Webstir began to complain that he was indeed tired, and that he was also the hardest working member of the band. However, after a suitable time of complaint the duck trailed skyward after Featherspark. Before the others had time to satisfy either hunger or tiredness, the two birds circled down to rejoin their friends.

"The bills of two waterfowl look to be uncommonly serious," observed Practicia.

"*Hronnkk!* That is because we saw something that neither of us liked!" responded Featherspark. "In the middle of this valley are set many painted-face warriors. The black-spotted jaguar skins worn on their shoulders make them to look very fierce. Dancing energetic circles in the center of their camp, they did not look to be hunting. Their much commotion has certainly scared away any wild..."

"*Qvaaakkk!*" interrupted Webstir. "That is not all! There must be at least one hundred wolves arrayed along a slanted line that cuts through the middle of this valley. The line of wolf sentries stretches from the edge of the river on our right all the way to the camp of the warriors."

"They know we are trying to return to the place directly opposite the deepest part of the river gorge where we fought Albarochk," baahed Rambuncture. "Since we are now fewer in number, they will not without bloodshed let us turn back toward the east."

"How can they know that we want to return to the deepest part of the gorge?" grunted the sow. "As we for three days traveled along the river we came not upon wolves or warriors. Nor did we today see any adversaries as we climbed out of the gorge."

"It may be, Naythorn, that the warriors and wolves know something else," offered Timidthy. "Something that we have neither seen nor scented."

As a lavender-blue tinted darkness fell that night over the valley, Naythorn paced back-and-forth.

"The blackmane is lost in thought," groinked Timidthy to Hamilton, Practicia, and Roothyford. "I wonder... do you suppose that somewhere out there the unicorn herd is moving toward us? If the unicorns have not yet found their new home, they recognize that winter snows will soon fall on them. What else could make our enemies, without knowing exactly where we are to be found, want to prevent our movement in the easterly direction that Naythorn wants to pursue?"

"Brother pig," answered Hamilton, "the wolf general knows that some of our band escaped his trap by breaking out in the direction of the morning sun. And, during these last days the wolves can estimate how far we traveled toward the evening sun. I will wager that Albarochk has his forces arrayed to prevent the two halves of our band from reuniting on this side of the river."

"Let us be practical about this," offered Practicia. "Compared to the slower speed of our half band, Albarochk probably found a faster way across the gorge, pushed hard, and is now found somewhere in this broad valley. One can also conclude that from this side of the gorge wolf and warrior spies observed our last battle, and know that Naythorn is intent on continuing northward travel. Having surmised that, I think that both of my pig brothers are right. Our enemies want to stop any and all of us from reuniting with each other... or with the unicorn herd. If our band and the unicorn herd remain in three separate groups, we can be surrounded and defeated far easier than if we were together united."

"Roothy, it is now the turn for your thoughts to be shared," groinked Hamilton.

"How courteous of my brother... to ask for my opinion. I was just thinking that the foal of Rayalas is also on this side of the great river gorge. That means that Naythorn's band is divided not into two parts, but into three. So that makes Naythorn's band and the unicorn herd to be found in four separate places."

As Naythorn and Rainsnow together settled to rest the night, Mama Pig approached and looked into the unicorn's troubled eyes.

"My captain needs to hear what my boarlings used their heads to think about." Naythorn and Rainsnow listened carefully to the report of what Hamilton, Timidthy, Practicia, and Roothyford had concluded about the unicorn herd, and the three parts of the band, that is if the third part being the foal was still to be found close to where battle had been waged and Rayalas had perished.

"Because we are blocked, we had best not enter into this valley," neighed Rainsnow with conviction sounding in his voice. "Even though the face of the mountain to our left looks to be more rough and difficult than is the one to our right, it makes horse sense to make our route up and along the high mountain ridge on our sunset side. Once we are beyond the wolves and warriors that search for us, we can circle back for your foal."

As Naythorn closed his eyes to sleep he convinced himself that surely the line of wolf defenders did not know of the existence of his foal, or the whereabouts of the bovines. That meant the line of wolves had been placed to stop him from reconnecting with the white herd. For the first time in more than a year of moons the blackmane glimpsed the hope of reunion with his animal kind.

CHAPTER 11

THE HAMMER IS THROWN BACK

Captain Avalcar was impressed, and for that said so, "Sir Cattle, I cannot well enough thank you for your splendid work carrying yesterday and today that great load of gold plates on your back. It will soon be dark. I say it is time you rest for the night."

"Sir Avalcar, you best save your kind words until even more distance has been accomplished."

"Thanks to your strength, Taurington, I am confident that we will continue to make very good progress toward the barges."

In light of the excellent headway made toward the enormous river where waited the admiral, Avalcar decided to enjoy the tabac leaves that he had come to much savor. Because the sailors knew that each taken step brought them closer to their barges, and so closer to Phoenicia and to their families, in spite of their physical tiredness the men were as well cheerful. While a long and possibly stormy passage awaited barge travel across the wide ocean, about this the men were unconcerned. From experience they placed high confidence in the navigational abilities of Admiral Zoumar. The important fact was that they were finally moving in the direction that led homeward. Talk that night around the campfire turned to the upcoming voyage.

"I truly believe the admiral is twice as good a sailor as am I," offered the captain.

"What you say, Sir, is based on false modesty," contradicted a veteran sailor seated nearby his captain. "While the Lord Admiral is a first-rate navigator, I commend to all that you are just as good a sailor as the famous Zoumar." At this comment was heard murmured agreement.

"Sir, we bring two intruders," interrupted a sentry. At that news sailors jumped up with weapons drawn and shields at the ready. The sentry held up his hands as a signal that all was well. "Two horses request permission to rest the night in safety with us. Just like Sir Cattle, they talk our speech." Taurington was immediately off to see who were these horses. After moorrawwing a loud hello to the visitors, the cattle escorted the two stallions toward the fire.

"Gentlemen sailors, I am acquainted with these fine young stallions. They are brothers of the valiant winged Rayalas, rest her spirit, that you have heard me to talk so much about. I am amazed that these two stallions are happened upon us."

"Sir Cattle," answered Avalcar with a pleasant ring heard in his voice, "because neither I nor my men have seen a horse in what seems ages, we heartily welcome them. Since they can speak the uniform tongue, they must tell us from where they come and to where they are bound."

"This is my brother next younger than Rayalas," informed the larger stallion. "I follow her next older in age. It was after our sister horse recovered from the terribly deep and treacherous wounds that were inflicted upon her by mean and vicious wolves, that we met Taurington. Had not unicorn magic healed our sister horse, the deep gashes made into her flesh by wolf teeth would have then and there ended her short life."

"We are the bearers of terrible news," neighed the younger stallion. "Warriors and wolves rent apart and scattered our horse herd. We do not know how many horses escaped. Fleeing without destination, my brother stallion and I have traveled long and far. Upon sighting your fire we knew this camp was not made in the manner of pursuing warriors."

"Do you by chance know the whereabouts of our sister horse, Rayalas?" neighed the older stallion looking about at the men and cattle bull.

"It grieves me to be the bearer of tragic news," answered Hammerclaw stepping into the light of the fire. "Your sister Rayalas no more runs and flies across this land. She died trying to escape from battle with her newborn foal. It happened during our band's last encounter with the wolf legion and its warrior allies."

"*Nyyeerrrarrhunh!*" responded with despair the younger stallion. "That is so sad! When I saw a ghost horse running across the night sky, I did not want to admit it but right then I knew that my sister filly was to me gone."

"We saw a brief flame of fire accompany her passage across the night sky," neighed the older horse.

"That flame signifies her undying love for her magic foal," concluded Hammer. "In flight from wolves and warriors, after giving birth Rayalas sickened and became weak. Her wings that had before carried my great heft, proved unable to carry the weight of her newborn foal across a deep river gorge. When the magic blue gold armor of the winged horse exploded in blue light, the spirit of Rayalas gave birth to a rainbow of the night. In honor of the mare's courage we now call the light that often colors the northern night sky, the Rayalas Borealas."

The Jeenista

Heartened by the presence of the two horses, the sailors began to brush equine sides and backs. Before much time had passed the horses began to cavort and show the jumps and twirls they could perform with their athletic bodies. In the light of the campfire a competition began to see if while remaining their bodies in place, the stallions could copy the jigging steps made by the men. In that contest the performance of the two horses dramatically improved. At last the camp became silent. Sailors, a blacksmith, a cattle bull, and two horses fell contentedly to sleep.

By the time breakfast was finished it had become evident to Captain Avalcar that a new feeling of camaraderie had spread over the camp. The men did not want to leave the side of the horses, and the equines in turn liked the attention given to them. The lone man apart was Hammer who seemed to have his thoughts planted somewhere else, somewhere far away.

Avalcar did not want to march off and leave the two horses behind. Nor after having just met them, did he feel comfortable proposing that the horses accompany onward his squad. Fortunately, his dilemma led to a creative solution.

"I propose that we here delay for the purpose of a late afternoon race between Sir Cattle and the horse brothers. Since the bull's legs carry far more weight, I further propose that Taurington be given a head start. I have one other request to make. But first, tell me which of you two is the faster horse?"

"I am sometimes by two paces faster than my older brother stallion."

"To my great disappointment, I must admit that my younger brother will likely win the race."

"Well then, older horse brother," continued the captain, "if you let me ride mounted upon your back, I say that we two together will beat the cattle and your younger brother to the finish line." Not understanding how adding more weight to his back could make him to run faster, the older horse shook vigorously his mane.

"A horse and his mount should find themselves in harmony with each other," continued Avalcar. "Through touches of reins, hands, and legs the rider communicates to the horse. With movements of head and neck the horse informs the rider of tactics that can accelerate hooves and win the race. To become a truly fast team they need to actually feel the beat of each others' hearts. Bonded together in support of each other, the team of horse and rider becomes faster."

Patting the neck of the older stallion the captain made a request, "Would you let me fashion a reined halter, and then spend with me a part of the early morning getting accustomed to the feel of me mounted upon your back?"

Sailors watched closely as the team of Captain Avalcar and the older stallion traversed gullies, and wheeled around trees and rocks. As the pace of the older horse smoothed and quickened, the men had to admit that the pair coordinated very well with each other. It was not long before the captain and his mount disappeared into the prairie. Meanwhile, Taurington and the younger stallion conserved energy by lazing in the shade of clumped trees.

With the halfway point marked by a boulder that stood as high as a man's head, the course went around and through an impressive variety of rocks, shrubs, and ups-and-downs. Spread apart helmets demarked the start, and the finish line.

As a late afternoon breeze began to freshen, Taurington advanced beyond the helmets to where he thought his lead would be fair to himself and to the horse brothers. With sailors crowded about the starting line, the younger horse brother jumped front hooves in excitement. Wearing a loose fit halter, the older brother horse stayed calm and relaxed. A sailor remarked that before Avalcar was promoted in rank, he had a reputation as a superb *jeenista,* which meant horseman.

When the flat side of a sword clanged against a gold shield, the race was on. Already far in advance of the brother stallions, Taurington took off very fast and extended his lead. However, the two stallions soon began to close on a cattle unable to maintain the fast pace he had initially set. With less weight on his hooves than his older horse brother, and no weight on his riderless back, the very fast younger horse settled quickly into second place. However, where the terrain proved difficult Avalcar maneuvered to close steps on the younger stallion.

As they approached the halfway mark the slowing Taurington still led by a substantial distance, the younger stallion came next, and the mount of Avalcar came last. Sailors cheered as they watched the younger and leaner horse continue to close on Taurington. More cheers sounded when Avalcar drew to within four lengths of the younger brother horse.

Coming down the home stretch the match tightened. Approaching the finish line, the winded Taurington slowed and was by the younger stallion overtaken. Slung low over his horse's neck, with the touch of his hands Avalcar urged on his mount. With a surprising burst of speed Avalcar's horse caught Taurington.

The men cheered for the captain and his mount, which motivated both to dedicate all remaining strength and energy to the final stretch of the course. Two stallions came to run neck-and-neck.

The consensus of the sailors was that Avalcar's horse won by a nose. Whether he really did win by a nostril was not clear to the always observant Hammerclaw, who readily admitted to himself that the decision was popular. At the conclusion to the race the older horse trotted easily, and his heavy panting soon subsided.

"Your encouragement, Captain, motivated me to run faster than I have in a very long time."

"My high-stepper ran a *magnificent* race," affirmed the captain placing his hands to the sides of his mount's long face. To his own step the captain added new spring.

"This is the best day I have known in years!" allowed an exultant Avalcar moving to place arms around the necks of the two stallions. "I can say that I truly *love* these brother stallions. And my mount today ran faster than any horse I ever rode in Phoenicia!"

"Sir, my younger brother horse ran very well today. The next time he will prevail."

"He has a very quick step. And I have never seen a bull run so fast," affirmed Avalcar moving to grasp the neck of the cattle. "You very nearly had us at the end."

"Of course I did!" snorted Taurington. "But *almost* did not for me win the race."

"Avalcar is a born jeenista!" shouted a sailor. "Our captain commands a great stallion even better than he commands a great sea!"

"Avalcar will in the future issue orders to trim the sheets while sitting on his horse," quipped another sailor. Men laughed at the thought of their captain seated on a horse that would have to develop sea legs to remain upright in heavy seas.

"We rest for the remainder of the day," repeated Avalcar his earlier order. As a tabac pipe was handed back-and-forth sounds of sailor songs rose to fill the air, and smiles were shared all around.

Hammer and Taurington

"Over there in the shade of those trees, do you notice how the captain rests content with the horses?" inquired Hammer of Taurington.

"The three are become fast friends," replied the cattle. "I find myself a little jealous of the affection

Avalcar shows to the two stallions. But since everyone knows that a cattle is not naturally made to carry a human person on his back, I really should not be jealous of the attention that the horses receive." After smiling wide at the smithy, Taurington added, "For this bovine there is one rider, and one only. And that my friend, is you."

"I am delighted to hear Taurington mraw that," replied the smithy clapping his hands. "I feel the same about you. In our day, Sir Cattle, we made quite a fighting team."

"I look forward to again fighting beside Master Hammer, next time in the army of his homeland."

"Unfortunately, Taurington, no cattle are to be found in the Phoenician army. And, for my part, I shall likely be posted to the forge. So, I am afraid that our fighting days... are for both of us ended." Between the two fast friends a heavy silence ensued.

"I surely like duty as a sire. Yet, Hammer, at my advanced age I would stay in better physical shape marching and fighting... and particularly so with you at my side. Left alone in a stable well supplied with hay and grain, my belly should become a great and perhaps overwhelming burden to my legs."

"I am truly sorry to say, Sir Cattle, that the chapters of victories that we together wrote... shall no more be composed."

"Hmph!" snorted Taurington. "I had not planned for those fighting pages to be no more written."

"The only way we can remain as a team on the field of battle is to... to not leave this land. While you gave your word when you assented to the exchange of yourself for Lucars, you have not yet been sworn into the army, and so you are not by a formal oath compelled to return on a barge to Phoenicia. Unfortunately for me, my past induction into the army binds me to return to my homeland."

"*Mrrwwoooaaahh!* Seeing as he is in such a fine winning mood today, I could at least have another chat with the captain to discuss my future." But neither Taurington nor Hammer moved. They instead lingered sharing an increasingly sullen mood.

"I wonder where Master Bison might now be found?" mused Taurington shifting his bulk.

"About that you and I can only venture to guess. But I dare to hope that not too many more suns will pass before Lucars and Buckmight again find themselves at the side of Naythorn. And the blackmane will be very pleased to see another unicorn. The arrival of the wind walker Belfloralex will cheer Naythorn."

"Remember how reassuring Mama Pig became when times were tough? On the other hoof, Hammer, there were many times that I wished one of the mountain sheep would *eat* Webstir. Eat the pesky duck, feathers and all."

"Our green-head duck could be very bothersome," replied Hammerclaw.

"And what about Hamilton Pig? I cannot tell you how many times he pestered me about my oversized girth."

"Yes, Taurington, that he certainly did. And the irony is that Hamilton is the most chubby of the four boarlings."

"And do not get me started on Trackler and Blackler. If those dogs nipped my heels once, they bit them a thousand times."

"No question about it, Sir Cattle. Those two dogs were incredible nuisances. And in my case I also found the pessimism of Rambuncture to grow very tiresome."

"Every single day that ram sheep tried to make everyone feel down and depressed... just like himself." Taurington slumped his neck into grass. "*Mmrraawww*, Hammer, what is the use? My complaints do not hide the fact that I deserted Naythorn. How can I forget that Naythorn stepped in to stop me and Buckmight from butting heads so hard that we were surely going to kill each other. And the blackmane that more than once in battle saved my hide still needs me, and I do not like to think that I am a quitter."

"Sir Cattle, the time of belonging to Naythorn's magical band is for you, over. Your future in a faraway land is to sire many strapping calves. Hence forward your one and only duty is to be a very prolific cattle bull."

Avalcar Decides

As the sun marked faster its decline, at the approach of the captain Hammer and Taurington roused themselves to stand. Over his shoulder Avalcar hefted a sack, of some sort.

"Sitting themselves apart, my worthy friends do not look to share the same jovial mood found in the rest of the camp. It may be that something troubles the both of you. Hammer, you and Taurington know that you can be honest with me."

The smithy and the cattle looked at each other, and without saying a word looked glumly back at Avalcar. When their grumpiness did not lessen, the captain ordered, "Accompany me on a ride to overlook the gorge."

The captain pursed his lips in a charged whistle. In response, two horses were soon at his side. The captain wrapped an arm around the neck of each horse and smiled big.

"Highstep and Quickstep... those are the names I shall give you. Let us ride out, all of us, to look at the river gorge. Oh, there is one thing more. I will have Hammerclaw to put on Taurington's suit of magical armor, as well as his own. Maybe the ride ahead will take the creaks out of the blue gold."

With the big blacksmith set comfortably on his back, the mood of Taurington began to improve. The shift into physical motion to be going somewhere, no matter where or why, took the minds of the cattle and blacksmith off Naythorn and his band. Hammer and Taurington began to think that a long gaze at the great river chasm would serve to revive their spirits.

A horse with a rider, a cattle with his mount, and a riderless equine were soon galloping abreast. For a reason known only to himself, Avalcar did not take a direct path to the gorge. He was intent on following a more circuitous approach. For the sake of pure speed, the two horses were soon running full-out leaving Taurington and Hammer in their dust.

"Humph!" Hammer was offended. "It is rude of the

captain to show off the speed of the horse brothers. Everyone knows that horses are built for running, and that cattle bulls are not."

"*Mrrawwnnnghh!* I know that this cattle is made for fighting, and running *into* danger."

The two horses finally came to a place on the rim of the gorge two leagues distant from the camp of the sailors. Before the heavily panting cattle gained Captain Avalcar and the two horses, he had slowed to a trot.

"Is not this a grand sight?" remarked the dismounted captain. "Early this morning I rode High Step to this very spot."

"It is rightly beautiful," replied Hammer. "I would even say the view is magnificent. Ahem... but Sir... we could have seen an equally impressive vista without the need to so far travel before the fall of dark."

"You make a good point, Sergeant. However, I ask you to study closely the gorge. Between the rim of the chasm at this spot, and the rim of the gorge adjacent to our camp, you will notice one difference."

"If you direct your eyes down to the bottom of the gorge, Master Hammer," interposed Taurington, "you might see to what the captain refers." Hammer dismounted from the cattle and peered into the steep chasm. His eyes lit up.

"Captain, far below where we now stand the river churned into the bend and washed away the bank. Because of that the ledge we stand on does not fall down onto rocks, but instead falls into water."

"That is precisely what I this morning realized. This hidden spot is the first place we have come to where one might jump off the rim of this deep gorge and splash safely down into water.

"Hammerclaw, Taurington, I brought you two here to let you freely decide if you want to with me return to Phoenicia. On the other hand should you desire to rejoin the blackmane and his band, and as well rejoin Master Bison and Lucars, then for both of you this is a moment of destiny."

"Sir, am I to understand that you would allow me to... to break my oath of service to the army and remain behind in this new land?"

"Here is my thinking, Sergeant Hammer. I can return to camp with the two brother stallions, not say a word to my men, and my sailors will simply see that Hammer and Taurington have departed my platoon. Yes, some of the men may surmise that your departure came with my blessing, but upon my return to camp it will be a done deed that cannot be changed. The men will not complain because after a mission met with much success they are marching homeward, and that is their focus entire.

"And since my two horse friends have agreed to take your places and return with me to Phoenicia where they will become superb war horses, the men will remind themselves that the stallions will freight on their sturdy backs the gold plate. Taurington is no longer needed by me or by my platoon. The addition of Highstep and Quickstep will allow my sailors to march fast with the full expectation of safety.

"So then, Hammerclaw, upon my return to the barges I will be purposefully vague about the circumstances of your departure. When a matter remains unspoken for days, weeks, and perhaps even during a long ocean voyage, the issue decays and diminishes in importance. It is sometimes better to not say anything that might later, at an ill-opportune time, be used against oneself. Just the same as for you, this matter might end up going well for me. I can never well enough thank you for bringing us the incalculable gift of the blue gold." The captain's voice softened. "If your loyalties still lie with the blackmane and the members of his magic band, then this is your final opportunity to follow above all else, the desire of your hearts. I set this sack of supplies here at your feet. That done, I leave Hammerclaw and Taurington here to think on things."

Avalcar gave a bear hug to Hammer, and then clasped arms about the big neck of Taurington. The captain mounted High Step, and without another word said rode into the last light of day with Quick Step trailing behind.

Hammer turned to look at Taurington. The smile they shared confirmed that between them no words needed to be spoken. At the same time that Hammer slung the sack of provisions over a shoulder, Taurington knelt for Hammer to mount. The cattle retreated fifty paces from the rim, turned, ran fast, jumped high, and dropped downward with front legs stretched out. During the long fall Hammer's hands clenched hold of the cattle's armor plate and his legs clung tightly to the bovine's sides. Hammer found that for all his great girth Taurington had excellent balance. All the way down to the river the bovine maintained his body in a level glide.

The large splash did no harm to either the cattle or his mount. Hammer was pulled through the current with one hand clinging tightly to Taurington's armor plate, and the other clasping firmly the sack of supplies. The two finally climbed onto the far river bank.

"Harr! Hurrah!"

"Mrrawwhahahhh!"

Finding themselves not caring a whit that they were soaked through, the blacksmith and cattle bull roared in laughter. Just as had happened to the weight of a ponderous cattle bull falling through the air, two hearts had lightened. At the advent of a clean beginning in a new land of plains, deserts, rivers, and mountains, their bodies and spirits felt fully revived.

"Welcome back, Captain," said a sentry saluting. "Where... are... the two..."

"As you were, Sentry." Returning salute, the captain's face scowled resolute and of conversation unwelcome.

As Avalcar later brushed down the horse brothers, the glow of a new thought relaxed his face. "Big fellow, what would you say to the receipt of a new name in honor of a departed friend?"

"Since I still have not grown accustomed to being called Highstep, a new name would suit me fine."

"The name Hammereins bespeaks much strength. You take the reins, and run with the power of a strong blacksmith wielding a hammer in his hand."

"Nyeerrheeh! The new name is to my liking. It shall always remind me of the noble Master Hammerclaw."

"Very good," answered Avalcar.

"The name Lucareins will tell all that your heart

pounds only in courage," said the captain turning to the younger stallion. "To be sure, I wish I had the exceptional athletic ability possessed by Lucars. Along with courage, the name Lucareins will for you signify great speed and agility afoot."

"*Nyeehrrreeheh!* I was told that Lucars moves his legs wondrously fast. In honor of the fleet apprentice blacksmith, I am well-renamed."

Hammereins and Lucareins trotted off to graze and Avalcar retired to smoke. After his pipe died out the captain spoke softly so that only he heard.

"Today by Master Hammer and Sir Taurington, I did right. What is more, their young stallion namesakes will be true to the integrity of the two blacksmiths that found the blue gold and defended in battle the blackmane. I have to believe that this trade of two horses for a blacksmith and a cattle bull will somehow end well for Naythorn Blackmane. Although one can never tell about these things, this matter may also not end badly for me."

A small smile came to set on the mouth of the captain as he added, "The idea of loyalty and obedience is not always so simple as instructed in a training camp for new soldier and sailor recruits."

CHAPTER 12

THE WHITE HERD TRAVELS OVER LAND

Because her calling was to be in harmony with the beauty of creation, most times the high escort Aneilee stood sparingly apart from the distractions of the white herd. The innocence of her heart was not to be sullied with gossip, small conversations that carried little import, or petty disputations. This day, however, would bring the high escort involvement in temporal issues.

"You see older stallions huddling together, young stallions jumping nervously about, and mares standing distracted," neighed quietly the matriarch to the high escort. "Observe that rather than being noisy at play, foals and colts are in aspect subdued. It is as if the white herd clumps together waiting for *something* to happen."

"I both hear and observe what you neigh, Elianor. Winter approaches, and with the shortening of daylight the grass for grazing discolors and diminishes."

"Our peninsular camp is not only *not* protected from the cold winds of winter," continued the matriarch, "it is also not defensible. Unicorn stallions and mares understand the strategic weaknesses of a winter camp boundaried on three sides by a river. A canoe attack could come from any one of the three sides fronted by water. Laying siege to our land side could bring attendant hunger and no avenue of escape."

"But Elianor, the admiral's barge now travels over water searching for the blacksmith charged with finding the blue gold. How can we from here depart without first communicating with Zoumar, and asking for the advice that comes from his great store of experience? Nor can we abandon Cabalblade, who is to soon return to us with his blackmaned offspring. I cannot imagine deserting the stallion that during so many years gave unblemished service in command of the unicorn guards."

"Faded and brittle leaves signal that hard winter is soon to come. The delay of our departure puts us at risk of being here trapped by ice and snow. Just consider that impatient young stallions may depart without you or me in their lead. The last thing we need is to contend with a revolt of young stallions. Aneilee, you who have always had the best horse sense of anyone, surely you must understand the gravity of the restlessness now felt throughout the camp?"

"All right," responded the high escort, "we will do as you propose. However, we must leave a message for Zoumar with the Phoenician sentries still found about us. The admiral will have to understand that just as he, upon securing his cargo of blue gold must depart for Phoenicia, so must we also depart this peninsula before the descent of winter imprisons the white herd. Do you with me agree that unicorns travel west toward mountains?"

"Just as a great volcano for a thousand years

protected Wittanor," neighed the matriarch nodding her head, "unicorn safety is now to be found in a new hold set amidst mountains that protect a hidden valley *and* a deep lake. But, Aneilee, something tells me that searching out that hidden place will for us not be easy.

"When Cabalblade and Naythorn return, they will have to follow our trail. I will warn mares and stallions to be wary of whatever may present ahead be it wolves, lions, warriors, or driven snow. And Aneilee, it will be well for the unicorns to see you much involved with the herd. Your active leadership, in support of me, will promote hope and perseverance."

"As without the powerful backing of the Phoenicians we strike out on our own, I will do as the matriarch requires."

The Unicorn Herd On The Move

With gait elegant Elianor and Aneilee trotted side by side out of the camp. Behind the two leaders came the sage unicorns followed by ranks of stallions, mares, fillies, and colts. Led by Lieutenant Hoovefort, the unicorn guard horses provided rear escort. Elianor fell back to make sure the herd of five hundred unicorns was orderly, looked alert, and was sharp in their movement.

Before the set of darkness fifteen leagues were traveled on a course that split an angle between sunset and the fixed star. Finding their legs and shoulders to be sorely out of shape, the pace of unicorn march slowed the second and third days to forestall cramping and limping. But by the fourth day of travel the horned horses had mastered the rhythm of trotting in a sustained fashion.

"I am starting to worry that our march proceeds too easily," neighed Aneilee to Elianor on the fifth day of travel.

"While I share the same concern, for now we will give thanks that the wind is at our back."

Before a thicket set beside a dry creek bed a decrepit looking wolf with brown hide matted in cockleburs was that afternoon seen to linger curiously stationary. Elianor neighed for a guard unicorn to see what the wolf was doing, and if he was alone. At the stallion's approach the wolf disappeared into densely matted thorns. No other wolves were thereabout seen. After hearing the report of the guard stallion, the matriarch nodded as she neighed, "We cannot be too careful. I do not want to find even one stray wolf out of place."

"We guard unicorns will stay vigilant," reassured the stallion.

That evening, of a sudden Aneilee quit grazing at the side of the matriarch and without neighing a word turned to gallop into softening twilight. In middle night the returned high escort awakened the matriarch, "Elianor, just *look* who I bring mounted on my back!"

"What on earth means this?"

"Your eyes, Elianor, do not deceive. Alexzana and Marsand decided to join us." The island girl rushed to hug the neck of the matriarch.

"After the unicorns left camp I could not bear that I remained behind, and Marsand would not let me to follow after you all by myself. I am so glad to have refound the magic white herd!"

"Aneilee, we cannot halt our march to escort these two back to the Phoenicians awaiting the return of the admiral's barges." That neighed the matriarch looked helplessly at the high escort, who in turn looked smilingly back at the matriarch.

"After all, Elianor, she is *the dream girl,*" responded the high escort. "Before her eyes ever saw a unicorn, Alexzana dreamt of the arrival of the white herd to her island, and then she bravely fought for us. And I will never forget that the drum playing of Alexzana and Marsand encouraged unicorns to dance." Aneilee turned to once more look kindly at the two interlopers.

"But Hoovefort will say that no human persons can be permitted to become guests of the white herd," observed the Matriarch.

"Yes, Hoovefort will again be irate."

"Well at that," replied the matriarch, "we both know that upon her return to us Belfloralex will be overjoyed to find her two close friends. So... it seems the white herd will tomorrow travel accompanied by an island girl *and* a Phoenician lad." Looking closely at the two youths Elianor instructed, "Understand that you will have to fend for yourselves. Unicorns will not be hunting rabbits for you to eat."

Spreading his blanket on the ground, Marsand smiled at Alexzana as he reflected, "Now, just like you I am an orphan without a people."

"I *so* love the smell of horses," answered simply the island girl snuggling into her blanket.

Puzzlement
The following day a guard stallion went to

investigate a new sighting of the decrepit looking brown wolf, seen once again on the left side of the unicorn procession. The stallion reported that before disappearing into bushes the lone wolf lingered long, all the while moving slightly up and down his head as if counting unicorns. The guard stallion was certain that the signs he found came from one wolf only.

The following morning the same thin brown wolf with an unkempt and burred hide again showed himself. When approached by two guard stallions the wolf vanished into underbrush, but on this occasion another wolf was seen loping away to the west.

"Why is that scruffy brown wolf trailing us?" worried Elianor. "And why is he today joined by another wolf?"

"The continued presence of that wolf does not strike me as coincidence," observed Aneilee. "The terrain roughens, Elianor. Through this unknown region we must chart carefully our course."

"I will send out five guard unicorns to scout ahead of us."

Upon return the scouts reported that distant bluffs marked where from west to east flowed a river that after turned southward.

"The unicorns are grown tired of dry vistas," neighed Elianor to Aneilee upon hearing the report. "It would be a welcome change to cross a river and feel cold water to refresh horse hide."

The approach to the river brought long descent through tree clad hills. From the height of low bluffs the unicorns looked down upon a waterway with the breadth of more than two hundred horse paces that did not look to be deeper than a grown horse's withers. Elianor and Aneilee watched as two wolves stepped into the water and began to paddle toward the far southern shore. Finding again the river bank, one wolf moved into the brush and was gone from sight. Upon seating himself, the scrawny brown wolf sighted on days previous began to again observe the unicorn herd.

"*Nyeerrhaaahh!* That wolf is truly intent on following us!"

"You are right, Elianor," answered the high escort. "But why would a skinny wolf follow us when by himself he can do us no harm?"

"Still, I do not like one bite to be pursued by even one untrustworthy animal person. Aneilee, we need to consider what that wolf is up to."

"On that I agree. But for now, Matriarch, please tell our herd to graze and rest... and to frolic if they are young-at-heart."

A Tiresome Wolf

"Hoovefort, Haltervor, what do you make of that brown wolf that plagues us?" inquired Elianor.

"It is but a lost wolf that can do us no harm," answered first Hoovefort as befit his higher rank.

"And your opinion, Sergeant?"

"I have been considering what purpose the lone wolf could have. If I were an enemy that for now remains invisible to us, I would want to determine to where the white herd was moving, how fast the pace, and the number of unicorns in the herd. Based on that intelligence I would then calculate where best might be carried out an ambush."

"Hmph!" neighed Hoovefort. "Sergeant Vor, can you really think that decrepit wolf is anything more than curious about a herd of strange animals trespassing his hunting ground?"

"I am no longer called Vor, Lieutenant. The name gave to me by Phoenician sailors is Haltervor. If as I believe that wolf is a scout, then his companion wolf could be dispatched as a messenger sent back to their leader with information regarding our whereabouts. Of course one or two wolves cannot do us harm. *If,* on the other hoof, in order to secure meat as scavengers the wolves converge on kills made by hordes of warriors, then we may be in danger from native tribes. I do know to be suspicious of a strange coincidence that day after day continues."

"Sergeant Haltervor," neighed Aneilee, "I find it odd that after crossing the river the one wolf disappeared into the brush while the other remained to watch us. In fact, the brown wolf still sits stone-like on the sand observing us."

"Dame Aneilee, if the lone wolf is providing intelligence on our movement, he appears to be reporting to an enemy force found on the southern side of the river. Along with other guard unicorns I yesterday scouted the bluffs that rise before us. I found that the river becomes a gorge that deepened as I followed it. Forward of the place we now approach, crossing the river will prove difficult for the mares and foals."

"As well difficult to cross for warriors and wolves?"

"No, High Escort. To our potential enemies the river remains passable."

"Lieutenant Hoovefort," neighed Aneilee. "I before wanted to here cross the river. But, that pesky brown wolf makes me think that we should proceed forward on the northern side."

"Since my guard stallions are swift, big, and strong not even a thousand wolves could do us great harm," responded the lieutenant. "Taking the south shore of the river would be conducive to warmer winter weather."

"Still, Lieutenant," continued Aneilee, "the more I think about the circumstances of this peculiar wolf, the more I want to err on the side of caution. Still, mind you, we really cannot know to which side of the river enemy wolves want us to go."

"*Nyreerrhrmhr!*" exclaimed Elianor. "Although it will disappoint our unicorn horses, we do not cross the river. By continuing travel on the northern side of the gorge I hope to lose the wolf spy."

"If I see him again, and I think that I might," added Haltervor, "my hooves will inflict a hard lesson to the hide of the scurvy wolf."

The guard lieutenant was not pleased at how his inferior had neighed so freely to the high escort and the matriarch, seemingly contradicting his authority.

"Back in Wittanor Hold," muttered Hoovefort, "Vor was my sidekick. Showing him too much attention and making him a halter, the Phoenician sailors ruined him. From here on I will have to closely watch my sergeant." Further resentful thoughts were interrupted by Elianor neighing his name.

"Wait, Hoovefort! I want you to right now organize a show of force by the adult stallions and mares. Put the fast unicorns first, and when they have galloped past the sight of the river wolf have them sneak back to rejoin the procession and close it out. Doing this can benefit us in two ways. The brown wolf will think our numbers are greater than we are, and prancing unicorn horses will themselves enjoy the show of force."

Following the display of force the well-watered, well-fed, and well-rested unicorn herd would resume march at daybreak.

Without Permission

Haltervor finished his watch well before the advent of new morning light. With no permission to so do, the unicorn sergeant was off to scout upriver.

"If I were a skinny wolf, where would I deploy to spy on the herd of unicorns?" Haltervor found the place he was searching for. "Right here is the perfect hidden spot for the conduct of illicit lupine surveillance." Haltervor sank himself down with his white hide camouflaged by the crisp tan colors presented by dry grass and prickles. He made certain that in that spot the wind carried toward him.

"Good enough," muttered the sergeant unicorn. "My scent will not betray my presence, and it will not be long before the white herd passes this way.

"I used to call the blackmaned colt *Thorny*. Huh! Now it is I that lie in a bed of thorns. As a former follower of Hoovefort, I used to bedevil the poor blackmane. But for some reason I find myself now missing him. It was wrong of me to belong to Hoovefort's gang of bullies that picked on Naythorn... just because he was different from other colts.

Considering it well, it would have cost me nothing to have been kind to the blackmane who cannot be as false as my former best friend Hoovefort has turned out to be. Hmph! Instead of being one more member of a gang of bullies, I could have been Naythorn's one and only friend." The thoughts of the sergeant unicorn turned back to his responsibilities.

"I truly hope that Lieutenant Hoovefort does not notice my absence without leave given. If outed, I will need to come up with an excuse that will sell. Failing that, I can expect to be marching a lot of extra guard duty as punishment. No matter what should ensue, at least I wear a fine halter of which I am very proud. I find that a loose halter is a comfortable thing for a horse to wear. I even imagine this halter makes my face to look... *distinguished.*"

When the morning sun was no more than five hooves high, a smart procession of white unicorns approached the grassy spot claimed by Haltervor. He turned his head slowly back to the bluff that to him offered camouflage. At that moment the long wait of the sergeant was rewarded by the sight of the decrepit looking brown wolf slinking toward the height of the river bluff. The wolf settled low into the grass. With no reason to tarry longer, the guard stallion charged a startled wolf unprepared to be run over by horse hooves. Shoveling under the body of the brown wolf, Haltervor's horn deftly propelled the lupine high in the air. The sergeant wheeled hooves in chase of the frightened wolf.

At that moment all the regrounded wolf knew to do was to scamper as fast as he could away from the charging horned beast. In consequence, the wolf was soon bearing down on the white herd. Too late the wolf realized that with a big charging stallion behind, and a wall of unicorn horses to his front, his position was precarious.

Unprepared to see Haltervor chase a wolf into their midst, the resultant confusion of unicorn legs and tails worked to the lupine's advantage. As the wolf dodged and turned this way and that unicorn necks craned, legs kicked out, and tails swished wildly. Haltervor braked hard his hooves in order to not crash into mares and foals. Then as fast as he had come into view, the brown wolf melted into bushes and scrub trees found on the other side of the unicorn procession.

"*Nyeeerrrr!* Sergeant Vor!" Lieutenant Hoovefort was livid. "What in blazes just happened? What were you doing out here? And where were you this morning when I looked for you? You used to be my closest friend and now you act... *crazy!*"

While Hoovefort continued to stomp and harangue, Haltervor lowered his head. Aneilee and Elianor joined the circle of curious unicorns that had gathered around the two guard stallions.

"Lieutenant, if you would let me explain..." To be satisfactorily understood by the lieutenant, Elianor, Aneilee, and bystander unicorns the explanation of Haltervor was three times repeated.

"You expect me to believe you somehow knew that same ragged wolf would be found hiding in exactly this spot and at exactly this time?"

"Lieutenant, it made horse sense to me. I tried to

think like a wolf set upon a spy mission. Rather than harm him, I only wanted to scare the dickens out of him. I surely did not know he would scamper under the legs of herd unicorns."

"Errm, Lieutenant," as she neighed Aneilee could not longer hide her smile, "the wolf did no harm other than to startle some in our ranks and cause them to land kicks on other unicorns, rather than on the intruder, as should have been done. From this frightened wolf we have learned something. We now know that we are by wolves being spied upon. We have also learned that our unicorn herd needs to be better prepared for when happens the unexpected."

"As for me," interjected Elianor, "I am appalled that our herd could not stop one pathetic wolf from raising havoc. I also disapprove of the fact that without permission a guard unicorn ventured out here last night. Haltervor placed himself in a vulnerable position. I do not want any unicorn stallion to unnecessarily risk his life in these unknown plains and hills. I trust that Haltervor will not again let that to happen."

Turning to the lieutenant of the unicorn guards, Elianor added, "Hoovefort, if there is a communication problem between you and your company of guard stallions, I want it right away solved."

"Thank you for the intelligence you today provided," neighed Aneilee nudging a shoulder against Haltervor. "You confirmed the brown wolf to be a spy. Because of your unpermissioned action we now know with surety that the movement of the white herd is being watched."

Hoovefort stomped off with his sergeant following

behind. As he walked after his lieutenant it seemed to curious onlookers that the sergeant's tail was arched up a little higher than it had to be.

"Leading a herd of five hundred unicorns across an unknown land turns out to be more complicated than I had imagined," neighed that evening the matriarch to Aneilee.

"You and I, Elianor, have from bitter experience learned that the purity and innocence of unicorn horses can attract a leviathan, death whales, sharks, and enemy warriors paddling war canoes. We have to recognize that no longer protected by the shelter of Wittanor Hold, or by Phoenician sailors, the white herd is very vulnerable. In that regard Haltervor was right to be concerned about the spy wolf. Hmph, Elianor, do you see grave trouble ahead for the white herd?"

"The high escort can herself best answer that question."

"Of one future thing I *am* convinced. The blackmane is destined to find and rejoin our herd. Naythorn will someday bring to our herd a kind of leadership that is new and vital."

"I wish that I could but glimpse the adventures of the blackmane as he makes his way toward where travels the white herd."

"Something tells me, Elianor, that since the day Phoenician barges sailed away without the misfit blackmane on board, his adventures have been many. I am convinced that Naythorn has learned much about himself, and that from us he is no longer so far removed."

CHAPTER 13

REUNION

Blown by a unicorn-made wind to splash down in a river, and made exhausted by a long upward climb out of a deep gorge, the trio decided to not worry about anything. After three days of grazing and food gathering Buckmight, Lucars, and Belfloralex made ready to recommence travel. A new morning found them motivated to find Naythorn.

"Looking at the great height we surmounted," brayed the bison, "I ask, Belfloralex, could you not have made the wind to blow the cloak tied to my armor all the way to this high rim of the gorge?"

"That, Master Bison, would have been too easy. You completed a climb that you will long remember, and be proud of."

"At least it is a cool morning," encouraged Lucars. "Let us drink one last time from this pleasant and comforting streamlet."

"I find myself ready to run very fast to refind Naythorn," brayed the bison.

Thinking that she could run twice as fast as the bison, the unicorn filly barely managed to stifle a laugh as she responded, "Errm, yes Buckmight, you are most built for speed."

"Well at that," continued Lucars, "I can say that I am

glad to not hear the groaning of Hammerclaw, or that of his companion Taurington, about our commitment to run fast and hard. If Sir Cattle were now found to be with us, he would insist on remaining here to savor the pleasantness of this place on the bank of a very impressive gorge." Travel commenced.

"Here, Belfloralex, is as far as I this day go," brayed Buckmight.

"But Bison, we have not gone far at all today," responded the filly.

"Yes I know, and for that there remains time for a bison to graze to his heart's content."

Twilight deepened into starlight. For the fulfillment of a day of travel meaningfully recommenced toward the blackmaned unicorn, Buckmight and Lucars began to recount remembrances of those remaining behind.

"I can tell you, Belfloralex, that the arms that stretch out from Hammer's shoulders are incredibly strong," said Lucars. "I have never seen a man with wrists more muscled than the smithy."

"The cattle has also huge shoulders," added the bison nodding his head in agreement. "You know, I found Taurington to be a very stubborn and difficult cattle. On the day we first met I gave my all to best him, and I could not. The worst thing was that no matter how hard I bruised his head, Sir Cattle refused to give up."

"Would that I had come to better know the smithy and the cattle," offered Belfloralex.

"Pretty filly, it is indeed too bad that you were not given more time to spend with them. Had that happened, I know that you would have come to count both Hammer and Taurington as the truest of friends."

"Of that, Master Bison, I am sure."

"Speaking of shoulders," continued Lucars, "I have never seen a horse more powerfully built than the blackmane. From neck to hips his lines bespeak strength."

"I would not want to take on the blackmane in an all-out fight," brayed Buckmight shaking back-and-forth his head. "The problem with a match against Naythorn is that he marries remarkable strength and quickness to perserverance and craftiness of mind. He will never relent in a fight, and he never repeats his blows, but instead lands new manners of stomps and thrusts.

"Hah! Let me tell Lucars and Belfloralex how works the mind of Naythorn. Fighting before a valley of tall trees from a position that we could not long defend, we once faced overwhelming odds. With much reluctance I told Naythorn that in order to save his band he must flee through the enemy line, and take after him into the desert the biggest wolves. Although the blackmane did not want to run away from the battle, he saw my point. Now I was convinced that the fleet and strong Naythorn would make good his passage through one hundred fierce wolves. What I did not imagine was that in the process Naythorn would lull Albarochk to drop his guard, and then manage to horribly wound the left shoulder of the monster wolf. To this day the wolf general still limps from the wound that day given to him by the fleeing Naythorn."

"Now that I think about it," reflected Lucars, "having more than once tasted unicorn blood, Albarochk's wounds can be expected to readily heal. That is, except for the shoulder wound he received from Naythorn. I wonder why that wound persists unhealed." No one volunteered answer to the young man's question.

The flames of the campfire ebbed. Belfloralex rose to take the first shift at guard. As she surveyed the sleeping landscape the filly decided it had been remiss to not have talked even more that night about the courageous Blackmane. As a filly in Wittanor Hold, she remembered well the misfit unicorn. Like other unicorns younger than Naythorn, she had teased him about his black mane, but only on two or three occasions. She now regretted having done even that, and hoped that when she next saw Naythorn he would have no recollection of her unkind teasing.

"What little filly in Wittanor was not a few times naughty?" muttered Belfloralex. "I am sure that Naythorn and I will come to be good friends."

Refinding Naythorn Blackmane

After having scaled countless rock ledges in the climb out of the deep river gorge, the previous day's trek that twisted through low hills could be said to have been, almost fun. An enormous grassy basin spread wide before Buckmight, Belfloralex, and Lucars. While on its far western edge raised a high and long mountain that slanted northward, lines of hills marked both the eastern and northern edges of the broad basin. Far to the north and west could be seen towering mountains with crowded peaks whitened by snow.

"The crispness of this new morning crowned by majestic mountain vistas, suits perfectly a bison's travel."

"But Buckmight," inquired the young warrior, "because many suns have come and gone since the *Battle before the Deep Gorge*, where are we now to find the blackmane?"

"Lucars, you and I both know that Naythorn wills himself northward. Now it seems to me that when crossing open plains, the five wild boars that go with our captain would be particularly vulnerable to attack. Even the mountain sheep and dogs would be hard-pressed to escape a wolf-surround invoked on flat land. Because wolves pursue best the hunt in valleys and plains, to avoid them as he travels toward the fixed star, Naythorn will take to the mountains."

"At the place of our last battle we saw a tall and very jagged mountain that faraway loomed on our left side," recounted Lucars. "Directly across the gorge we observed a second very long mountain fingering upward toward the north. During our escape to the east we passed the peaks of a third long mountain that as well leaned northward. From this spot we can see to our left the heights of that third range that now stands the closest to us."

Lucars began to mark the ground with the point of his sword.

"This spot denotes where we now sit. These wide-swathed lines represent the three separate long mountains that to our west finger northward. These two squiggled lines represent the hills seen on our right and directly to our north. The wide east-west line scratched at the top left of this crude map marks the snow covered peaks of what I will call a range of blocking mountains.

"From the way the peaks of the three finger mountains stretch away in pattern consistent with each other, I can guess that they will together spill down into a great valley. Because the three north-south mountains cannot penetrate, but must end before the blocking mountain range, I am sure a valley providing closure to the three parallel ranges, must there be found."

Lucars held up his open left hand with three fingers extended, and the thumb and little finger folded back.

"It is as if the three mountain fingers that stretch north are anchored by the folded-back thumb of the snow-tipped peaks that we see far beyond this great basin. Since travelers in these parts are by the flow of mountains and valleys drawn northward, the place to find and reconnect ourselves with our band is where *end...* the three mountains. That said, our best chance to find Naythorn is to follow northward the proximate finger range."

"So then, Lucars," clarified Belfloralex, "because it is too dangerous for Naythorn to stop and wait for the return of the missing members of his band, he will follow one of the three mountain fingers northward to keep distance between himself and the monster wolf."

"And that means that if we were to follow the deep gorge toward the afternoon sun, we would only find where Blackmane... *had been,*" brayed Buckmight. "We would eventually find where the unicorn had crossed the gorge, but not find where he now moves."

"That is so," replied Lucars. "Our captain *will not* halt his advance toward the fixed star."

"Then it seems to me," mrawed the bison, "that we should take a path across the heart of the basin in front of us. Once the plain is crossed, we can climb up the first finger range of mountains and there find protection from wolves as we continue our travel northward."

"The sky begins to darken with clouds that look to carry rain or snow," observed Buckmight glancing upward. "Hmph! Thinking too much, tires me out. Lucars, Belfloralex, let us forage here the remainder of this day that promises to bring a storm. Then early tomorrow we will venture into the wide basin."

"To that I will *gladly* agree," replied the youth cheerily. "Having now a plan, and knowing that soon enough we will be reunited with Naythorn Blackmane, I am going to rest, eat, and then rest again."

Hostages

Beneath a sky sown in silky gray clouds the morning breeze exhaled sweet freshness. Travel into the grassy basin became an easy walk through low descending hills... until a commotion arose. Along the near edge of the basin natives ran fast toward the river gorge.

"We have no trees or ravines for cover," mrawed the bison. "They will see us."

"No they will not," rejoined Belfloralex.

The unicorn filly reared front hooves high, scratched them against her horn, and so made sparks to fly. The effect was immediate. A whirlwind began to kick up dust on all sides of them. The unicorn had commanded a small wind to envelop them.

"The fast-running natives cannot see us," assured the filly. "From out of this whirlwind we can see them, but their eyes cannot penetrate my wind magic. And they cannot hear us."

"Well, I am... *astonished!*" exclaimed Lucars.

"Me more!" mrawed the bison.

"The natives move as if they are scared; each one with thought only for his or her own flight," observed Lucars.

"They rush to find protection in the difficult to reach cliffs of the river gorge," added Belfloralex. "Natives in flight can readily disappear into the recesses and caves poking the walls of that huge chasm."

"That is so," assented Buckmight. "But of what are they afraid?"

"We may not like those that pursue after the fleeing natives," cautioned Lucars. It did not take long to find who it was that came after in pursuit.

"The adornment of black raven feathers on their chests and shoulders make those warriors look darkly ferocious," asserted Buckmight.

"Their number is seventy or eighty," calculated Lucars.

"That makes a lot of Raven warriors," offered the filly.

"*What? Look!*" exclaimed the bison. "At the end of the warrior column! The Raven warriors bring three prisoners, two women and a young brave. Why do they drag three hostages along with them?"

"Those three were surely captured in a raid," answered Lucars. "I hate to see women pulled along by their hair, and it is cruel to kick a young brave made defenseless with hands tied. Now it stands to reason that the natives we saw in flight escaped the raid. The raiders intend to use the three hostages to later negotiate for even more hostages, or else to provoke the losers to show themselves from their hiding places in a soon fight to reclaim the three prisoners."

"So then," brayed Buckmight, "we can presume the hostages are important members of the defeated tribe. I do not know what the two of you think, or how you see this situation, but a few seeds of Naythorn's philosophy to protect the helpless have been sown into my hide. Lucars, Belfloralex, help me wrest those hostages away from their captors. In that regard, I could on my back carry away both the young warrior prisoner and Lucars."

"And the two women prisoners can both fit on my back," neighed Belfloralex nodding her head in agreement. "I can carry them until we have placed a good distance between ourselves and the warrior band. Breaking into the plain, two big four-legged animal persons can surely outrun the Raven captors."

"I am... *agreed,*" answered Lucars with resolve sounding in his voice. "This protective whirl of wind allows us to observe closely the hatred that consumes the faces of the captors, and that makes it impossible for us to not have sympathy for the plight of the hostages. Just consider one thing. Most times there is a price to pay for doing good to another. A kindness is seldom rendered without exacting a cost to the giver. This rescue will likely create another enemy for our band."

"This bison comprehends full well your concern, Lucars. But I do not much care if we come to count another enemy that hates us. There are already so many wolves and warriors set against us, that one more angry chieftain is just another name added to a long list of adversaries. Still, let us make effort to not kill or maim the raiders. Having no casualties to report from the skirmish we are about to author, Raven warriors will save face."

The swirling cone of wind lifted to show a bison and mounted warrior, both clad in shining armor, and a half horned unicorn running full speed at warriors found at the very end of the Raven column. Swinging his great head to knock aside a half dozen startled warriors, Buckmight was the first to enter the fray.

After jumping off the back of the bison the first thing Lucars did was to sever the binding at the wrists of the young brave. The youth immediately grabbed a discarded Raven sword and proceeded to defend himself.

The first thing Belfloralex did was to touch her half horn to the head of the hostage girl and so give her the gift of uniform speech. The second thing the filly did was to order the girl to jump onto her back. That was no sooner said than by the native girl done.

The second thing Lucars did was to grab the waist of the startled captive woman and place her behind the girl on the filly's back.

The third thing Belfloralex did was to promptly charge off into the plain. The unicorn filly felt herself very grown-up to be carrying on her back not one, but two riders.

After jumping on the back of the bison, the third thing that Lucars did was to pull the young hostage brave up behind himself onto Buckmight's sturdy back. That accomplished, the bison raced after the unicorn filly.

Warriors rushed back to see what had caused fighting to erupt at the end of their column. Spears and arrows were sent flying toward Buckmight and his two riders.

Hanging tight to neck armor, Lucars slid his body down on Buckmight's side to make of himself as small a target as he could. The just-rescued young brave locked a knee to Lucar's leg, grabbed hold of Lucar's armor, and slid to also protect himself against the side of Buckmight. Although every spear point missed its target, a plenteous number of arrow points bounced off the bison's armor plate. Once out of danger's way, Belfloralex slowed her pace allowing Buckmight to catch up.

"Ha-hah! We pulled it off!" exclaimed Lucars. "You both were magnificent back there. Buckmight, I have never seen you to move so fast, and Belfloralex ran even faster. We made successful the escape of the hostages, and not one warrior was gravely hurt. The gentleness of our attack must be reckoned to our benefit."

After proceeding two leagues into the plain the riders jumped off to allow the unicorn filly and bovine to recover breath and strength. Soon six escapees, for three native hostages and three rescuers had all eluded capture, trotted together in silence.

The Eagle Feather Tribe

"The sky darkens more. We have come far, and for that my legs tire," brayed Buckmight. "I would welcome a rest."

"We all would," agreed Belfloralex.

"My name is Amaluna. My mother is Shawnee and my brother is Scarlet Point." The native maiden with penetrating eyes, delicate forehead, cheeks smudged in dirt, and long tangled dark hair continued, "Before he was killed in the raid, my father was the chief of our clan. Because my grandfather is the big chief of our tribe, we three were taken as valuable hostages."

"Is the big chief the father of your..." began Lucars.

"He is my mother's father," clarified Scarlet Point. "The people fleeing ahead of our enemies were the ones that survived the raid. They know where hard to reach places in the wall of the river gorge can hide them."

"It offended us to see you three treated so brutally by your captors," offered Buckmight.

"For my mother the loss of her husband is devastating. For myself and Scarlet Point the loss of our father is tragic." Showing trust in the unicorn, the young girl leaned against the side of the resting Belfloralex.

"This defeat at the hands of the Raven Tribe is for our people shameful," continued Scarlet Point. "Just like eagles hate ravens that destroy their nests, so does the Eagle Feather Tribe hate Raven warriors that kill our children and destroy our lodges."

"The dwellings of our clan were totally demolished," added Amaluna. "But because the remaining lodges of the Eagle Feather Tribe stand strong, we must find where leads my grandfather the main body of our people. With this enemy Grandfather had hoped to find a way to dwell in peace. Now with the destruction of our village and the death of my father the opportunity for peace, like grass covered by falling snow, has vanished."

"My heart aches for the loss of my husband," said Shawnee softly. "But for now I need to rest, so that I can tomorrow be strong for my children." To be sure, the idea of rest sounded good to the other five gathered on a dark night in a bouldered place. Until the sun stretched out welcome arms of warmth and light, Lucars stood guard.

The push of travel was the next morning less strenuous. Amidst shrubs that crawled about a small spring a unicorn filly, a bison, and four human persons paused to rest at midday.

Upon rousing themselves to complete the last five leagues of their trek across the basin, the six member squad was startled to notice in the distance a warrior column following their trail. Lucars jumped onto the bison, stood upright, and studied the movement of the warriors.

"We are far enough ahead to gain the protection of the mountain before the pursuing warriors can waylay us." The young Phoenician shaded his eyes with a hand and added, "Huh! What is this I see? The Raven warriors turn from pursuing us. Hmph! There is another visitor to this plain... no... there are two of them. Like us, the intruders entered the valley from the east. How about that! The warriors are more interested in the two newcomers than they are in us!"

"Can the two new arrivals flee back to the gorge?" asked Belfloralex.

"Having not enough time to outrun the warriors,

they do not turn back," answered Lucars.

"I do *not* like the looks of this," fumed Buckmight. "Who can the interlopers be?"

"I also have a bad feeling about what is to happen next," seconded Scarlet Point.

"There is something strange about the way the intruders move," continued Lucars.

"My half horn tells me that we have to rescue them."

"All right, Belfloralex," responded the bison, "but not all of us. While Lucars and I attempt a mission of rescue, you are to lead our three friends into the cliffs ahead. You must help Scarlet Point to there protect his family."

Bending her neck toward her side, Belfloralex began to twirl fast her body. For that, a strong current of wind shot out from her hooves to hasten the bison's gallop toward warriors now in pursuit of two new victims.

"Run faster, Buckmight!" exclaimed Lucars pointing his sword. "The warriors are about to catch the intruders. Look! The armor of Hammerclaw flashes in the sunlight! I would know that armor anywhere!"

"And our cattle bull is with Hammer! Ready yourself, Lucars, to see more bison kicking and horn slashing."

Head lowered, and horns thrashing from side to side, the bison smashed warrior arms and legs while the whirling sword of Lucars drew blood. The men ornamented in raven feathers were obliged to give way, and the bison and his mount achieved the place where Hammer and Taurington were besieged. Confronted by the two stalwart reinforcements, the clutch of warriors around Taurington and Hammer hesitated their attack, and so permitted an interchange of greetings by the bovines and blacksmiths.

"By heavens am I glad to see again my apprentice!"

"But, Hammer, I cannot believe you are returned!"

"This blacksmith's duty will ever after be to Naythorn Blackmane."

"Your eyes do not deceive you, Buckmight!" continued Hammer. "You and this cattle shall again walk in front of the blackmane's platoon!"

War cries resounded and the passion of battle rekindled. Unlike the first skirmish for three hostages that left unscathed the Raven raiders, this time the bison's fighting tactics did mortal damage. Buckmight threw himself forward twisting his armored back to angle kicks deeply into crowded adversaries. Impressed by this maneuver, Taurington amplified it. When Buckmight stepped back to again launch himself, the cattle propped his great back against that of his friend. Using the power of his back and hips, Taurington propelled Buckmight deeper into the enemy. Grasping immediately the tactic of Taurington, the bison returned the favor timing perfectly his push against the cattle's back so that it coincided with the moment of Taurington's outward launch.

Hammer and Lucars brandished their swords in defense of themselves and the rear quarters of the bovines. As the fray became more bloody, the resolve of the Raven warriors finally lessened. They feigned charges, and then without risking loss of life or limb, quickly withdrew. However, the sturdy braves would not unblock passage toward Belfloralex and her three companions.

"I grow tired of this conflict," brayed the bison. "If we take the path of least resistance toward the hills at the top of this basin, we can outrun our enemies and then circle back to regain Belfloralex and our new friends."

"What new friends?" asked Taurington.

"Three hostages that we yesterday freed from this same column of warriors."

"Well, Buckmight, *of course* that is so," mrawed Taurington. A bison and cattle, mounted by two Phoenician blacksmiths, sped away from angry and incensed Raven warriors.

At the break of dawn, as he cast his eyes toward the skirts of the enormous mountain before him, Buckmight saw a white unicorn filly rearing in greeting.

After a joyful time of introductions and reunion, Amaluna proved to be talkative. Slowly, but surely, her questions came to focus on the Phoenician youth.

"Is not your golden armor heavy? It must slow you down so that you cannot run very fast."

"You know, Amaluna, the magic blue gold is so light to wear that I swear it hardly slows me at all."

"I hope that someday I might come to wear armor so beautiful as yours," said the girl tracing fingers over the chest plate of Lucars.

"With the hands and eyes of a great workman, Master Hammer fashioned the metal so that it well-hugs my body, and at the same time does not interfere with the movement of my arms or legs. When he works at his forge my sergeant transforms into both a master metal worker, and a subtle artist."

"But Lucars," interjected the smithy, "since my recent

release from the army, I can no longer claim to be your sergeant."

"You will always be my superior officer, but now first in friendship. By the way, Master Hammer, was your discharge officially authorized?"

"I will ever insist that it was."

Shawnee had a question for the master smithy.

"The wife I once had is forever departed from me," answered Hammer. "Without children I am a man alone and all by myself. Hah! However, given his high opinion of me, I am thinking to adopt this young Lucars." At Hammer's answer Shawnee smiled shyly.

Noting the native youth's interest, Lucars handed his sword over for inspection. Scarlet Point promptly began a sword fight with an invisible adversary. Upon observing the youth's keen interest in wielding a beautiful sword made of blue gold, Hammer challenged Scarlet Point to a good-natured contest with sharp blades. The boy's beaming smile was Hammer's reward for losing at sword play, where of course he could have won.

"To these two men I will know only loyalty," declared Scarlet Point to his mother.

"For my part," offered Amaluna turning to her brother, "I will show equal loyalty to Buckmight, Lucars, and a pure white unicorn filly whose magic dance made a whirlwind to blow."

The vast mountain now claimed by two bovines, two Phoenicians, and three natives provided food, forage, water, and positions of defense where a handful of fighters could deny passage to twenty times their number advancing upward through rocks and boulders, or attempting to penetrate a narrow ravine.

Buckmight, Taurington, Hammer, and Lucars felt sure that Naythorn traveled northward along the crest of one of the two high mountain fingers to their west, and that the blackmane would be refound at the place where ended the three parallel mountains.

Belfloralex could not stop wondering in what place Naythorn's little foal was learning to run, and perhaps as well to fly. The half-horned filly felt in her heart, actually her heart knew full-well, that both the blackmaned unicorn and his foal lived on.

CHAPTER 14

A FOAL INTO MOUNTAINS

Cabalblade was thankful that from the rim of a deep gorge he had rescued his grandfoal, that she possessed surprising wings, and that the presence of the foal meant that the blackmaned colt he searched for was somewhere not so far away.

Because the grandsire unicorn could not risk that a vulnerable foal should travel through wide plains infested with wolves, he had immediately led into the mountain. Once she knew where exactly the big unicorn stallion wanted for her to climb the foal made sure, if not on her first try then on her second or third, to reach the next designated spot. The captain of the unicorn guards gave the foal credit for being plucky.

Cabalblade had worried that the foal much required sustenance. Lacking her mother's milk, whenever and wherever the chance availed the foal bit off grass headed out in grain, and nibbled on certain select colorfully petaled flowers. Knowing the nectar of flowers could not replace a mare's milk, Cabalblade decided it was his duty to substitute a grandsire's love for that of the mare that the little one so lacked.

On any given day he neighed to the foal twenty times more than he had neighed to Naythorn after he was newly born. During the course of one day he neighed more to the foal than he in a month spoke to the entire company of unicorn guards under his command. But that was not a fair comparison to make, for all he had to do was nod his head or look hard at a guard stallion to be immediately understood and obeyed. Cabalblade smiled at the thought that he had never before minded, not even a little, that he was more feared than loved.

"Little one, do you truly understand what I neigh to you?" asked Cabalblade one afternoon.

Swallowing her mouthful of purple and blue flower petals, with the shake of her head she responded... *yes.* The grandsire was amazed that one so young could already, after a manner of speaking, converse with an adult stallion.

There could be no argument with the idea that the foal was indeed bent on growing fast, for with every passing day she grew enough to horn-scratch a higher height mark on a tree trunk. Each day she stretched wingtips further out from her back.

Since the stallion had never before seen a foal with two appendages grown from her back, he was fascinated by how the foal extended, fluttered, and folded her wings. While the stallion swished bothersome flies with tail only, the foal fly-swished with a tail and two wings. Finding them to be softer than any horse coat, Cabalblade liked to nuzzle the little foal's wings, whose white feather covering seemed to thicken more from one day to the next.

In the passage of not so many suns the little one had transformed from newborn to independent foal.

Wherever led Cabalblade, her objective was to clamber hooves in front of him. The springs in her legs had more coil than the stallion had ever before seen in any foal or colt so young. She crouched down, and then from a still position leaped hooves higher than she held her head when standing. She would then decide to leap and jump even higher.

Her manner was so natural and confident that the guardian stallion began to scarcely worry about danger confronting them, or an enemy attacking them. However like a thin layer of snow on the sunny side of a rock, too soon freedom from worry melted away. A black panther came to stalk the grandsire stallion and the winged foal.

Cabalblade hated panthers. In all his years with the unicorn guards no mountain lion had ever trespassed into Wittanor Hold, but the same could not be said of panthers. It was as if a lion could somehow sense the magic invested in the white herd, but a panther could not. Or, more likely, panthers chose to simply ignore the presence of unicorn magic.

Upon sighting the panther a memory returned to haunt Cabalblade. The stallion told himself that had the attack not happened in his first moon of duty as a novice unicorn guard, his hide would not have been deeply scratched and torn by the big black cat's sharp claws.

As he watched the big panther slink through rocks and trees, the heart of the unicorn stallion pounded. However, this time he would not fear the panther. He would never allow a black panther to attack his grandfoal. A sudden thought occurred to Cabalblade.

Perhaps the fright and fear so long ago felt from the attack made upon him by a black panther, had contributed to his disdain for the black mane worn by Naythorn.

With knees locked as he stood guard that night over the foal, the grandsire unicorn did not once permit his eyes to rest.

Yellow Wolf and Great Lion

Instead of a black panther, a wolf with a dingy yellow hide followed the next day the trail made by a unicorn stallion and his grandfoal.

"Oh well, better a wolf than a black panther," muttered the captain of the unicorn guard stallions. Cabalblade knew he could well-handle any wolf, even a very big one. However, when seen openly on a rock ledge they had passed only two hundred horse breaths earlier, the wolf was confirmed to not only have a drab coat, but to be abnormally small.

As the wolf slowly but surely drew closer, Cabalblade observed something unusual in his demeanor. It was not only that the yellow wolf wore a deeply scarred face that made his visage to appear crooked, his eyes shone with intelligence. Strangely enough, the bent and crooked face looked to entrance a mind made to think deep thoughts.

"I had considered that intelligence was supposed to look attractive and appealing, but it seems that may not always be so. Smart or not, I can at the same time confront ten wolves like that one, and lick them all."

After staring briefly at the yellow wolf, the foal took to nipping the sides of her grandsire. About the dingy wolf she was blissfully unconcerned.

That night one big and one little unicorn found an opening into rocks where they slept against each other, with Cabalblade's ears twitching at every sound by darkness registered.

Finding himself the following morning to be in particularly good spirits, Cabalblade told the foal that it was a grand day for her to be scrambling about on a mountain. Unfortunately, that afternoon found the tawdry wolf trotting in front of the stallion, as if in his wolfly arrogance he had appointed himself to lead onward the two unicorns. Cabalblade was affronted by the cavalier attitude of the wolf that without any excuse, or much less invitation, had imposed himself in the way of an equine path.

Through and around rocks, trees, and cliffs two sets of hooves pushed higher into the mountain. After the night air grew chilled, in a rocky recess the grandsire and grandfoal again warmed sides against each other. The presentation of new morning, patented off the previous day's success of plenteous sunshine, found the foal beginning to dominate her wings. In advance of Cabalblade's hooves she was by midafternoon half trotting and half flying.

The wolf compounded his insolence by inviting a mountain lion to join his travel. The curious pair of half sized wolf and oversized lion plodded nonchalantly ahead of Cabalblade, who now felt truly offended at the presence of the uninvited guests.

"What in tarnation is that mismatched pair of wolf and lion up to?" neighed the grandsire to the foal. "No matter if there were ten wolves and lions confronting me, this unicorn stallion will not back off a trail which I feel to be owned by myself alone."

The path of the old and young unicorns reached a Y-juncture. Between two paths that each continued forward, a needle formation of slender rocks raised fifty horse paces upward. The wolf and lion chose to follow the left arm of the juncture. For that very reason Cabalblade chose to take the right arm of the path that divided in twain.

"Maybe we can now leave behind that dirty hided wolf and his big lion partner, *for good!*" neighed the stallion to the foal. It was not so to be. When the right arm of the divided path proved to be impassable, the mood of Cabalblade turned sour.

Upon returning to the juncture in the trail the grandsire unicorn found the wolf and lion seated in wait for him. The stallion made up his mind to once and for all have it out with the strange pair.

"Away from my mountain!" ordered Cabalblade with all the forcefulness his neigh could muster. "That you two follow my trail *angers* me! Get you gone away from here!"

"Lianvil and Danseyclono, mind you those are our names, do not follow but rather lead," answered calmly the wolf.

The stallion had counted on the angry tone of his neigh to instill fear into the wolf and lion; he had not counted on their precise comprehension of his neighed words.

"We mean you no harm," barked more the wolf. "We

happen to be friends, albeit unusual sorts of friends, of your colt Naythorn. Believe it or not the blackmane has quite a number of friends that are exceptional. Take for example a bison and a cattle."

Upon hearing this, Cabalblade jumped and shook his head *no*. For a stallion that had bordered his whole life by the cut and dried discipline of the elite unicorn guards, news of such strange friendships was shocking to hear, let alone to comprehend.

"*Grrrarr!* You... and the foal... are in danger," growled Lianvil picking his words slowly. "The valleys on each side of this mountain fill with enemy wolves and warriors. Should they discover that you and the winged foal are here, and alone, upon you they will fall."

"You do understand that this great lion and I make sure that no enemy obstructs your path," continued Danseyelono. "Might I add that in that regard you surely have noticed that a certain black panther no longer follows you."

"If what you say is so, how did you know to find us on this high mountain?"

"Hmph! I was waiting to hear a thank you to the lion for making the panther to leave off your trail," responded the wolf. "It was Lianvil and I that devised the plan that ended the *Battle before the Deep Gorge*, and so permitted Naythorn and his band to escape. In that battle this lion and I managed to smash the mouth of the monster wolf Albarochk."

"The wolf general found that with a broken mouth it became no longer convenient for him to inflict orders on his inferiors," added the lion.

"*Nyeeerrrr!* I heard the noise of that battle, and saw the sky to light up. Out of colored light flew this foal to land on the rim of the gorge."

"Yes, that is exactly so," affirmed Danseyelono. "After the battle and the death of the foal's mare, with the purpose of reaching the winged foal before did wolves, we two ran off as hard and fast as we could. It took some time but we finally found a way down, managed the dangerous descent to the bottom of the great gorge, completed the difficult crossing of a swift current, and without injury climbed out of the gorge. However when we came to the place where the foal was supposed to be, she was not there, but along with her's, your scent was there about.

"We at last found you leading the foal up the slopes of the mountain. After carefully studying you to be sure of your intentions, it became clear to us that you were the foal's grandsire.

"At the Y-juncture where you on purpose took what anyone could tell was a path that led to a dead-end, you tried to leave us behind. That proved to be the worst idea you have had since we spotted you."

"The time came for us to reveal ourselves as friends of Naythorn," interjected Lianvil.

"One thing more," yipped the yellow wolf. "You need to be aware that the warriors and wolves that Lianvil spoke of are gathering for a great battle to come. The wolf general brings new columns of wolves and warriors for the final showdown with Naythorn. If he is to prevail, the blackmane will need to count on every one of us. So, in sum, we lead you and the foal forward to reunite with your courageous blackmaned colt in his time of need."

"While I still cannot comprehend all that you tell me, I have no choice but to accept that you speak the truth. Otherwise you could not know these things. So for now it is up to this stallion to follow, and for you to lead on."

The lion and wolf comprised a consummate advance team with the lion taking an approach to trail blazing that was cautious and methodical, while the wolf's approach was more creative. Together they solved problems of where to, and where not to climb, so that Cabalblade and the foal had only to follow the least difficult route identified for them.

It was not long before the lion, wolf, unicorn stallion, and foal found themselves traversing a difficult place where cliffs plummeted downward, that after opened to the highest part of the huge mountain. While the three grown animals carefully tested each footing, the foal made her wings to lighten her hooves so that she walked the treacherous trail as gingerly as would a butterfly that in addition to wings, possessed durable legs. Drawn close to the high apex, the spine of the mountain narrowed. The wolf cautioned the stallion and foal to try not to show themselves visible, for the scouts in the valleys on both sides of the mountain could clearly observe the rocky high point where sprouted no trees for cover.

With the ascent completed, Cabalblade crouched down his legs and relaxed to enjoy spectacular views. To the west a long file of warriors, who from his high vantage point individually looked to be the size of small spiders, was moving northward. Wolves trod the perimeter of the column of human persons. Upon finding that the valley floor on the other side of the mountain displayed a similar formation of warriors and wolves, the unicorn muttered, "Truly we are surrounded."

"I see that too, grandsire," answered the precocious foal with a tone delicate. "And we must thank our escorts for warning us of the danger present."

Upon overhearing the foal's response, Danseyelono smiled and thought to himself that as well as possessing a gift of extraordinary natural beauty, the foal was a creature intelligent and gracious.

The next morning found the crest of the mountain broadened with flat parts that upon the great height spread wide.

Red Intruder Wolf

As the sun progressed more westward, with suddenness northward travel was interrupted by the appearance of a trespasser upon the mountain. Lianvil cornered the half size red wolf and herded him to Cabalblade and Danseyelono. After sending the foal off to graze, the unicorn touched his horn to the wolf's head. The nervous wolf was astonished to find that by horn sparks he had received the gift of uniform animal words.

"Ouch... that hurt! But really... *only a little.* Yikes! I hear myself to talk a new tongue! I can actually speak to a horned horse... and a lion. I will right away assure you that I am an innocent wanderer upon this high place... and that is all I am... and nothing more than that."

Danseyelono sat his rump down before the red wolf and looked him square in the eyes, which since the interloper wolf was equally small was practical and convenient to do. "So then red wolf... you must be... hunting rabbits?"

"Exactly so!" came too quickly the reply.

"Because the rabbits on this mountain are skinny, devious, and very well hidden that is quite unprofitable for you," responded Danseyelono tilting quizzically his head.

"Yes, of course the yellow wolf is right about that. If I had brought another wolf to hunt with me as a team, I would not now be half starving."

"How many lone wolves in these parts hunt in very high places bereft of game, while at the same time dangling a leather pouch at their neck?" The interloper wolf glanced downward at the purse that he wore.

"Now that the yellow wolf points that out, I doubt that many so do."

Danseyelono grabbed with his teeth, yanked, and broke the thin strap of the pouch. With his paws he then proceeded to spill its contents on the ground.

"Hmm, let me see. The red wolf is carrying... a bent back eagle feather... a broken arrowhead... a clump of bison hair that happens to be smeared with dried blood... and several fragments of white stone. I wonder now, could it be that these items comprise a message to the warrior chief in the next valley. You would not be conveying orders sent from the wolf general Albarochk?"

"*Rrrowowwrr, yripe, yrelp,*" whimpered the intruder wolf cowering down. Having no patience for the wolf's sniveling, Lianvil batted the wolf onto his side and planted a great lion paw to the wolf's throat.

"You will with the yellow wolf... *cooperate,*" grrrd the lion in a tone of voice made to sound menacing. The lion took his paw off the red wolf's neck, grabbed the wolf's head in his teeth, and dangled the wolf's body up to resume a sitting position. The red wolf squirmed to better situate himself on his rump, clutched two front paws to his throat, and coughed once, twice, three times. With Lianvil gaping wider and wider his teeth, the wolf intruder decided not to cough a fourth time.

"Having now nothing to lose, I will confess everything." The wolf slumped his shoulders. "Just as you surmised... the items are a message to the chief in the next valley." The small red wolf pawed toward himself the doubled over eagle feather and the half arrowhead. "These signify that the Eagle Feather Tribe approaches. That tribe that comes down from the north is the enemy of fierce Raven warriors that travel on the sunrise side of this mountain. The feather and arrowhead are bent and broken to signify that the northern tribe must be stopped, and that their arrows not be permitted to take flight in the battle that is soon to come."

"This clutch of hair refers to a bison that is reported to be traveling toward the mountain positioned across the valley on our sunrise side. With the bison walk a unicorn and a man wearing metal armor. The blood that stains the bison hair instructs that he and those with him are to be found and killed."

"How about *that!*" Danseyelono's face lit in an

incongruent smile that reached from one crooked wolf ear to the other. "Bison, and either Hammer or Lucars travel on our east. But the unicorn that goes with them cannot be the blackmane. *Yip, yripe!* Master Wolf, what good news you bring. But, we are not yet done. You have not accounted for the white pebbles. What do these broken bits of stone signify?

"*No wait!* Let me for a moment think on this. Now, what do I know that is white? Let me see. It comes to mind that the hide of Cabalblade is pure white. Hmph! I think that the stone fragments signify... *unicorns.*"

"The smart yellow wolf is not wrong," barked the intruder. "Hundreds of unicorns approach on the plain that lies above these mountains. The brokenness of the white stones conveys the order that the white herd is to be scattered, and not permitted to join to the blackmaned unicorn and his band."

"So then, can I suppose that the blackmane travels the crest of the long mountain oppositional to the valley from where you came?" After looking toward the mountain to the west, the intruder wolf nodded.

"Lianvil did well to apprehend this red messenger wolf before his mission was completed," yipped Danseyelono swatting forepaws at the air in a gesture theatrical. "With this information we can surmise the battle plan of the monster wolf, my former commander that continues my cousin.

"So, Albarochk knows that along the top of the mountain to the west travels the blackmane northward. The monster wolf also knows that a bison, warrior, and unicorn are climbing up the mountain to the east. But the wolf commander still does not know that the four of us travel on top of this middle mountain.

"To our benefit the unicorn herd approaches on the plain above these mountains. The warriors of the Eagle Feather Tribe also move toward us with promise to become the blackmane's allies. There can be no doubt that the wolf general wants to destroy us while we are separate one from another, before the blackmane's platoon has a chance to reunite and join to the Eagle warriors and the white herd. *Yripe!* I think that... it falls to us to help reconnect the parts of Naythorn's band, and with the Eagle Feather allies spring a surprise attack upon Albarochk's forces."

"Everything I cherish faces destruction, ruin, and death," neighed Cabalblade. "Why does the wolf general and his warrior confederates lust to destroy unicorns? What harm have unicorns done to those that now count themselves to be our bitter enemies? Now, since I have always been a unicorn of action, I further ask what precisely we can do to unite together my unicorn herd, my blackmaned colt, and my little winged filly?"

The yellow wolf paced back-and-forth. After pausing to stare long at the messenger wolf, Danseyelono resumed once more his pacing. Finally he turned to the unicorn stallion and the lion.

"I know what I must do... and I know what you must do. Lianvil, you are to escort forward along the mountain Cabalblade and the foal. With this red wolf in your tow, you must travel fast. As for me, I am going to do something uncharacteristic of myself, for what I am going to do requires... *courage.* And because Albarochk cannot expect that from me, my scheme has a good chance of succeeding.

"*Yripe!* I will travel in place of the messenger wolf. But, instead of reporting to the war chief that is allied to Albarochk, I will slip unseen through and across the valley to our east. Then, I will climb the mountain beyond the valley and find Buckmight. I will instruct him and his party to make all speed northward along the mountains. Before we are attacked we need to get in front of our enemies and there unite with the Eagle Feathers, or the white herd, or both.

"After I deliver my message to Buckmight, and confirm his agreement to my plan, I will again with all speed make my way back over this mountain and descend into the valley on our western side. I will once more climb upward a mountain, find Blackmane, and tell him what I have done. Since I will by then be exhausted, I will remain with Naythorn while he moves full-out northward. If fortune smiles upon us, three parties loyal to the blackmane will join together at the far end of these three mountain fingers to there present a united front. If we are truly fortunate, we will join to our reunited platoon two strong allies. When we surprise Albarochk, the ambusher will become the ambushed."

"Because my colt is our commander, why not travel first to alert Naythorn of what we have discovered?"

"I see your point, Cabalblade, but time is of the essence. Naythorn needs to know as soon as possible where Buckmight now travels, and where to rendezvous with him. I can only provide that information to our captain if... I go first to find the bovine. And the bison needs to be told to move fast ahead. Wherever it can be gained, time must be saved."

"Although time is short, your plan is our best hope," grrrd the lion. "Witnessing a second time your clear thought and courage, I am proud to call the yellow wolf my friend. I will lead fast along these high places and make sure no harm befalls Cabalblade and his grandfoal. In that regard, while he goes with me the red wolf had best behave himself, or he will not walk off this mountain alive."

"I believe there is more to this messenger wolf than what first meets the eye," responded Danseylono looking closely at the newcomer. "I think that somewhere hidden inside this interloper's pliable personality is a prickly edge, and that the information the red wolf freely divulged will come to sting sorely his general. For that I am going to right now give him a name. Calling this prickly wolf by the name Thistle is easier than saying *Hey, you, red prisoner wolf.*" Heads, including that of the newly named Thistle, nodded in agreement with what the yellow wolf had barked.

"Now be off," grrrd Lianvil. "Run like the wind and alert Buckmight to our plan. Tell him that Lianvil prepares for battle to take place in three or four suns time. In that conflict, with the bison I will fight side-by-side."

After raising a hoof to signal Danseylono to hold, the stallion neighed for the foal to rejoin them. "I am going to show this brand new filly something important that a unicorn can do." The big stallion turned back to

Danseyelono and ordered, "Sit straight up and extend your forepaws toward me."

When the yellow wolf did as he was commanded, the unicorn stallion bent his head down and with his horn touched wolf paws, which in turn reached to grab hold Cabalblade's horn. At the same time that the horn glowed blue, and sparks traveled from horn to wolf paws, the unicorn pronounced, "The full measure of my magic will make you faster on your feet than you have ever before been. Since he is pressed for time, this is my gift to the yellow wolf."

Without barking a single word of thanks, Danseyelono bounded *extra fast* toward the east. He was soon lost from sight.

"Thistle, as my prisoner of war you must obey your captor," growled Lianvil in a low and threatening tone. "I will have you to run right at my heels, and I will not tolerate you falling behind, not even once." Lianvil led off with Thistle, the foal, and Cabalblade following behind.

"Can unicorns decide what exact gift they are to give?" inquired the foal of her grandsire.

"That question, my little foal, shows you to be very perceptive. Since I have never before touched my horn in blessing to anyone, not even to my own colt Naythorn, I trust that the large store of magic built up inside my horn permitted me to give the precise gift of fastness to Danseylono."

"Grandsire, with your extra magic will you touch your horn to me?"

"I will be more than glad to do that, when the right

time is come."

It was not long before the prisoner wolf resumed his normal personality, which meant that he became a talker.

"Great lion, I love to hunt rabbits. What do you like best to hunt?" Although no response came from Lianvil, Thistle was undeterred.

"Have you a brother lion as big as you? Although mind, as big as you are I hardly think it is possible for any other lion to duplicate your size." When again no response came from the lion, the red wolf tried once more at conversation.

"My two favorite things are the sky and green trees. What are your favorite things?"

"A proper prisoner is not chatty," growled Lianvil.

"Even more than I love the sky, I love the color blue," volunteered the foal drawing beside Thistle. "Since I like to neigh lots of things, you can talk with me."

"Even among wolves Lianvil is known to be an illustrious captain," yipped the red wolf addressing the foal as if she were a grown-up. "Because of his renown, I actually mind little being this great lion's prisoner."

"What games do wolves play?"

"Hmph, well little foal..."

"But I stand more than twice as tall as you do."

"I only call you little because compared to how big unicorns grow to be, you are still small. Now, let me see. Because I was born smallish the other wolf cubs made my tail to suffer lots of bites. For that reason I hated the *Grab the Tail* game. Hmph! My favorite game has to be *Rabbit Chase*. Without meaning to brag, I must say that

I have become very good at it. The most elusive rabbits are always surprised when after I catch them, I let them go so that there can occur a next round of chase the rabbit."

"Are those the only games you play?"

"Well, I also like to roll head over heels down a hill. After the big battle is finished we will, little foal, do that together."

"Do you promise?"

"Of course *I promise.* It will be great fun to with you tumble down a big hill."

"Why are you and your friends fighting against my sire? The first time I saw my sire, he saved my mare and me from painted warriors."

"I am very glad that Naythorn rescued you, and I look forward to soon meeting your sire who I really do not regard as... *my* enemy."

"I do not want to have an enemy, and besides I am too young to have a real enemy. But, I could have a make believe enemy."

"Since I am a young wolf that is no more than a messenger in the army, about war I know little. Wolves like me just do as we are told. Because Albarochk is a wolf giant that gets his way about whatever he wants, he gets to decide who is and who is not his enemy."

"This war *does not* make any sense to me!" exclaimed the foal jumping upward her forelegs. "Maybe you should not fight for Albarochk. I know what! You can do what Danseyelono and Lianvil did, and change your allegiance to Naythorn!"

"Little foal," a smile began to wrap about the jowls of

the messenger wolf, "I shall have to take some time to think on your proposal." The red wolf put new spring into his step. Even Lianvil noticed that the young wolf was beginning to relish his prisoner of war status.

As advancing afternoon light took on a softer hue, the little red wolf grew silent. He could not stop thinking about the straight-forward suggestion posed by the foal. Thistle began to weigh the pros and cons of changing sides in a war that, without asking his permission, had come upon him with the promise to bring battle and bloodshed to all found about him. Changing his allegiance seemed more and more to be the red wolf's best option.

"I have been thinking to whom I most owe my allegiance," yipped Thistle to the foal. "This, little one, is how I see the matter. The yellow wolf, the lion, you, and your grandsire have treated me honestly and fairly. In fact, I would rather be captured by this great lion and this big unicorn stallion, than to be made a friend of Albarochk. And even if I were to successfully escape from the lion, upon my return the wolf general would be furious with me for having been by Lianvil captured. A great paw of Albarochk would fling my little body hard against a rock or a tree, and then I would no more be."

"Then, Thistle, you must right away change to our side."

"You can satisfy my curiosity about one thing. What does it feel like to have wings?" At that question the foal bounded away and began to practice flight.

CHAPTER 15

THE YELLOW WOLF RUNS FAST

Danseyelono propelled himself so fast down mountain slopes that he imagined his body, like the foal of Naythorn, to have wings. When the thoughts of the yellow wolf turned to the task ahead of him, he muttered, "In order to slip unnoticed through many wolves and warriors, and then find Buckmight, in addition to gifted speed I will have to keep all my wits about me."

Upon reaching the valley floor the yellow wolf came upon too many wolves and warriors moving all about. While he hid he again and again reminded himself that should he be captured the big wolf would put two and two together, and so guess that his cunning and traitorous yellow cousin had come into possession of the plan to surprise Naythorn's friends while they were divided and apart from each other.

At dusk the yellow wolf ventured into the valley. To his immense satisfaction Danseylono passed through one enemy line after another without being sighted. Because the night provided no starlight to guide his path, climbing up the chest of a big mountain proved painstaking work. Still, the yellow wolf stayed positive, "Being so skinny my bones do not carry extra weight on this climb, and the touch of Cabalblade's horn speeds on my paws."

"Who goes there?" from out of the darkness came the sound of a familiar voice. "Be it friend or be it foe?" It was the unmistakable braying of Buckmight.

"It is me! Danseyelono! You cannot have forgotten how I and the lion captain helped Blackmane and his band to escape the conflict at the great gorge?"

"Of course I have not. So then, welcome yellow wolf. How come you here to us?" Roused from sleep to sit around a small campfire, Buckmight's companions soon listened attentively to the wolf's intelligence report.

"What a comfort to learn that the three parts of our band are safe," mrawed Taurington, "that each group travels by itself along mountain tops toward the north, and that where end the finger mountains the band will reunite and find the unicorn herd."

Well acquainted with the lay of the three finger mountains, Scarlet Point described how at their northern ends they spilled into a great plain with ample grass and water. He was certain that the unicorn herd would travel on the far side of that grassy valley through flinty rock hills that followed a river. For the lateness of the season the native youth also hoped that his Eagle Feather people would be following southward the same river before it coursed eastward into the flint rock hills.

When Danseyelono described item by item the contents of the pouch hung on the messenger wolf's neck the two bovines, Belfloralex, and the five human persons listened so intently that they seemed to stop breathing.

"So I was right," responded Scarlet Point.

"Grandfather brings his warriors to punish the Raven raiders. Since Eagle Feather warriors are the best fighters, the great wolf is rightly worried about having to do battle with my tribe."

"Scarlet Point's grandfather must come as fast as he can to join the battle that awaits," observed Hammerclaw.

"I am the fleetest animal person here," neighed Belfloralex. "With the wind always at my back, I will run fast to relay that message."

"And since Amaluna knows our trails," said Scarlet Point motioning to his sister, "she can ride on the filly's back. With my sister's help, Belfloralex will straightaway find our people."

"Well then, it is fortunate that unlike me the maiden is slight of frame," spoke again Hammerclaw smiling wide at Amaluna. "She is a slender rider that will little slow our filly."

"While the filly and Amaluna alert the Eagle Feather tribe," brayed Buckmight, "Scarlet Point will stay with us to protect his mother."

"*Arrouuhaqqhaqq,*" Danseyelono cleared his throat. "Err, not having authority over anyone or anything, I do hope that Naythorn's generosity of spirit will overlook the fact that I decided to share my information with you first, and him second. But before I leave I want you to know what my message will be to our leader."

Heads nodded in agreement.

"I will tell the blackmane that Belfloralex and Amaluna speed north to request her grandfather, the big chief, to make all haste to uphold us in the soon to come battle. I will next inform that Master Bison, Sir Cattle, Master Hammerclaw, Lucars, Scarlet Point, and Shawnee travel fast in one squad. I will identify Lianvil, Cabalblade, his grandfoal, and the red wolf as comprising a second squad. Both groups have the goal of arriving at the valley on our north before Albarochk's columns. I will also inform Naythorn that his unicorn herd approaches from the east."

"Yellow wolf, when this night you arrived I initially doubted your constancy and the depth of your commitment to Naythorn," confessed Buckmight. "I let myself question if hidden deep inside your heart still clung a measure of loyalty to your huge cousin wolf. I let myself question if in the last battle you had changed over to our side, only to someday betray us. In you I now place my full trust, and as you journey back across mountains and valleys to find Naythorn, I wish you much speed. On the plain that lies ahead of us, in less than three days a bison will fight as a brother to a yellow wolf."

"Although I have fought beside two black dogs," continued Hammer, "I have never gone into battle allied to a wolf. Master Danseyelono, with you Lucars and I must do a session of practice to see what style of fighting befits the three of us teamed together. The yellow wolf could push quickly up my back and from my shoulders spring onto an enemy warrior."

"Or, the yellow wolf could jump from my shoulders to the shoulders of Hammer," interjected Lucars, "and then spring upon a foe."

"Be careful, Sister!" yelled Scarlet Point as Belfloralex

179

struck out with Amaluna mounted on her back.

"I will! And brother I will bring strong Eagle Feather warriors back to help Naythorn!" Into darkness disappeared the filly and the girl. The yellow wolf began his return descent, and the bison and his squad recommenced journey.

"Although I was not born for battle," muttered Danseylono, "fighting as a team with Hammer and Lucars would warm my blood. I do take some pleasure to imagine myself growling as I jump off the smithy's shoulder to grab hold a warrior arm raising a war axe. Who knows, perhaps I could become a very frightening wolf adversary. But enough of that. So, Hammerclaw *trusts* me. Good for him to tell me so whilst looking me in the eyes."

Under the cover of darkness Danseyelono again moved fast. Scampering over and around boulders, and through steep ravines, made wolf movement perilous. Fortunately, near-falls did not count. With only minor scrapes and bruises the traitor to his monster cousin reached the valley floor.

As he shot through a gap in a long column of warriors, a brand new sun began to warm his hide. Running in broad daylight, Danseyelono knew he had by warriors been seen, but thinking the yellow wolf to be no more than a curiosity, they had shown him little regard. When a sentry wolf picked up his scent and began to trail after, Danseyelono's safety became precarious. Doubling back and leaping off the trail to slink into a sprawl of dusty rocks, the traitor wolf managed to confuse and lose the wolf sentry. While he crouched hidden, the yellow wolf fervently hoped that his passage through warriors and wolves would not be reported up the chain of command to Albarochk.

At last the valley was crossed and the yellow wolf began to climb the mountain where traveled Lianvil and Cabalblade. He hoped to with them share the news that Buckmight and Hammer had agreed to the strategy of fast march to gain entrance to the northern valley before the arrival of Albarochk's reunited army.

Danseyelono's calculations were not far off. To be safe he made the intercept of his trajectory further to the north then he thought Lianvil and Cabalblade could have gone since he had from them departed. But, instead of intercepting them in their lead, he crossed their trail a thousand wolf paces behind the four member caravan. With new motivation the yellow wolf ran fast to catch up with the great lion.

"Yap, yripe! Wait for your friend the yellow wolf!" A rest was welcomed by the stallion and his grandfoal, but less so by the great lion whose tightly kneaded muscles never seemed to tire.

"I found Bison, Bull, Hammer, Lucars, a unicorn filly named Belfloralex, and three rescued natives being a mother, son, and daughter. Belfloralex and the maiden now gallop north to find the Eagle Feather warriors. The maiden is the grand-daughter of the big chief of the Eagle Feather Tribe, and that chief wants revenge against the Raven warriors that now hunt Naythorn. Buckmight leads fast the others toward the valley where end the three finger mountains.

"Whew! I am tired of traveling so far alone. Can

Lianvil be spared to accompany me on the return to find Blackmane? To be honest, it would also help if two of us reported the plan to Naythorn instead of just me. Of course if this complex plan fails, I will alone shoulder the blame."

"There is nothing I would rather do than with you travel, and so offer my strength in support of your plan," grrrd the lion as he touched a great paw to the yellow wolf's head. "But, that I cannot do. I am here needed to protect Cabalblade and the precious winged foal. I have not before seen anything like this foal, and doubt that I ever will again. I must make sure that her blood is not, and shall not, be spilled."

As Danseyelono nodded his head in agreement with Lianvil, the disappointment in his unkempt and scarred face was visible for all to see.

"What say you... to the red wolf accompanying Danseyelono?" offered Thistle sauntering to where stood the lion next to the yellow wolf. "If by my lips Naythorn is told the contents of my message pouch, he will better understand how Danseyelono contrived his plan."

"Hmph!" A smile grew on Danseyelono's jowls that almost made the mottled wolf's scruffy face to look somehow handsome. "Oh! I just remembered something! I was told by Buckmight that the proper name of the bay foal is Isabaya Estraya, which means Bay Beauty of Starlight."

Proud to have her very own name, the foal jumped and flitted about in pure happiness.

CHAPTER 16

WOLF ACTOR BORN

"So Thistle offers to join me in the dangerous journey to the western mountain to find Naythorn. Now, it would not do for him to escape the company of a yellow wolf and spill my plan to Albarochk."

"Yes, it would be easier for me to escape a scrawny yellow wolf than to flee the great paws of Lianvil. But if I were to escape, I would have many uncomfortable questions to answer, and mind you not a single one of my answers would satisfy the wolf general. Albarochk would not let me hide the truth from him, and he would not forgive my having shared the meaning of the contents of the messenger pouch I carried. In the great wolf's eyes my life would be forfeit for failing my mission. So you see, Danseylono, my only option is loyalty to my former enemy Naythorn, and to Cabalblade, Isabaya, and you." The smiles of both wolves spread from jowl to jowl.

"Mind, I captured Thistle once," grrrd Lianvil. "If he betrays our newfound trust, I will do so again. The red wolf does not want to find the full force of my anger loosed upon him.

"So it is that we travel on as a party of one lion and two unicorns. Tell the blackmane that if my travel is not beset by conflict, in less than two days I will run out of the mountains and onto the plain. May two partnered wolves have safe passage."

Traveling as a wolf pack, even a very small wolf pack, requires teamwork. The lead wolf sets the pattern of jumps, climbs, slides down crumbly cliff sides, and scrambles through and over rocks of all shapes and sizes. The follower wolf observes exactly where and how steps the lead wolf, and then makes an improved pattern of steps that takes into consideration any mistake or false step made by the lead wolf. When Danseyelono grew tired and slowed his pace, the prisoner wolf took the lead and so allowed his captor wolf to conserve energy. With cooperation and mutual encouragement given, the red and yellow wolves traveled faster than either one could have done alone. Upon reaching the valley floor, Danseylono found their course more filled with wolves and warriors than the valley to the east.

At the same instant the red and yellow wolves froze. The way ahead was suddenly thick with adversaries. Danseylono and Thistle jumped into a thicket and hoped no traitorous breeze would give away their scent.

"We are here hard stuck," whispered the yellow wolf. "And I do not like that the blackmane's enemies move so fast northward. Their progress needs to be slowed to give us time to set up an ambush."

"Our timing to reach this place was terrible," responded the prisoner wolf. "We arrived at this spot when the movement of our enemies became very active."

"If the wind but a little shifts, our scent will be carried to wolves accompanying the warrior column. If that happens, you will then no longer be restrained by me as my prisoner. In fact, I am right now powerless to hold Thistle here."

"Actually I would rather be your prisoner, than their wolf private," wuffed the red wolf nodding toward passing enemy wolves. "Ahem, not to change the subject Danseylono, but what do you remember about Albarochk's first encounter with the blackmane? They say the whole fight was about nothing more than a bear, and that Naythorn refused to let Albarochk kill the bear. Might I inquire the color of that bear?"

"Treestandbear, as he was originally named, wears a black coat. When at the Battle of Spire Mountain I last saw Tristanbear, as they now refer to him, he had grown to become a very big bear. In fact, Tristan is the largest bear that I have ever seen. I would guess that in his whole life Albarochk was never so deeply humiliated as he was the day that Naythorn stepped between him, his five wolf companions including myself, and that bear that was at the time less than eighteen moons old."

"You know what, Danseyelono? An idea just came to me. I know how to get you out of this trap and again on your way. Mind, it will be tricky for you, and even trickier for me."

"What are you thinking?" asked the captor wolf.

"Only about a big black bear," came the elusive reply. "Now, yellow wolf, pay close attention and use your head. Since it was you that gave me the name Thistle, I am going to take a liberty with your name. From now on you will by me... be called Dansey." Thistle smiled slyly but confidently. Then as subtly as flashes a strike of lightning against a sky patched blue, Thistle was gone.

Tall Tale Told

Dansey lay on his belly as if paralyzed, and even worse for him, shocked speechless. The yellow wolf had never before lacked for words, not even once. When he had many times found himself to be mired in a situation fraught with danger, he had managed to quickly come up with a scheme to ungrasp himself from the clutches of harm. On this occasion the prisoner wolf had turned the tables on the yellow coated veteran conniver of schemes. Dansey crouched down lower. The yellow wolf watched as the red prisoner wolf ran fast in one direction, slid to a stop, turned, and sprinted in reverse direction.

"Rrrarruuu! Yrripp! Rrrarruuu!" howled Thistle. "Bears! Bears are after me!" The red wolf was by strong paws bowled over and pinned to the ground.

"Get a hold of yourself!" barked a big sergeant wolf. "What is this you say about bears? And *who* are you anyway?"

"Am I made safe?" Thistle struggled frantically against restraining wolf paws. "Tell me that I am really safe! If I am... then let me up on my paws!"

Dansey crept out of his hiding spot and went in search of mud. Finding puddled ground, the yellow wolf rolled about until his coat no more shone yellow. That accomplished, he eased himself into the rear echelon of the many wolves that had gathered about his former prisoner.

"Yrripe! Yrraaipse! All right! I am calm now. Let me stand up. *Please...*"

Danseyelono had to admit that Thistle was quite an actor. While only a few moments earlier he had calmly inquired about Tristanbear, the red wolf looked now to have become unstrung and abject.

"Not so fast," continued the sergeant wolf. "First tell me who you are. And what is this talk of bears?"

"You really do not know me? I am the red messenger wolf that Albarochk sent over the mountain and into the next valley. At my neck I carried a pouch with secret information for the chief of the Raven warriors. I was sent back to provide new intelligence to Albarochk. But just as I was getting close to reporting back to our fearsome wolf commander, I was attacked and bitten by bears. There were *twenty* of the big brutes! Well... at least fifteen bears pursued me."

"That is strange," answered the big sergeant wolf. "I have not seen any signs of bears. Are you positive they were... *bears?*"

"Not were, *but are!* Lots of them! The hugest bear called himself TreeStand... something. I understood some words that the huge bear growled... like *Naythorn.* He also growled about Albarochk. Everyone knows that Naythorn is our grayback general's great enemy."

"Never mind that! Where are these bears?"

"They are back there on the cliffs that edge this valley. Sergeant wolf, do not make me go back there, *please* do not do that. I have to deliver the message entrusted to me by the Raven warrior chief for General Albarochk."

"That you shall do, and right now. My general will determine if this little red wolf is who he says he is. And if you are who you say you are, I will bring you back to hunt down your so-called bears." The big sergeant wolf smiled gruesomely. *"Grrarr...* it has been too long since I led a bear-kill."

A procession of enemy wolf soldiers, a muddied yellow wolf, and the red-haired former wolf prisoner of the now discolored Dansey, headed toward Albarochk.

"Gosh, there really is more to Thistle than what first meets the eye," muttered Dansey to himself. The yellow wolf was torn. He should take advantage of the confusion generated by his former prisoner to escape into the mountain where traveled Blackmane. But, he was riveted to the performance of the red wolf. No wolf thought to care one bite that the muddied Dansey tagged quietly along at the very rear of the sergeant wolf's procession.

"Ggrrarrff! You dare, Sergeant, to disturb my nap? If this is not something... *important..."*

"Commander Albarochk, this half sized red wolf tumbled right into my sentries. He claims to be a messenger wolf that returns with important intelligence from the chief of the warrior column in the next valley."

"Ahhrrrr, yes, I do remember now. To him I entrusted a pouch. So, you delivered my message?" The messenger wolf groveled low, and for pure effect rubbed back-and-forth his lower jaw on the ground.

"Yes, General, *that* I did. And I bring the message sent back to your lordship."

"Out with it. I have little time for the likes of a pathetic wolf like you."

"The chief asks you to grant him one day of delay

before he joins up to you in the valley ahead."

"What? Impossible! I gave that chief strict orders to be there two days from now."

"Your Lordship, the chief has concluded that a new circumstance must be met with, immediately."

"*Grarrooo!* I authorized no... *circumstance.*"

"The chief discovered that the enemy squad that gained the mountain has grown in number, and needs to be right away destroyed."

"Hmph! Who and how many move along the eastern mountain?"

"You before knew about the armored bison, the armored man, and the unicorn. With those three now go an armored cattle, another armored man, and three native hostages stolen from your Raven warrior allies."

"Decrepit wolf," Albarochk put on what for him was an extra sly look, "since you were told information that I only just learned, that three hostages, another man, and a cattle had joined to the bison, I was wrong to suspect you as a traitor. You are a truthful wolf. Is my allied chief certain that he can destroy all of them?"

"The chief will set a trap to spring shut on all sides of your adversaries."

"Destroying the bison, the cattle, and the two armored warriors would cut the blackmane's strength by half," grrrd Albarochk as he rubbed his jowls with his one good front paw. "Still, I did not authorize that the destruction of the bison should cause any delay to the march of the Raven chief, and I despise the thought of having to delay my surprise attack by one more day." The enormous wolf relaxed his shoulders as he added, "I will reprimand my allied chief for disobeying my order for speedy march, but for killing those particularly powerful enemies I will show him a measure of clemency. Is that all?"

"Yes, Sir, other than the matter of the bears that attacked me. Sir, the big one knows you, intimately."

"What is this nonsense? Not since the last moon have I seen a bear."

"All I can say, Sir, is that the extraordinarily large and smelly black bear, that was leading the other bears, did a lot of growling. I heard him say your name, and the name Naythorn. Now that I think about it, the bear called himself Treestandbear, or Tristanbear. He bragged that when he was not even eighteen moons old he defeated you and five more wolves, including a small yellow wolf."

At that news the eyes of Albarochk glowed red and his body stretched more huge than it had been just moments earlier. The monster wolf jumped high and clawed upward as if he would scratch stars hidden behind the thick covers of a clouded night. Landed back to ground, Albarochk pegged Thistle's shoulder with his good paw, knocking over the red wolf. As Albarochk calmed himself his mouth widened into a salacious smile.

"With my own claws I will make end of the bear I have hated since the blackmane first stopped me from killing the brute. I knew that bear would again return to fight me, and it is far worse that he brings with him the other obnoxious bears that at Spire Mountain cost me a great victory. Sergeant! Since it appears that I now have an extra day's time on my paws, get me now that bear! Drag that black bear back to me so that I may tomorrow kill him. Destroying the huge Tristanbear will make the other bears to relent and go away.

"*Rrrraaouu!* Along with the death of the bovines, the destruction of the black scoundrel Tristanbear will make the next battle to be won before it even begins. Sergeant, all my forces must arrive together at the same time to do battle. For that we will remain here one more day to permit the Raven chief to destroy the armored bovines and foreign men. Now go bring me Tristanbear!" Albarochk slowly drew gigantic wolf limbs back into the earthen hollow he that night claimed as his den.

The trusted sergeant led many wolves toward the cliffs identified by Thistle. Made to run directly in front of the big sergeant, the red wolf knew that from the company of wolves intent on killing and capturing enemy bears, he could not escape. At least not for a while.

No wolves took notice of a small wolf with a muddied coat breaking off from the rear of the bear chase. Dansey turned in the direction of the western mountain ridge. As he sped on he could not help but feel proud of his new friend the red wolf.

"It is not slight praise to say that I could not have acted the part better than my former prisoner. When Albarochk learns how his prickly messenger wolf played him for a fool, he will with Thistle be furious. For sticking so hard Albarochk with his farce about Tristanbear, we could have better named the red wolf

Cactus. So long as Thistle's luck holds, he will sooner or later find some way to break away from the wolf sergeant and rejoin me at Naythorn's side. That means that I shall soon have the opportunity to thank the noble Thistle for his grand performance on Albarochk's stage." As Dansey ran on, the prickly wolf's tall tale coursed back-and-forth through his mind.

"The red wolf and I will someday laugh about the trickery he just played on my great cousin wolf, now become my blood enemy."

Following Thistle

Thistle led the wolf sergeant on a wild goose chase. Wherever rocks were more jagged and ravine walls more sheer, that was where Thistle took his escort. The wolves in the sergeant's company began to struggle to keep up the pace; some found they had doubled back on wolves in the same company traveling against their direction.

"I want to kill bears!" growled the big sergeant wolf. "Where are the big dumb bear oafs you told me about?"

"You just now came to the place," responded Thistle. "I saw them exactly above that big cliff that looms before us."

"*Grraarrwww!* The face of that cliff is almost straight up and down!"

"Tell me about it! I would now be dead if the branches of the tree against the cliff had not cushioned my fall. Since the bears would not follow me off the cliff, that is how I escaped them. It is a very good thing that my luck held, or I would *not* have been able to relay the Raven chief's intelligence to Albarochk, and you would not now be pursuing victory over brutish bears."

"*Grrarrarrr!* I am Albarochk's most fearsome wolf sergeant. Even if others cannot, the wolves I command can and will climb that cliff."

In the lead of a large company of wolf privates the big sergeant wolf began to claw his way upward. Wolf finger nails scratched hard to purchase each hold. It was no matter that when paw grips slipped, wolves fell off the face of the cliff. The lupines regrouped and kept pushing higher and higher. The top of the precipitous height was almost gained when Thistle slipped and fell onto the wolf next below him, whereupon both wolves sandwiched between them a third falling wolf.

Thud, whomp, crack, thud... thirty wolves fell either onto hard ground at the base of the cliff, onto the bodies of other wolves, or as in the case of Thistle had their fall cushioned by tree branches. For the hurt of the precipitous fall wolves lost their tempers and started biting any wolf found to be too close by, especially if the too close wolf was sprawled on top of an even angrier wolf. The collective animus of bruised and bleeding wolves directed at the scrawny red wolf that had instigated the chase after bears.

"*Grrarrrarrghhh!* It is the red wolf's fault!" exclaimed loudly the sergeant wolf. "The clumsy oaf made everyone to fall!"

Thistle yipped, howled, and generally made a huge ruckus as he dodged enraged wolves. The diminutive red rabbit-chaser soon demonstrated that he was, indeed, well-practiced in swerving and darting. The little red wolf also proved expert at tucking his tail between his legs so that the game of *Bite the Tail* could not be won by pursuing wolves.

Above the collective howling of many furious wolves, and the pathetic barking of the pursued Thistle, the sergeant wolf's voice was once more heard.

"Get back here, now! All of you! Get up this cliff or I myself will snap your backs harder than could any rock!" As obedient wolves once again tackled the cliff, in the distance Thistle's yipping grew faint. During the final chapter of the difficult climb no slipping or sliding wolf tumbled either himself or other wolves back to ground.

"*Damnation!*" swore the sergeant wolf. "The day I catch the clumsy little red wolf will be the last day his chest gulps air. That scrawny messenger wolf was not worth much anyway. I cannot imagine him holding his own in battle. I say *good* riddance! Now wolf privates, we are almost to the top. *Climb harder!*"

When the sergeant wolf finally surmounted the rock wall he found that only disappointment awaited him. Of bears, the top of the cliff was bare. Even worse, no paw prints or scents indicated that bears had been there on that, or on any recent night.

"Darn it all!" grrrd the sergeant. "Now I will have to report that not only did we not find the enemy bears, but that half my wolf privates were injured on this treacherous and slippery climb. And to top it all, the craven red wolf disappeared on me." The sergeant wolf quieted as he began to consider how to dismount the treacherous cliff he had just climbed.

"I hate nothing worse than reporting bad news to Lord Albarochk. For the failure of this mission my general will cuff me hard. Unlike the red wolf, for me there is no escape. For not finding the cursed Tristanbear it will be me that suffers cruel abuse. That is the way Albarochk runs things in his army."

Into the western mountain ridge to where he directed, Thistle followed the bed of a stream whose wetness would make it impossible to track him. After the tumult at the cliff, the red wolf was thankful that to his ears the evening had become gloriously quiet. Leaving off the stream he inclined paws upward through pine trees that stood like silent straight-backed sentries.

Thistle caught the whiff of a scent. Dansey had recently passed that way. Thistle smiled each time his sensitive nose reaffirmed Dansey's presence somewhere ahead of him. And the wider he smiled, the less tired grew his limbs. The red wolf began to think how he would boast to Dansey of his canniness in making the feared sergeant of the wolf guards to swallow his tall tale about the nefarious, and elusive, Tristanbear.

Refound

Dansey was accorded a welcome that made him to feel what he thought a famous wolf must feel like. Mama Pig called him the hero of the *Battle before the Deep Gorge*, which stretched the truth a little considering the hard fighting by Buckmight, Taurington, Naythorn, Hammer, Lucars, and on down to the dogs, sheep, and water birds.

"Naythorn, I have much to report... but first let me apologize for the muddied look of my hide." The yellow wolf abruptly turned his head; he had heard something. *"Arrrouuwharhwarh!* Well, well, it seems that both my prisoner and I have much news to report to you." The yellow wolf darted back down the trail that only a short time before had led him to Naythorn. It was not long until he bowled over the oncoming Thistle in a demonstrative and energetic greeting.

Mama Pig noticed that the yellow wolf sauntered as he rejoined the unicorn captain. "Let me present to one and all the great wolf actor Master Thistle, who incidentally shortened my name from Danseylono to Dansey. His story begins with a carried pouch, including a full description of its contents."

The diminutive red wolf duly explained that after Albarochk sent him as a messenger to deliver military intelligence to the Raven chief traveling in the eastern valley, he had suffered the bad luck to encounter Lianvil. His situation was made worse when the messages encoded in the contents of the pouch that swung from his neck, were discovered. When the doubled-over feather, broken arrowhead, bloodied bison hair, and fragments of white stones were explained, their logic became clear to all gathered. Clear even to a duck with an attention span shorter than the width of his wings.

"Oh, I failed to mention one thing," continued Thistle. "The touch of Cabalblade's horn not only gave me the uniform animal speech, that touch of magic compelled me to be honest and to confess everything."

At the mention of his sire's name, Naythorn reared high and flashed forepaws. Deeply felt emotions had an immediate effect upon unicorn blood, and could not inside unicorn horse bodies be hidden or suppressed the way human persons make to quiet their emotions.

"Naythorn, that is not all," interjected Dansey.

"Lianvil and I not only guided forward Cabalblade along the mountain ridge, we also performed service as bodyguards to keep safe from harm the loveliest young thing I have ever seen... *your winged foal!*" Upon hearing this totally unexpected news Naythorn again jumped high, kicked, and for happiness twirled about his body.

"Your foal grows fast," added Dansey, "and she is determined to fly. I became entranced watching how she twitched and fluttered her wings."

Upon learning that Hammer and Lucars had made the delivery of the blue gold to the Phoenician Captain Avalcar, Naythorn stomped with contentment because the unicorn pledge had been fulfilled. Upon next learning that Lucars and Hammer had made a deal with their commander involving two horse stallions so that they might rejoin his band, and that Taurington and Buckmight had also found a way to return to him, Naythorn shook about excitedly his head. An exuberant Naythorn approved all that Dansey had thought to organize and communicate to the bison and lion.

Needing to think about what lay ahead, Naythorn quieted. He began to worry about the role the unicorn herd would, or would not take in the upcoming battle.

"Not believing in the idea of war, I think that the unicorn matriarch and high escort will not want to become involved in what they will say is a fight that pertains only to the wayward unicorn with a black mane. Of course I, myself, do not like or welcome battle. The two unicorn leaders will not understand that once Albarochk's anger and covetousness were unleashed, I could do nothing to stop his march to conflict."

Turning to Thistle the blackmane inquired, "Red wolf, what made you to fight? What promise of adventure, or betterment to your position in life was by Albarochk offered?"

"Not so at all, Captain Naythorn. The privates in Albarochk's wolf corps were given one choice only, enlist in the ranks of the great wolf, or have their necks broken in his jaws. I myself was a very reluctant recruit. I would much rather be running stream banks and up and down hills in the hunt for rabbits. Do you know how clever rabbits are at hiding and dodging? More than anything else in life I enjoy the challenge of matching wits with rabbits. Most times the rabbit outsmarts me."

"By way of introduction, my name is Rainsnow. So what made the red wolf to become a traitor to Albarochk and pledge loyalty to Naythorn?"

"Well, to begin with, I found the treatment afforded me by Lianvil and Dansey was fair. It also seemed to me that in the upcoming fight Naythorn's side faced insurmountable odds. I always prefer that the underdog, even an underdog rabbit, should have a chance to win. Hah! Sometimes I even *pull* for the rabbit to out-dodge my chase. I will add that I do not like Albarochk, or like the wolf sergeants with whom he surrounds himself. And I detest Albarochk's ideas about right and wrong. I came to despise the very ground on which walk the enormous paws of the wolf general."

When Timidthy raised a paw, the direction of the conversation changed. "I commend our two wolves for the idea of a forced march to enter the northern valley before the arrival of Albarochk's forces."

"We must now make of ambush our own device," neighed Naythorn. "We will race to the valley ahead of us and make camp at the foot of the middle mountain range. We there join our three forces together to plan the strategy and tactics of our ambush.

"Webstir and Featherspark, now that your wings are from injury recovered, I need you to again become my ever present eyes from above." As Naythorn shifted his gaze to look closely at each member of his band found with him, his somber regard bespoke the gravity of their situation.

The blackmaned unicorn reared, shook his head, and without neighing another word began to trot along the crest. Five wild pigs, two sheep, two dogs, two fowl, two wolves, and one roan uncle horse followed after Naythorn.

Mama Pig moved next to the hopping and fluttering Webstir and Featherspark. "You heard our captain, no more crying and moaning about your hurts. Without your flighted scouting we may not survive the next days."

"*Qvackk!* Oh, all right. But Featherspark is more healed than me."

"While my feathers are not perfectly straight," rejoined Featherspark, "I have to agree with Mama Pig's insistence that we return to the work of flying far and fast. I do say, Webstir, that from a high flighted perspective the plan of a big battle will be very interesting to follow." The goose chugged a wing at his smaller friend. "*Hrronkkhaha!* During the next few days our intrepid duck can focus upon the art of spying, and not have to all by himself kill cruel wolves and ferocious warriors."

CHAPTER 17

LIANVIL, CABALBLADE, AND THE WINGED FOAL

The trio of a lion, a unicorn, and a foal came to a place where mountain ridges presented a vista of a big forward leaning plateau.

"Now that we see the plain ahead," neighed Cabalblade, "we have earned a rest." Isabaya immediately sank into a patch of grass to sun herself. For comfort she extended legs and neck in the manner of napping foals. Cabalblade began to graze near Lianvil who had sprawled his belly on a high boulder that provided a perfect place of lookout. Become bored with sentry duty, the big lion for the first time engaged the unicorn stallion in a conversation that did not have to do with the progress and circumstances of cautious but speedy travel.

"It might please you to know that I found your blackmaned colt to be a most difficult and dangerous opponent. No one else has in battle gotten the better of me."

"How came you to fight for Albarochk?" responded Cabalblade moving hooves toward the big feline.

"That choice was precipitated by the entrance of Naythorn into the canyon of blue gold. My lion clan had forever known Shining Canyon to belong to us alone.

When Naythorn and Lucars were chased into our mountain, their enemies became our, albeit unnatural, allies. The yellow wolf made himself by me to be understood, and through his arduous efforts forged the pact that allied my lion clan to wolves."

"How then came the great lion to change sides?"

"From the start the alliance with wolves had compromised my independence. While I had found Danseylono to be not false, his general proved unendingly duplicitous. My lions always fight from out of our mountain, but for no reason the monster wolf made my lions to battle on level ground away from our mountain. The giant wolf saw every one of his wolf and lion soldiers as things to use and then cast aside. The day came when the yellow wolf became convicted that at the side of Albarochk, his days were numbered." The lion paused to scrutinize all four directions. When the unicorn stallion did not neigh anything in response, the lion continued.

"After suffering defeat in the *Battle of Spire Mountain*, the yellow wolf and I found ourselves to have on the one paw acquired trust in each other, and on the other paw to have lost all confidence in Albarochk. Danseylono convinced me that once the monster wolf had drunk all of Naythorn's blood and consumed his flesh, I would lose my authority as a lion captain, and would sooner or later be destroyed by the monster wolf's all-consuming quest for power. So, Cabalblade, you might conclude that it was out of pure self-interest that I am come to be here found with you."

"To be honest Lianvil, it is not just because I am the

sire of Naythorn that I myself am found here. I was never a good sire to my colt. I was too proud to accept the fact that the only black marked colt in the unicorn hold was my progeny, and for his part Naythorn was too honest to feign love for an aloof and uncaring sire.

"You see, when the Phoenician barges left Wittanor I should have stayed behind to search for Naythorn. But instead, I abandoned my own colt to embark with the unicorn herd. I chose duty to my herd over my tepid love for my colt. So, great lion, the real reason I am here is not because Naythorn is my colt, but because I am now forced to recognize that what the high escort of the unicorns has told me is true, Naythorn's destiny is to someday rescue the unicorn herd." A frown spread over Cabalblade's muzzle.

"A big, strong, and ambitious unicorn by the name of Hoovefort has in all but name become the true captain of the unicorn guards. Left to his own devices Hoovefort will destroy not only me, but also the matriarch and the high escort. Our leaders are both convinced that my stubborn colt is the only horned horse that can stop Hoovefort from doing irreparable damage to the white herd. While I did not before need my own colt, the leaders of the unicorn herd now require Naythorn."

"After committing to enter a battle under the command of an odious wolf, I and my lions suffered defeat. For that I no longer lead my clan of lions. Instead of obeying me, the lion who is anvil hard, the young lions now follow only themselves. When I joined myself to the monster wolf, instead of gaining more power I planted the seeds that grew to strangle my power and take from me my lions. The irony is that had I been smart enough to immediately ally myself to Naythorn, I would not now be in exile from my mountain of magic gold."

"Sir Lion, because I could not recognize that you were leading me in the right direction, I was made to retreat and thereafter join myself to you and Danseylono. So, just like I stubbornly did at the fork in the trail, you chose the wrong path to travel. But now that I think about it, I would rather be here with you than commanding unicorn guard horses. For me it may not be such a bad thing to find myself bereft of power."

"And now that I hear you neigh that, Cabalblade, I will admit that commanding surly lions is not the most pleasant work. I am going to decide to be content commanding only myself. And I will be satisfied that my only true friend is a lone yellow dancer wolf."

"Not just Danseylono. While this unicorn guard stallion does not show well his feelings, he is also become your friend."

"All three of us are friends!" neighed the foal.

"I had not seen you to join us, Isabaya." That neighed, with his horn the grandsire nudged the chest of the foal upward so that her feet tussled the patch of mane on his forehead. "Yes, little deer with wings, Lianvil and I *are* your great friends."

"And I will protect these two unicorns as if they were my own blood."

"Grandsire, how am I to find my sire?"

"Your sire travels the mountain over there," neighed Cabalblade pointing with his horn. "He, and the other friends of your sire that travel along the other mountain, will soon come to join us."

"I cannot wait to again see my sire. He is just as big as you."

"So, Isabaya, that means that since I last saw him my colt has grown. Do you think Naythorn will still remember his sire?"

"If I can remember my sire, then of course he can still remember his sire. I even remember my mare. She had such big wings. Grandsire, will I become a great winged horse like my mare?"

"Hmph! Because your horn makes you to be a true unicorn, you will come to be twice the winged horse that your mother was."

The foal did not respond to what her grandsire had neighed, but instead broke to run down a hillside. Then happened a miracle. The wings of the foal for the first time took her skyward. Isabaya flitted about beating hard her wings. But when it seemed that she was about to gain full control, her wings forgot to obey, and the foal fell back to the ground.

"Do not bruise yourself! Naythorn will not forgive his grandsire if he finds his foal to be hurt." The foal paid no mind to the words of Cabalblade. Running more down the hill she again achieved the required momentum to regain the air, and this time she did not tumble back to ground. The flight of the foal was soon circling above a smiling grandsire. In recognition of the gift of the foal's flight, even the dour lion managed a smile.

"All by myself I flew!" exclaimed Isabaya setting her hooves back to earth. "And it would be the *very* best thing if Lianvil could right beside me fly!"

"You do know, Cabalblade, that by touching me with your magic horn and so giving me wings, you can satisfy the wish of your grandfoal."

"Make the lion *to fly!* Do it grandsire!"

"Both of you listen to me. Some unicorns can with the touch of their horns only once or twice bestow magical gifts. To the yellow wolf I already once gave away my horn magic."

"Just try it, Grandsire! Do it for me!"

"Isabaya, the big lion is only joking about wanting wings."

"Not so, Cabalblade. This lion readily gives his consent to be sparked by the horn of the unicorn guard captain."

"Firstly, Isabaya was born with her wings. It would take a long time for wings to grow big enough to lift skyward the body of a great lion. Secondly, a unicorn stallion cannot always precisely control what the magic that sparks from his horn will make to happen. Should a gift of magic be given to Lianvil, the exact outcome will as well depend on what the lion's body wants to do... with what is bestowed."

"Try, Grandsire!" neighed the foal in her crystalline voice.

"Hmph! Well, I suppose I am not too old to do a thing outrageous. For my foal and our lion friend I will do something, that if it works, will drain all my strength to make it happen." The big unicorn moved to stand before an imposing lion seated on his bottom. When Cabalblade lowered his horn to touch Lianvil's head, many sparks *zzzzdd*. The grandsire unicorn relaxed his body.

"Now, Isabaya, you must be patient. Some magic gifts take time to happen. We at least know that something magical is beginning to occur in the body of this great lion."

"I do feel magic to stir inside me," grrrd the lion shaking back-and-forth his head. "I cannot say what is happening to my body, except that it is something that will bring to me *change.*"

"I want the lion to fly with me!" With much anticipation the foal jumped about flapping wings to make herself glide from one boulder to another, and from one spot of grass to another. Isabaya launched upward and neighed, "Perhaps my sire is close by. I shall soon return."

Before Lianvil and Cabalblade had traveled one more league downward, the foal returned flying in the lead of a green necked duck and a goose whose dark wing feathers hinted a blue glow of magic. Webstir and Featherspark followed Isabaya to land before a lion and a unicorn stallion.

The goose opened wide his black beak to speak, but before he could honk anything his bill was batted shut by the duck.

"*Qvackk!* Naythorn is close by and..."

The goose, in return, plugged with a wing his friend and interjected, "I am going to send Webstir and Isabaya back to lead Naythorn to the unicorn stallion and the mighty lion. You will soon see the blackmane to approach."

After pointing a wing at Webstir, Featherspark added, "Tell Naythorn that after I find Buckmight and his platoon, I will bring them to where these hills connect to the plain."

"*Qvackk!* That is a very good idea! I should have thought of that. But, that means that while I and the foal go together, I get to give Isabaya a flying lesson, and of course I can do that better than any goose."

"For some strange reason my body feels that it wants to walk upright," grrrd Lianvil. "So that is what I shall do."

"*Nyeerrr!* So the touch of my horn made Lianvil not to fly, but to walk on hind legs. But how can a lion think to walk like a human person?"

Paying no attention to what concerning him had been neighed, the lion ambled ahead on two legs only. Before long the unicorn stallion was trotting fast to keep up with a lion that had learned how to run on two, instead of four great feline paws.

CHAPTER 18

UNICORNS TOWARD MOUNTAINS

With Lieutenant Hoovefort at their side, Elianor and Aneilee walked westward in the lead of the white herd. Absent Cabalblade, the lieutenant had been quick to assume command responsibilities for the guard stallions whose number he insisted on increasing. Elianor was sure the motive for this was to expand Hoovefort's prominence in the white herd. As could be expected, newly selected guard stallions were most loyal to Hoovefort.

"We must turn our path to follow on the north side of the far mountain range."

"You before wanted the white herd to travel southward to achieve a more warm winter place," commented Elianor. "It is curious that the lieutenant now wants us to strike northward."

"No, Hoovefort," neighed Aneilee. "Since we do not know what lies on the far side of those mountains, the path of the white herd will for now follow these flint hills westward toward a clear and open horizon."

"You play games with me! You think that by not striking northward it will be easier for the blackmane to find my herd. Every unicorn in Wittanor Hold saw that you before did not like Naythorn, why the sudden change in your attitude?"

"It was not a matter of Aneilee or me disliking the blackmane," answered Elianor for the high escort. "He was an immature and insolent young stallion that needed constant discipline. Having survived a long journey over deserts and mountains to find us, surely Naythorn will have come to be a more mature stallion.

"And of course Aneilee is right. It is more prudent to follow a path that we can see will lead us far westward, and not risk a detour into country that may be cut by impassable rivers or mountains. By the way Hoovefort, this herd is *not yours*. Nor does the white herd belong to me, to Aneilee, or to any one unicorn horse."

At the rear of the herd a commotion began. The three leaders sped hooves to find out what had happened.

"Beyond the rise where advance the brown spy wolf and twenty natives adorned with panther skins," reported a guard unicorn, "come many more natives in pursuit of the white herd.

"This is terrible!" exclaimed the matriarch flashing up her hooves. "The last thing we need is to be pursued by hostile natives who know nothing of the goodness of unicorns. And I do not *like* that the spy wolf leads on the warriors!"

"What is worse," neighed Aneilee, "on this plain we have no Phoenician sailors to tender protection to our herd. Our one advantage is that unicorn hooves move faster than warrior feet."

"But, Aneilee," replied the matriarch, "although slower, warrior feet can pursue over very long distances."

Fear and Confusion

The white herd found itself in flight from Panther warriors intent on destruction. As the horned horses galloped fast, the line of the herd began to elongate, and slower of foot unicorns fell behind.

"So it is to be white unicorns against black panthers," neighed Hoovefort. "I must make sure that guard stallions keep the formation from scattering wide."

"I will stay back to make sure that unicorns travel in an orderly way," neighed Elianor to Aneilee, "and do not become a divergent mob."

"Just be careful, Elianor. Since you stay back, I will go to lead at the front of the herd."

As the formation of running unicorns lengthened further, the matriarch began to worry. Then it happened. A limping old unicorn mare fell out of the fast-running formation. A heavily breathing old stallion was the next unicorn to falter.

"Old and infirm unicorns fall away!" exclaimed Elianor upon refinding Hoovefort. "You must do something!"

"What, Matriarch, can I do? If we slow our pace the entire herd will come to be in danger."

"We can stop running away and instead create a protective shield for our herd, just like we did at sea."

"We have not the time, and besides that would place the whole herd in danger of being surrounded and destroyed. We cannot stop! Those left behind will have to fend for themselves!"

"Hoovefort, *No!* We cannot abandon old unicorns... to be slaughtered!" Instead of answering the matriarch, the guard lieutenant sped hooves ahead.

"Find strength! Do not slacken!" neighed Elianor to a faltering old mare. "You *must* stay with the herd!" Nonetheless the mare fell more behind.

"Stop! Haltervor!" neighed Elianor to the sergeant guard stallion as he ran toward the laggards trailing the herd. Haltervor did not stop. In the space of a long moment Elianor decided; she would join Haltervor and perhaps with him... perish.

"Take heart and do not falter! Haltervor and I will protect you!" Little by little, Haltervor and Elianor pushed the unicorn laggards into their own compact and slower moving formation.

"Elianor! We need more guard stallions to present a barrier," neighed Haltervor. "There is no other way but to confront the Panther warriors that are gaining on us!" That neighed, the hooves of Haltervor sped to regain the main herd.

A guard stallion soon found Elianor, then another stallion came, and then another. By the time Haltervor had returned, he and nine guard unicorns were to be found with Elianor.

"To buy time we guards must charge at the warriors," neighed Haltervor.

Led by the brown spy wolf, the fast running Panther warriors in the lead of their war party suddenly found that *they* were now the pursued. Galloping toward them at breakneck speed came Haltervor in the lead of Elianor and nine stallions. Unicorn hooves and horns decimated the ranks of the forward party of warriors.

Haltervor's squad of unicorns did not stop until they

had pathed through half the entire battalion of native warriors, whereupon Haltervor led his line of fast galloping unicorns to break out of the broken column of Panther warriors and return back to the rear of the unicorn herd. Eleven unicorns reformed with the new intent of holding their ground. The brown wolf was now nowhere to be seen.

Arrows were sent skyward toward the rear guard formed by eleven unicorns.

"Haltervor! Join your horn to mine!" ordered Elianor. "If we are this day fortunate, our horns will bring forth a magic shield to stop arrows from striking our bodies. Even a small barrier shield is better than nothing." Two horns began to glow. In currented magic the air enveloping the line of eleven unicorns began to bend.

Upon finding their arrows to strike a magic shield that could not by the eye be seen, and then watching their arrows drop like stones to the ground, Panther warriors stared in bewilderment. Elianor and Haltervor would not let falter or fail the compacted magic unicorn shield. While the stalemate between the warriors and Haltervor's line persisted, the main body of unicorns drew further and further away. Panther warriors finally conceded that, at least for this day, the herd of unicorns had made good their escape.

"I say, Haltervor, unless we run fast we shall be left behind... even by the laggards that we today well-defended."

"Then, Elianor, let us be off!" responded the sergeant unicorn. When Elianor, Haltervor, and the laggard unicorns they protected caught up with unicorns come to rest, the greeting given by an irate Lieutenant Hoovefort was not kind.

"You two placed at risk the entire white herd! I gave no permission to Vor or the guards that went with him to abandon our herd. You were incredibly fortunate that your haphazard shield this time worked, and this is the second time that Vor has willfully disobeyed my orders. There better not be a *third* time."

"Haltervor did what I required." Elianor would not be intimidated. "And, I repeat that he no longer answers to the name Vor. Without his courage my life and the lives of many old and infirm unicorns would have today been forfeit. Does that outcome matter nothing to you?"

"The matriarch must accept the fact that the white herd's only chance to survive is for the guards to be a disciplined unit solely under my command. It is unfortunate that the enemy now knows the secret to our defense. To the next ambush the Panther Chief will bring warriors from two or three directions, and so make it impossible for us to well-establish a protective shield.

"Because he was with the matriarch, I will not this time punish Haltervor. But be forewarned that no stallion in the unicorn guards will again listen to the haltered stallion. They will obey me alone!"

Observing tired unicorns rest the night, Elianor neighed quietly to Aneilee standing beside her, "Lieutenant Hoovefort daily subverts my authority. In so doing he also threatens your position as our herd's high escort. It has for Hoovefort become very convenient that the captain of the guards went away to search for his blackmaned colt. What, Aneilee, are we to do about Hoovefort?"

"There is more to Haltervor than I thought," mused the high escort.

"But I am worried... *about Hoovefort.*"

"Given the benefit of hindsight, I now think that the concerns I have long felt for the constancy of our herd had more to do with Hoovefort, than with sharks or death whales. I have never before seen a unicorn so ambitious to hold authority that he would sacrifice old and infirm unicorns... as if they mattered nothing. I ask you, Elianor, how can a true unicorn be entirely consumed by power and the lust for control?"

"The stallion with the black mane is a truer unicorn than the mighty and beautiful Hoovefort."

"You did well to by yourself establish a protective shield for the benefit of slow afoot unicorns," responded Aneilee relaxing her neck and shoulders.

"That was not by me, alone, accomplished. Absent the surprisingly strong magical power of Haltervor's horn, no shield could have been raised. As well as to you, Dame Escort, it has become clear to me that two things are needful. We must soon find Naythorn, and then find him to be a changed unicorn."

"It has always been comfortable for me to be the high escort," observed Aneilee. "Every unicorn showed respect for my position. In turn, with my authority unquestioned I focused on the higher and nobler things that presented to my heart. That elevated spiritual dimension of my life now lies behind me. I have to find the courage to with you stand for what is true, or if need be, to stand alone.

"Matriarch, the same as you did on the barge when with his hooves Hoovefort struck your head and drew blood, today you were unafraid to show true leadership. Had it not been for the bravery you showed by standing with the faltering unicorns they, and with them their magic, would now to us be lost. I can never repay you for what you today did, nor can I disregard the example of courage you showed to me.

"It occurs to me, Elianor, that time is like a barge that billows immutable sails through the sea of life. That barge begins to leave me in its wake. No longer young, unicorns now look at me as if I am an anachronism. I wonder if I am to be the last high escort of the unicorn herd."

"Everything now depends on finding the blackmane."

"I feel him to be not so far away. In that regard, Elianor, have the guard sergeant to be sent to us. It is become time for me to show Haltervor that I am not quite yet displaced in time and place."

CHAPTER 19

STRATEGIES FOR AMBUSH

At the endpoint of the middle mountain range Buckmight, Taurington, Hammer, and Lucars found Cabalblade, Lianvil, and the winged foal. The former hostages Shawnee and Scarlet Point were introduced, and the manner of their rescue was recounted.

Much had transpired since the *Battle before the Deep Gorge*. Hammer told how the two stallion brothers of Rayalas took the places of himself and Lucars for the return voyage of Phoenician barges. By the time Buckmight finished describing how Belfloralex caused a wind and a great cloak to float him and Lucars down into a deep gorge, Naythorn and his half band were seen to approach. The reunion of the three parts of Naythorn's band became a time of heartfelt celebration.

Upon the return from her mission to the Eagle Feather chief, Belfloralex found the band of Naythorn reunited. She brought the news that Amaluna had remained behind to with her tribe travel toward Naythorn.

"Upon finding his granddaughter Amaluna to be safe and sound, Chief Walking Tree shed tears of joy. So that he will be able to talk to Naythorn, and to the rest of us, I touched my horn to his head."

Hearing of the chief's tears, Naythorn wondered why

after so many moons apart his own sire had not that day shown tenderness upon greeting his one and only colt. In fact, upon her reintroduction to the blackmaned unicorn that she had heard so much about, the greeting of Belfloralex had been ten times more enthusiastic than had been the greeting of his own sire. Still, every member of the band was truly elated to be once again united with their captain, and with each other. With the exception of Naythorn's sire, the newcomers all wore big smiles.

Hammerclaw, Lucars, Lianvil, Belfloralex, Dansey, Scarlet Point, Shawnee, and lastly Thistle pledged an oath of loyalty to Naythorn.

"Now then, Master Smith, where is my armor?" inquired a smiling Thistle. "Having joined myself to the band of Naythorn, I require magic to protect my thin shoulders."

"With this big hug my arms take your measurements," responded the blacksmith grabbing the red wolf to his chest. "As soon as this next battle is done, I promise that Thistle will have blue gold armor that suits him... perfectly."

The next morning the entire band, grown to number well more than Naythorn's previous complement of five wild boars, two bovines, two sheep, two dogs, and two waterfowl gathered to consider that an enormous battle was to soon take place against Albarochk, his wolf legion, and many hostile warriors.

"I can feel that the unicorns are come close to us," confirmed Cabalblade to Naythorn. "Still, it is unfortunate that the matriarch will not consent for unicorn stallions to enter the looming battle, and still more unfortunate that Lieutenant Hoovefort will heartily sustain that prohibition. You see, Hoovefort now commands the unicorn guards. By the way, a young stallion called Haltervor, who you will remember by his old name Vor, has become Hoovefort's nemesis. It could happen that four or five of the guard stallions will disobey Hoovefort, and with Sergeant Haltervor come to join your force." At that news, Naythorn's mood noticeably improved. The addition of five unicorn stallions would bring the strength of his band to number about thirty animal person soldiers.

"Featherspark and Webstir confirm that we are to face a pincer movement from two separate columns of warriors and wolves," informed Naythorn. "In support of Albarochk and his many wolves, the Jaguar Tribe comes at us from the valley to our west. At the same time the Raven Tribe pushes up the valley to our east. As each enemy column travels through separate valleys, their intent is to corner us between them. We cannot permit Albarochk's two armies to join as one. If we convincingly crush the enemy wolves and warriors, this will be the final time we do battle against Albarochk." That neighed, the blackmane turned his head right and left to look at each member of his band. He took heart at the physically tough appearance of the bison, cattle, smithy, and his apprentice.

"Lucars, you show even more confidence in your strength than when we were last together."

"I will do my part, Naythorn. And with your platoon increased by so many, I am confident that we shall prevail. I continue impressed that the yellow wolf traveled across two valleys and into three mountains to reunite your band."

"And I could not have done that without the dramatic flair of the red wolf."

"For my part," offered Thistle, "I count it an honor to call Dansey my friend."

"In my times of absence this bison led very capably," continued Naythorn. Along with Buckmight, I need Lucars and Dansey to develop a strategy to defeat Albarochk and his warrior allies."

Lucars grabbed a stick, and after sharpening its end with his sword began to scratch marks into dirt. After glancing briefly at the blackmane, he pointed the stick at a place marked in his ground map.

"This spot represents where we now find ourselves." He pointed twice more. "Out of these two narrow-ridged valleys come the forces of Albarochk. The enemy armies intend to join together where we now find ourselves. Naythorn is right. We cannot permit that to happen.

"Before at the side of Albarochk, and now at our side, the yellow wolf proved himself to be a born tactician. So, Dansey, how does Naythorn's band stop the two oncoming armies from joining together?" The scrawny yellow wolf with bright eyes immediately walked a circle around the lines that Lucars had drawn.

"The greatest part of our force needs to front... the monster wolf," yipped Dansey gesturing with a paw. "Thanks to the sharp claws of Lianvil, the wolf general was made to lose his voice, and I think still cannot clearly bark commands. Without receiving timely orders from Albarochk, enemy lines can be made to become confused and to break apart, just as they did at the close of the *Battle before the Deep Gorge.*"

The yellow wolf moved closer to the map Lucars had scratched, and carefully placed one front paw, and then the other. "At these two quite narrow places we can block the progress of Albarochk's columns, and prevent the monster wolf's two armies from entering the plain and joining forces. From a strategic standpoint, both bottlenecks must be held."

"We are not strong enough to fight on two fronts at once," baahed Rambuncture.

"We are favored by the wondrous armor that Hammerclaw for us fashioned," reassured Timidthy. "And the new recruits to our band make us far stronger than when we last faced the wolf general."

Balanced only on hind limbs, to the surprise of almost everyone Lianvil began to pace with an upright posture. He turned to Naythorn and grrrd, "If we ambush the enemy from a place of rocks and ravines that give to a lion advantage, I can assure you that in the battle to come I will do *more* than my part."

"I am grown tired of being ambushed by the wolf general," neighed the blackmane. "For the first time it will be my band that surprises Albarochk. So, how do we divide our force to conduct two separate ambushes?"

Band members again directed gazes at Lucars.

"First off, it must be Naythorn that goes to face Albarochk and his accompanying jaguar warriors."

"It is very fitting for a black spotted unicorn to lead the fight against black spotted jaguars." At that comment from Naythorn, Lucars smiled.

"With the exception of Blackler and Trackler," continued the youth, "I would place the strength of soldiers wearing blue gold armor at Naythorn's side. That means that with the blackmane go Buckmight, Taurington, the five wild boars, the two mountain sheep, Hammer, and myself. Although unarmored, Rainsnow and Dansey fight as well with Naythorn.

"On the other hand, the incredible scenting abilities of Blackler and Trackler will best serve those who fight at the site of the second ambush made upon the Raven warriors."

"I want to fight at the side of my friend Dansey," yipped Thistle.

"The two wolves can fight with Naythorn as a team," brayed Buckmight.

"Because I am most worried about the tricks that Albarochk will surely invent in the fight to come," yipped Dansey, "and because both Thistle and I know how Albarochk thinks, I also agree that the red wolf should go into battle at my side."

"To both Naythorn and Cabalblade, the scouting intelligence provided by Webstir, Featherspark, and Isabaya will prove invaluable," added Buckmight.

"May I?" interrupted Dansey walking over to Lucars. The youth handed his pointer stick to the yellow wolf.

"You might be the only wolf that can grasp tight a pointer stick," mused Lucars.

"Since the captain of the guard stallions is well-experienced at command, Cabalblade should lead the defense against Raven warriors," declared Dansey.

"There can be no doubt that Sir Cabalblade is the obvious choice to lead against the Raven warriors," agreed Buckmight.

"So then, to block this eastern pass through which the Raven warriors attempt to advance onto the plain," Dansey pointed with the stick, "will go Cabalblade, Lianvil, Belfloralex, Scarlet Point, Shawnee, and the two dogs. I remind that Amaluna brings her father and the Eagle Feather warriors to reinforce Cabalblade in the fight against their hated Raven enemies."

"Amaluna, Scarlet Point, and I will exact revenge against the Raven warriors that killed my husband their father, and destroyed my village."

"I am content to go with my friend Sir Cabalblade," grrrd Lianvil. "Lions loathe despicable pesky ravens."

"One thing more," continued the yellow wolf. "The unicorn herd must be quickly found and told of the battle that is soon to come. If at least a few unicorn stallions were to join the fight, they would best contribute under the command of the captain of the unicorn guard."

"It would be very helpful," interjected the bison, "if bears or some of the horse brothers of Rayalas tomorrow joined us in our attack. I keep thinking that Tristanbear must somehow have sensed that we need him. Hmph! It is unfortunate that we do not have time to spare so that the duck could once again search out Tristan and bring him to us."

"Rar...aahhrrmm..." After clearing his throat the red wolf yipped, "I found it extraordinary to learn that Belfloralex commands the wind. You know, I used to hunt rabbits in the narrow pass where Cabalblade and Lianvil will make their stand. A high ledge provides an open command of that pass. From that height Belfloralex might current a gale into the faces of enemy warriors. That wind would give a strong helping hoof to the charge of Sir Cabalblade."

"That, Thistle, is an *excellent* idea!" exclaimed Lucars. "I will never forget when Belfloralex hid me and Buckmight in her whirlwind so that passing warriors did not see us. And after the filly twirls a whirlwind that makes Cabalblade's ambush to be invisible, she can cause dust to blind the eyes of the Raven warriors."

At that moment was heard the very welcome sound of equine hooves. With necks arched and heads held high, ten vigorous young unicorn stallions trotted into the camp. The unicorns proceeded to crowd around Naythorn... as if he were a prince among them.

"I am Sergeant Haltervor. We come to join the fight of Captain Naythorn."

"Vor... err... Haltervor... how did you find me?" neighed the astounded blackmane. "Does your presence here mean that the herd of unicorns is close by?"

"Feeling your presence for many days past, Aneilee insisted the unicorn herd travel westward toward you. Mind you, Naythorn, when she and Elianor only yesterday crossed horns and pictured you in their minds, a vision presented showing where you were and that battle would soon be upon you. Based on her prescience, Aneilee asked me to recruit guard stallions, and with them gallop toward the lost blackmane to provide help in the conflict to come. The nine stallions with me are now proven in battle. They are the ones I could trust."

"I am to soon reunite with the white herd!" exclaimed Naythorn. "But, Haltervor, I remain confused. You see the matriarch never approved of me, and the high escort cannot condone the behavior of a war unicorn."

"Many things have changed, Naythorn. The white herd is now pursued by hostile Panther warriors. The leadership of the matriarch and the high escort is also threatened by Hoovefort, who seeks for himself all power over the unicorn herd. You cannot have forgotten Hoovefort?"

"He delighted in making me miserable."

"Captain Naythorn, given the dire nature of these two threats, Aneilee has come to believe that you are the stallion destined to rescue and preserve the unicorn herd. Now there is one thing that I require. I will have the two armored warriors to wet dirt and smear it onto my mane." Realizing that soon Naythorn would no longer be the only blackmaned unicorn, Lucars and Hammer grinned big at each other.

With his head, Haltervor motioned for Cabalblade to join the line of unicorn stallions that had formed before Hammer and Lucars. When the captain of the guard stallions hesitated, all eyes came to focus upon the sire of Naythorn, and an awkward silence prevailed. Finally Cabalblade surprised even himself by neighing, "The sire of Naythorn will tonight wear the color of his colt's mane."

Joined by eleven unicorn stallions including

Cabalblade, with freshly blackened manes, the mood of the camp soared. From that moment all those in Naythorn's company began to truly believe they would triumph against the many wolves and warriors soon to be thrown against them on two fields of battle. After a day of much activity, the camp of the blackmane quieted.

"I wonder where Tristanbear is this night to be found," muttered Naythorn to himself as he stretched out his neck on the ground. "I will bet his arms are grown even bigger than before. Hmph! I am tonight... not the only unicorn... with a black mane..." Given that the exertion of terrible battle would be soon upon him, it was well that Naythorn fell quickly asleep.

Later while pacing the perimeter of the camp, Lianvil paused before a sleeping Cabalblade and his grandfoal. "I told him I wanted to grow wings and fly; he instead made me to walk upright. I wonder if fighting upright, my paws will tomorrow know to wield swords."

After the yellow and red wolves relieved Lianvil of guard duty, the powerful lion slept the remainder of what he found to be a strangely hopeful night, at the side of the winged foal.

CHAPTER 20

WALKING TREE, CABALBLADE, AND TEN UNICORN GUARDS

As new light hinted in the east the camp of the blackmane stirred awake. Grown more in number by the arrival of ten unicorns that now wore dried dirt in their manes, the company of animal person soldiers assembled to hear Naythorn neigh final encouragement.

"The strategic thinking of Lucars, Dansey, and Buckmight has inspired an innovative battle plan that will surprise and give pause to our enemies." Naythorn nodded at his sire and continued, "It is well-fitting that the experienced captain of the unicorn guards command the ten unicorn stallions. My fellow helpers, triumph over cruel and relentless enemies will this day require all the strength and courage saved-up within us."

"Captain Naythorn," grrrd the muscular lion standing up on hind paws, "seeing Cabalblade reinforced with the platoon of unicorn stallions, I will change to fight at your side. I hate jaguars even more than bothersome ravens."

"We wild boars are proud to go with Naythorn," groinked the mama sow. "The blackmane saved my pig family from being ground up in the teeth of Albarochk. Even the same, if today the monster wolf survives he will not stop until he destroys the entire unicorn herd.

Cabalblade and Haltervor, if you are broken through then we who fight with Naythorn will find ourselves assaulted from behind. Today unicorn stallions *must* prevail!"

Buckmight, Taurington, Hammer, Lucars, five wild boars, two mountain sheep, two wolves, Rainsnow, and Lianvil followed Naythorn toward the place where ambush would be sprung upon the monster wolf Albarochk.

Allied Warriors

The Eagle Feather braves crossed the flint rock hills. At the side of her grandfather, the fit and fleet Amaluna kept up with the fast pace set by his warriors. Chief Walking Tree was proud that the heart of a girl whose laughter had ever been filled with innocence, showed no fear. He could not permit harm to befall a young girl's life so precious.

Come to meet them as she saw approach her daughter and her father the chief, Shawnee's heart parted with emotion. Grasped in the safety of her father's embrace, the grief she had felt since the loss of her husband came to be replaced... by new hope.

Shawnee led her father and the Eagle Feather warriors into a deep ravine where horned horses awaited them. The warriors were mesmerized by the beauty and strength of the unicorn guard stallions.

"I just had to do that!" exclaimed Scarlet Point after jumping upon the back of Haltervor. "I could not let my sister ride Belfloralex, and me never to have the chance to mount the back of a unicorn."

"The fit on my back of this young brave feels to be

right," neighed Haltervor. "The sight of a unicorn carrying a warrior armed with a spear and hatchet will instill fear into the enemy."

It did not take long for all the unicorn guard stallions, excepting Cabalblade, to acquire riders and form into a cavalry with Belfloralex and Amaluna, and Haltervor and Scarlet Point.

Cabalblade Leads into Battle

As the afternoon sun shoved westward, Raven warriors advanced toward the terminus of the tight-walled canyon. When the Raven fighters reached the place where a vista of the valley to the north presented before them, a big and slow moving whirlwind approached, and then the loud barking of dogs was heard.

At the canine signal, from out of the whirling wind Cabalblade and ten unicorns with mounts broke upon the Raven warriors. Behind those unicorns ran Belfloralex who brought with her the wind. The forceful gale spit dirt and sand into Raven warrior faces, and made it impossible for the enemy to with accuracy launch arrows or throw spears. Raven warriors were struck, buffeted, and thrown aside by the unicorns and their mounts. As they crashed upon and through Raven warriors, the quickness of the stallions to break one way or the other was amazing to behold. The young natives that clung to the backs of the unicorn stallions seemed to have been born to ride. The unicorn and its rider could talk to each other and feel each other's instant worry for a false step or a slow reflex.

The force of Raven warriors reset, and once

established, made to stall the advance of unicorn stallions and their mounts. At that early point in the battle hundreds of charging warriors led by Walking Tree broke upon their Raven enemies, and to them dealt devastation. It was not long before Walking Tree led his infantry after an enemy in retreat. The battle became a rout. While the warriors that fled the battlefield were allowed to escape, others of the enemy that remained behind fell on the valley floor with their honor intact.

"Where," inquired Scarlet Point approaching his Grandfather, "is the body of the great warrior chief of the Raven Tribe? That chief has killed very many of our people. Afraid of no one, surely that chief is not a coward to run away. And none of us saw him to flee away with the small-of-heart enemy warriors. How is it that the body of the enemy war chief is not anywhere found?"

"Are you certain the Raven chief's body lies nowhere in this place?"

"We have looked everywhere; the chief's body is not here."

"Can the numbers of our enemy fallen and fled match the full strength of the Raven Tribe?"

"No, Grandfather. Including even those that we saw to flee, we can account for less than half of the warriors of the Raven army."

"To my ears that is very bad news," responded Walking Tree with a frown. "That can only mean that the chief and more than half of his force of braves have climbed out of the canyon and over the mountain. The reason the Raven Tribe did not use all their great strength against us today, is that they have another objective in mind. Of this matter I will talk with Cabalblade."

With their dismounted riders at their sides, the unicorns gathered together amidst Eagle warriors.

"Cabalblade, the body of the chief of the Raven army is not here found," alerted Walking Tree, "and that fierce chief would never flee a battle. Eluding the attack of my warriors and the unicorn horses, the Raven Chief secretly took more than half of his army out of this valley. If the enemy chief did not betray the monster wolf, what objective could for him be more important than defeating my warriors and these unicorn stallions?"

"Which victory would be greater for our enemy," asked Scarlet Point, "to kill Naythorn and his band, or to destroy the entire herd of unicorns?" Knowing immediately the answer to Scarlet Point's question, the young unicorn stallions began to stomp excitedly and rear upward on hind legs.

"Many times the monster wolf tried and failed to defeat Naythorn," answered Cabalblade. "It is at the same time both a greater, and an easier victory to destroy the herd of unicorns."

"I will lead fast my Eagle warriors after my Raven enemies that cannot be far ahead of us. I will push them westward in the direction of the lands I know like the palm of my hand."

"Exactly so," answered Cabalblade. "You and I will do our part to rescue the white herd."

"Our enemy has stolen a march on us!" exclaimed Walking Tree addressing his braves. "We will run fast as the wind to protect the white herd from ambush!"

"As the advance attack force, we must reach the unicorn herd before it is too late, and all is lost," ordered Cabalblade. Immediately Amaluna, Scarlet Point teamed with his mother Shawnee, and nine more native riders flung their legs onto the backs of unicorns. Accompanied by Blackler and Trackler, Haltervor, Belfloralex and the other mounted unicorn guard stallions left with Cabalblade the canyon on the east side of the middle mountain where a half battle had been won. All understood that something great waited to be accomplished.

Mounted on Belfloralex, whose speed surpassed every young stallion, Amaluna sped past Cabalblade. The darkness of night came to muffle the sound of galloping unicorns.

CHAPTER 21

AGAINST ALBAROCHK, WOLVES, AND JAGUAR WARRIORS

"Where in tarnation does Albarochk find so many warriors and wolves to do his dirty work?" brayed Buckmight to Taurington as they watched the enemy host come into view.

"*That* is a mystery," answered the cattle. "And although it seems impossible, Albarochk's frame is grown even bigger than when we last fought him."

"Sir Cattle, this fight promises to be even more difficult than when we battled with our backs against the precipice of the great gorge."

"With the wolves held in reserve," commented Hammer to Lucars, "the vast weight of the fighting will for now be upon the shoulders of the thousand warriors that Albarochk commands. I suppose it is fitting that warriors representing jaguars, the largest predator cats in these lands, go with the giant wolf."

"Although the jaguar skins worn by the warriors are impressive," observed Lucars, "today we are not to battle real jaguars. And you are more practiced in battle against human persons than spotted lions."

"Nice of you to remind me of my illustrious service in the Phoenician army. By so doing, Lucars, you restore my confidence." That said, the two Phoenician soldiers exchanged small grins.

Battle Begun

The blackmaned unicorn crashed into the advance phalanx of the enemy. Launching their massive bodies into the Jaguar warriors, Buckmight, Taurington, and Rainsnow elected the same tactic. The initial thrust of the four big beasts opened a large gap in the front ranks of enemy warriors. Lucars, Hammerclaw, the red and yellow wolves, and the mountain sheep attacked the warriors found on one side of the opening made in the line of the enemy force.

Attacking on the other side of Naythorn the wild boars and Lianvil made the bodies of enemy warriors to buckle and fall. To their dismay Jaguar warriors could not stop the onslaught of the sword wielding Lianvil, and many braves found their ankles torn by the teeth of fierce wild hogs. When enemy reinforcements wrested the time required to set a new line, for Naythorn and his band the fight became not easier, but harder.

Albarochk held himself and his legion of wolves in reserve. The monster wolf's strategy at the beginning of the fray was to sacrifice as many warriors as need be.

"Brother Timidthy," groinked Hamilton, "two enemy warriors wait at the ready for each one that falls!"

"Their greater numbers offset their tactical disadvantages against our armor and spirit."

As nightfall approached the fighting became noticeably less sore. The forward thrusts of the Jaguar warriors seemed half-hearted, as though the braves were just following orders rather than fighting with their full strength and conviction. The fighting ceased.

"I can barely move my legs," gasped a weary Hammer. "Thank goodness that Albarochk finally gave the order to pull back his force of soldiers."

"Albarochk usually has one initial goal in battle, that being to wear us down," answered Lucars. "That said, the monster wolf no doubt has something else prepared for us."

"I share the same worry, Lucars. My gut tells me that Albarochk will soon bring to us an unwelcome surprise. No matter what is next thrown at us, you and I need to be at the ready."

"Albarochk is a crafty foe," answered the youth nodding his head. "The trick he is conniving will in some way involve his own entrance into the fray."

The Battering Ram

From out of deepening shadows overlaying close canyon walls, Albarochk's trick came into view. It was a war machine, simple in design, which Naythorn and his band had not before seen.

Two hundred of the biggest and strongest enemy warriors marched in a long wedge that broadened at its base. On the shoulders of the twenty files of warriors rested long and straight pine poles sharpened to have piercing points. Cadenced by the beat of enemy drums, each new step taken thrust ahead the heavy platform of tree spears.

"Look! They intend to impale on pointed poles our big-bodied Naythorn, Buckmight, Taurington, and Rainsnow!" exclaimed Hammer. "The warriors hold with one hand the enormous spear poles, and with their free hand wield a war axe to smash the legs, feet, and hooves of any that should jump upon the poles."

"They are intent on ramming their way through our defense and into the valley," added Lucars. "Should the war machine break through, the rest of Albarochk's army will scramble past us."

Behind the wedge of poles, and towering above everyone, walked Albarochk. At his right and left advanced many sturdy wolves. The general and his wolves were the rear guard protectors of the pointed battering ram.

"We low-legged soldiers must lead the attack against the pole bearers," growled Lianvil. "Wild boars, mountain sheep, and wolves can penetrate below the tree points."

Not waiting for an order from his captain, Lianvil charged the wedge of tree shafts. The great lion's reflexes made him to move twice as fast as the awkward defensive moves of the warriors hefting the poles. At the sides of the fierce lion the wild boars, mountain sheep, and the red and yellow wolves did more damage to the pole bearers. Before he was overwhelmed and beaten back, the teeth of Lianvil had torn the flesh of twenty Jaguar warriors. Still, as new Jaguar warriors shifted ahead to take the place of fallen comrades, the menacing poles continued to be held high, and step by step the pole bearers fought ahead.

"For the first time Albarochk's army fights with true coordination," neighed Naythorn. The company of the blackmane was forced to grudgingly fall back.

Standing on hind legs, with his forepaws wielding two swords, Lianvil joined a new attack led by Hammer and Lucars against the front edge of the wedge. Still, the push of the many warriors positioned at the rear of the war machine made to advance the battering ram. Naythorn crouched to leap onto the poles and crash them down.

"If you lose your balance and fall through the poles," cautioned Mama Pig, "enemy warriors will club you to death. Your band cannot afford to lose you."

"I cannot let Albarochk advance more his war machine."

"Captain Naythorn," grunted the sow, "just as we have always done, we will think of some way to stop them."

It suddenly seemed that ten things happened at once.

Approaching where the canyon narrowed at its bottleneck the cadence of the drums quickened to hasten warrior steps. Albarochk jumped up onto the poles, as if they presented to him an elevated throne. In coordination with their general's advance, wolves rushed through the legs of the Jaguar warriors bearing the pointed tree poles. At the front of the wedge soon crowded a phalanx of veteran wolf soldiers.

Buckmight vaulted over the lead wolves to place himself upon the forward part of the poled platform. As best he could the bison clambered toward the waiting Albarochk. With a great upward blow struck by his undamaged right front limb, Albarochk batted Buckmight off the platform of poles.

Undeterred, the cattle followed after the bison. Unable to withstand Taurington's great heft and pounding hooves, poles splintered. Still, the heavy cattle bull secured footing and launched himself at Albarochk. Once again timing perfectly the blow from his powerful right front paw, the giant wolf knocked aside Taurington.

Not able to be longer restrained the blackmane leapt upon the platform, lost his footing, and accompanied by splintering wood fell into and onto enemy warriors wielding war axes. Seeing the deadly danger to his leader, Lianvil leaped after Naythorn. He jumped about the damaged but still raised platform whirling and swinging both his swords, and so kept at bay Jaguar warriors attempting to converge on the prostrate unicorn. Taking advantage of the disarray and disorder, Rainsnow charged with lowered shoulders, banged forcefully into the wedge of wolves and warriors, and with his hooves sowed havoc all around him.

The swift reactions of Lianvil and Rainsnow gave Naythorn the chance to gather himself and clamber away. The bovines, Lianvil, and Rainsnow joined Naythorn at the side of the great platform of poles where they coordinated shoulders, heads, claws, and horns to tear into warriors sustaining the platform of tree trunks. Wood splintered and broke, and the platform of poles came no more to be.

In the resulting chaos, Albarochk sprang forward over the collapsing battering ram, and with many Jaguar warriors vanished into the night. Even if he had ultimately lost the *Battle of the War Machine*, the giant wolf had gained entry into the plain that opened wide before him.

A crisis was upon Naythorn. The blackmane could not permit the giant wolf, with a numerous army behind him, to advance across the plain toward the herd of oncoming unicorns. Perhaps the mere sight of the monster wolf would cause the white herd to stampede and break apart. Blackmane neighed for his friends to follow him in pursuit of the monster wolf. The unicorn and his band left behind the fight against remaining wolves and Jaguar warriors.

CHAPTER 22

A PLAN DARING AND DIFFICULT

"Wait! Blackmane! Stop!" groinked Timidthy. "Look upward! A light made of beautiful colors comes out of the darkening sky to shine down the promise of renewal. It is a sign that if we keep faith in the grace of a benign heaven, a lasting triumph will come to favor us." Reluctantly, Naythorn halted his hooves.

"Rayalas calls to you from above," continued the boarling. "Her calming presence tells our Captain that we cannot just chase after Albarochk. That together we have to out-think him."

"But the monster wolf rushes to attack the unicorn herd!" neighed Naythorn excitedly.

"Yes, but the cut once dealt by the point of your horn to his left shoulder will slow the monster's travel toward the white herd," rejoined Hammer. "That gives us time to prepare. Captain, our plan of battle closed tight the bottleneck at the end of the canyon. However, in the making of our strategy the invention of a war machine was not by us countenanced. Timidthy is right. We need to take some time, no matter how precious, to make an even better plan."

While the brightly colored lights shafting the night sky came to hover directly over the blackmane and his band, everyone sprawled bodies down. A time of rest was by all sorely needed.

"Timidthy... is right," neighed Naythorn untensing taut muscles. "The spirit of Rayalas fosters the light of encouragement."

"Do you know, Naythorn," groinked again the extra smart boarling, "that when the Rayalas Borealas shines down I find that I value more highly you, and everyone in the band including even myself."

"*Aherm,* Captain," mrawed Taurington, "I was just now thinking about how the poles of the battering ram splintered under my weight. Those flying wood shards were... *very dangerous.*"

"The combination of your sharp hooves and your heavy bulk made the poles to split," interjected the bison.

"Did Naythorn also notice," continued the cattle, "that as you struggled upon the poles to right yourself, Albarochk had a chance to fall upon you, but he hesitated."

"I think to know at what hints Taurington," groinked once more Timidthy. "The great wolf likes to fight from an open position, not body-to-body close with sharp splinters flying all about. But consider that in so doing Albarochk leaves open his chest to be penetrated by a sharp splinter of wood, or a spear."

"Timidthy," neighed the blackmane, "I will do anything to save the herd of unicorns, and I will not permit past failure to stop me. I right now need my friends to tell me *what* I must do to vanquish the monster wolf."

"Well," answered the boarling, "we have all heard the

story of how Belfloralex left half of her horn buried in the neck of the leviathan, and so chastened the sea monster to change from evil to the side of doing..."

"To puncture the chest of the wolf, I would sacrifice my horn," interrupted Naythorn.

"*That,* my captain, would be a drastic measure for you to endure," neighed Rainsnow pawing the ground.

"Hmph! Still..." the bison nodded his head slowly up and down, "it is interesting to conjecture what would happen if a long shard of unicorn horn were to be lodged in the heart of the wolf monster. When Taurington saw tree poles splinter before the chest of the great wolf, that idea occurred to him. Perhaps it also occurred to Timidthy. If a big and long sliver of your horn were to traverse Albarochk's heart and there remain, you would gain control over and dominate the monster."

Naythorn began to slowly nod his head up and down.

"Did Master Hammer and Lucars also notice how the tree poles set before the monster wolf splintered beneath the pounding feet of Taurington?" inquired Buckmight.

"I could not but take note of the dangerous splitting of those tree shafts," responded the smithy.

"It was loud to my ears," agreed Lucars.

"Well then, Master Smithy, thinking on that image could you with your sharp chisel cut the length of a unicorn horn from its tip to its base?"

"Master Bison, with the sharp edge of my chisel I can lengthwise sever a long hair pulled from the top of your head."

"That, Master Blacksmith, is something valuable to learn," answered Buckmight nodding his big head.

"Master Bison," interjected the blackmane, "if in some way I could thrust into the heart of Albarochk a shard that encompasses the entire length of my horn, the monster wolf would be unable to dislodge it. And, the fresh cut magic... of my horn... would be too strong for the great wolf to cast aside. Not for one moment could the monster forget that my horn shard was there set inside him to nullify his hideous evil."

"This, my captain, is how the deed could be done," mrawed the bison. "It would be me running with my head held high, that first springs upon the monster wolf. While his left limb hangs useless, he will follow his habitual tactic and strike upward with his enormous right forepaw. When Albarochk's great right arm remains momentarily extended upward, before he lowers it, his chest will be vulnerable. That is the exact moment when the horn of our captain, who will be running close upon me, comes to pierce the chest of the monster wolf."

Lost in thought, Naythorn set himself to pace. Finally the blackmane turned back to his band and neighed, "Taurington, Lianvil, Rainsnow, Mama Pig... tell me if you believe the plan just set forth by Buckmight can finally bring defeat to Albarochk."

Heads nodded; no one in the band of the blackmane voiced disagreement.

"Know, Naythorn, that I would hate for you to lose half your magic horn in the conflict," grunted Mama Pig.

"I will be saddened to not again see whole the conquering horn that has led our band through many battles. But I recall that after losing half her horn, Belfloralex retained intact her magic gift."

"With my own eyes I have seen that the filly still powerfully commands the wind," agreed Lucars.

"Then perhaps this blackmaned unicorn will, in that regard, be as fortunate as Belfloralex," offered the sow. "Albarochk grows stronger, and I can think of no other remedy to end his malevolence. If we do not soon destroy him, the monster wolf will annihilate every last unicorn in the white herd."

"I *will* do this thing," neighed softly the blackmane. "In fact, possessing but half a horn I will think to value it more highly. Now if it turns out that the pessimistic Rambuncture agrees with this audacious plan, then I am *absolutely* decided."

"*Of course* my ram cannot disagree with such a brave sacrifice to be made by our valiant captain," answered Ewelissas for her mate.

"So long as it is Naythorn's horn that is hammered and chiseled," baahed Rambuncture, "and not one of my own."

"Understanding well the goodness signified by the sacrifice to be made, I am sorry that I ever fought for Albarochk," yriped Thistle. "In the battle to come I will make whatever remedy I can for my past grave error."

"Thistle was not the only one to commit that grave error," concurred Dansey. "Guilty of having also served the monster wolf, in the battle to come Lianvil and I will also make amends for the error of our former ways."

"You must take heart, Naythorn," groinked Roothyford. "By the warmth of her light Rayalas Borealas tells us that it will go well for our captain. From out of the sky above her blue, orange, and purple shafts send down hopeful promise."

For the words groinked by the most sensitive wild boarling, Naythorn took heart.

CHAPTER 23

FOR SOLDIER FRIENDS

Four wings intersected the brilliant shafts of light shining down on Naythorn's band.

"Back to report, Sir!" saluted Webstir after whipping up dust with his wings.

"And there is *a lot* to report!" hronkked Featherspark.

"Because it has been a very trying day, your news had better be good," responded Naythorn. "By the way, I am impressed to see you stand so properly at attention."

"You will make soldiers out of us yet, Captain," answered Featherspark. "So much is happening that I do not know where to..."

"Then I will go first," interrupted the duck. "Walking Tree and Cabalblade carried out their ambush attack on the column of Raven warriors, and whipped the enemy army. That is, they defeated one half of the army. Playing a trick on our allied chief, many of the Raven warriors escaped over the mountain and now cross the valley to stop the westward progress of the unicorn herd. Chief Walking Tree and his Eagle Feather warriors are hot in pursuit of their raven enemies. And right now Cabalblade and the young guard stallions with their warrior riders travel fast toward the white... "

"*Hrronkk! You quacked enough!*" interrupted

Featherspark. "The most amazing discovery that was made by me..."

"But Goose, I saw them first!"

Featherspark chugged the duck with a big wing. "The most unexpected thing that I really did see first, was another enemy column traveling from the direction of the morning sun. They had war paint on their faces!"

"They wear panther skins, and wolves go in their lead," interrupted Webstir.

"That makes them to be enemy panther warriors that now follow behind the unicorn herd!" exclaimed Featherspark.

"It was clever of Albarochk to block the white herd from behind with Panther warriors," neighed the blackmane, "and shrewd to have Raven warriors block the herd of unicorns at their front."

"And it was nice of your foal to wave a wing at us as she fluttered above the white herd!" interjected the duck.

"That is all we have to report, Sir," hronnked the goose.

"So we now know that we confront three warrior armies," neighed Naythorn. "Does my sire Cabalblade know about the Panther army that comes out of the east?"

"Yes, Sir!" exclaimed Webstir. "On our way back to you we detoured to report the Panther danger to Cabalblade. He said to tell you that the unicorn guard stallions will stop the Panther advance from the east, and that Walking Tree will stop the advance of the Raven chief from the west."

"Very well done! I knew that I could count on my two waterfowl. Since Walking Tree and Cabalblade will not relent until the Raven and Panther warriors are beaten back, that leaves it up to our band to once and for all stop Albarochk and the Jaguar warriors."

"It is particularly fitting that the blackmaned unicorn stops the black spotted Jaguar warriors," hronnked Featherspark.

"Yes, exactly so," answered Naythorn. "Fortunately for us, Albarochk must slow his travel so that the rest of his wolves and Jaguar warriors, that are still behind us, catch up with him."

"Captain," barked Thistle, "once you are positioned with Cabalblade on your left, and Chief Walking Tree on your right, defensive reinforcements will be close at hand to counter an enemy break-through on one or the other side."

"Right you are, Thistle," agreed Dansey. "And Captain, the more I think about all the enemy warriors and wolves that we will contend with in the upcoming battle, the more I am sure that it is your horn that must deliver the fatal blow to Albarochk."

"Webstir and Featherspark, it is time for you to lead on my band to the unicorn herd."

The cattle with Hammer on his back, and the bison with Lucars, ran on opposite sides of Naythorn. The lion, the uncle stallion, five wild boars, and two wolves comprised the next file behind the blackmane. The mountain sheep moved about at the rear making sure that no enemy was sneaking after in the darkness. At the band's right and left scouted Trackler and Blackler.

When Naythorn slowed his pace, Buckmight came to be in a talkative mood. "You there, Sir Cattle on the other side of our captain, can you hear me?"

"As if you were trotting right next to me."

"I have been thinking on all the fighting that you and I have together done. Have we battled only because we like to fight? Would not you say that we enter the fray to stay the goodness of unicorn magic in this land?"

"I have now come to fight more for purpose than for enjoyment," agreed Taurington.

"But that is not the entire reason that a cattle and bison this night travel together toward battle."

"Not so? I am afraid, Buckmight, that now you have lost me."

"The real reason that I will enter gladly our next conflict is because I go... *with you*. I go with the blackmane. I go with the strong lion, our two crafty wolf friends, the intelligent and sensitive wild boar family, our smiling dog friends, the half silly duck and goose that pester us to no end, and the stalwart mountain sheep."

"I still do not catch your drift, Master Bison."

"So soon after the last conflict, the reason that I again commit my scarred hide to another battle is that you and the rest of the Naythorn's band have come to be for me... a family of friends. And so I defend my family."

"About that, Master Bison, you are right," concurred the mama sow overhearing. "I go again to battle because each of you are now to me *family*."

"In Albarochk's army," grrrd the lion, "I fought only because I was commanded to fight. Here this night with you Master Bison, and with you Sir Cattle, I can say that I also fight out of loyalty to my new friends found in this band."

Out of respect for the kindness of their expressed feelings of loyalty, Naythorn at first neighed nothing. Instead, the unicorn trotted forward with a new realization of the love he bore for those that followed him. The blackmane knew that what in his heart he shared for band members, was shared back to him.

"Because impressed upon my heart is the love of Rayalas," neighed at last Naythorn, "and the love held for me by those found beside me, if tomorrow were to be my last day I would die knowing that I did not live in vain. And I ask you Buckmight, is it not beautiful to travel under the light of the Rayalas Borealas?"

"It is at that, my captain."

Cabalblade on the Move

Cabalblade was panting. His run into the night was at breakneck speed that the captain of the unicorn guards did not know he was able to for so long sustain. The impetus for hard travel was the intelligence provided by Webstir and Featherspark that from the east Panther warriors pursued the white herd. Ahead on his left Cabalblade came to glimpse Raven warriors traveling north to attack his unicorn herd. He knew that not far behind them followed Chief Walking Tree.

"The escaped Raven warriors constitute a formidable brigade. Not the captain of the unicorn guards, but Chief Walking Tree and his Eagle Feather braves will stop the remaining half of the Raven army. My charge is to confront the Panther warriors... and I *hate* panthers!"

CHAPTER 24

CABALBLADE IN COMMAND

When shafts of brilliantly colored light came to illuminate the flight of his grandfoal, Cabalblade knew he had been right to not delay his return to the white herd by contending again with the Raven warriors. He could best protect the white herd standing at the front of his entire company of unicorn guard stallions.

Of a sudden, memories presented from his former life in Wittanor Hold. He could now admit to himself that even when surrounded by his guard stallions, he had always felt himself to be alone, and that he had ever before felt himself to be less than content. Cabalblade decided that his wonderful grandfoal, who from above now led him onward, symbolized the reason his spirit had changed.

"I was born to fight hard for my herd. In the Hold of Wittanor there never presented a danger that forced me to recognize and fulfill my destiny *as a war unicorn*. My colt Naythorn was as well born to be brave in battle."

A sudden revelation struck Cabalblade. It had been the restlessness of unsatisfied calling that had made him to be a difficult sire to Naythorn. Finding himself to be unhappy, he had every day brought discontent to the life of his only colt.

"My captain, watching Isabaya's wings waft above must fill you with pride," neighed Haltervor interrupting Cabalblade's thoughts.

"*I am* very proud of my beautiful grandfoal. It is for her and the other unicorn fillies and colts that I, you, and the guard stallions will tomorrow shed our blood."

"Yes, Captain, we will give our all to save the white herd from destruction authored by pure evil."

Spreading wide its shafts of light the Rayalas Borealas lit the north half of the heavens, and so permitted Cabalblade to see farther into the land of night. From the summit of a flint rock hill he beheld in the distance, discord. The entire white herd had lost all semblance of direction and organization. Darting wolves presented danger beyond the ability of a mare, with a foal at her side, to dominate. Unsure from which direction came the attack, the guard unicorns in their defense of the white herd were even less effectual than Belfloralex and Amaluna.

As his hooves brought him closer, Cabalblade heard mares shrieking in desperation. He suddenly realized that the wolves were focused on achieving a surround of the unicorn herd. Like sharks marshalling a school of darting fish, the objective of the wolves was to herd the unicorns into a tight constrictive circle. More and more wolves came to run on the periphery of the herd. It was inevitable that when the surround had been fully achieved, and wolves rushed the herd from all sides, that the hides of many unicorns would be punctured by sharp wolf incisors.

"Halt!" neighed Cabalblade to his platoon. "Those

guard unicorns that remained with the herd have forgotten how to form up in defense. We must organize the guards into a long line to intervene before the enemy. Snort and neigh loudly, and about our strength and numbers let us present worry to enemy wolves."

Cabalblade's platoon of guard stallions promptly put on an impressive display of neighing that could be heard from afar. As they charged ahead the guard unicorns zig-zagged back-and-forth to further create the illusion that their numbers were more than they actually were.

He had almost achieved the herd of unicorns when, in an instant, Cabalblade grasped the true purpose of the wolf surround. Enemy warriors had run over a rise, formed in a line, and shot shafts high so that arrowheads penetrated the area where crowded unicorns wheeled about in confusion. The reason wolves had not long pursued one or another vulnerable foal or mare, was that their one objective was to corral and immobilize the white herd for assault by the flighted arrows of many Panther warriors.

Ignoring wolf predation, Cabalblade led his platoon of stallions and riders onto a knoll that intervened between his herd and Panther warriors come from the east.

"Captain," neighed Haltervor, "the warriors will soon be close enough to use their spears against us."

"From their adornment we see the enemy warriors purpose to fight like panthers. From long experience in Wittanor Hold, guard stallions despise black panthers. We will show these warriors that of panthers we have no fear."

Led on by Cabalblade, as Haltervor and nine more unicorn stallions with their mounts ran at the enemy the Rayalas Borealas curtained shut her fading light. The line of unicorns took advantage of the dim and elusive time between night and new dawn to obscure the forward charge of their line, all the while dodging the whirring darts sent from Raven warriors with eyes now forfeit of skylight. Veering right and left, unicorn hooves abetted by the war axes of their Eagle warrior mounts, struck and flung aside the remaining wolves set before the Panther warriors.

"I go to recruit more stallions to join us," neighed Haltervor.

By the time the stallions led by Cabalblade penetrated through the front line of enemy warriors, a second line of twenty stallions led by Haltervor was speeding to follow after. It became the turn for both the captain of the unicorn guards and Haltervor to plant fear and anguish into the chests of Panther warriors.

Stealing glances in the direction of their captain, the guard stallions advanced their line. Observation of Cabalblade's fighting style served to both inspire and instruct. The stallions returned ruin to warriors rushing to engage at close quarters. Where accompanied by the cutting axes of their mounts, unicorn hooves introduced an involvement of war that veteran Raven warriors knew not how to withstand.

"Nyeeerrrr! Push back the Panther warriors and do not relent!" ordered Cabalblade.

For the over-confident warriors that had only a little while before held victory within the grasp of strong hands wielding bows, the battle became confusion. Panther soldiers shifted feet backwards, and then turned to flee. Tails tucked between legs, wolves scattered to the winds. The countenance of the battlefield changed its look from one of unicorn disarray, to one of hard-pressed enemy warriors and wolves in flight. The conflict ended as a breeze came to freshen the dawn.

Standing over the unbreathing body of her foal felled by a sharp arrow point, a mare was inconsolable in her grief.

"How did this come to happen to our herd?" inquired Elianor of the high escort as they turned away from the grieving mare. "How is it, Aneilee, that stampeded by wolves, our hearts became so frozen in fear and terror that we did not know to protect ourselves?"

"Our eyes, Elianor, have been opened to clearly see the great evil that surrounds and is upon us." The matriarch and high escort gladdened to see Cabalblade trotting toward them.

"When hope to us became lost your example restored discipline, procured fortitude, and saved us," neighed Elianor. "Your rescue teaches us the dangerous consequences of uncontrolled fear beset by wanton disorder and panic."

"We thought we were prepared for danger," added Aneilee. "As you saw, we were not. From out of our confusion one thing was learned... for the unicorn herd to survive we must better prepare for the battle, before it is fought. For if we do not, even in desperate victory much enemy blood on our hooves and horns will destroy our very identity as bringers of hope."

"As you look closely upon this field of battle, you will here find few unbreathing warriors and wolves," answered Cabalblade. "More than killing them, Haltervor and I today struck fear into the enemy. By the way, something has been made clear to me. I realized that I was born to be a war unicorn. The will to do battle flows in my blood and hardens my spirit. After I organized my line of unicorn stallions to advance, about myself I came to know another thing. I do not fight because I want to, I attack because I care deeply about the survival of the unicorn herd."

"But do you hate those that with your hooves you strike?" inquired Elianor.

"Being honest with myself I have to neigh, *yes*. When charging at my enemies I am satisfied that they suffer much."

"For that I am sorry," responded Elianor with her eyes softening.

"Sir Cabalblade," interjected Aneilee, "you must reach out beyond the guards and train every unicorn stallion to think of himself as a keeper of the peace, who like you fights as a war unicorn when so called upon. You see, Captain, when our very survival is at stake new ideas must be found, accepted, and followed."

Pausing to look closely into the eyes of the two unicorns she needed the most to hold her trust, Aneilee added, "Cabalblade, Elianor, you two are born leaders. For unicorn goodness to persist we together must change the mentality of the unicorns toward the always unfortunate and regrettable circumstances of war."

"I will do all that is within my power to make

unicorn stallions the first line of defense for the white herd. And, Aneilee, I assure you that when he fights wolves and warriors that kill for enjoyment, this captain of the unicorn guards will keep unseen the hate that consumes his heart. And one thing else, I have come to desperately want Naythorn to again present himself into the space he left unfilled."

"That Naythorn helped the Phoenician blacksmith and his apprentice to find the blue gold they sought," neighed Aneilee, "and so repaid the exceptional debt incurred for the rescue brought to us by barges, bespeaks his nobleness. That the blackmane now leads a band of lowly animal persons shows his gentleness of spirit." After bowing to Cabalblade, the matriarch and high escort turned hooves to impart healing where it was most in need.

"From high above I saw your entrance into the battle," neighed the winged foal as she landed dainty hooves. "My grandsire was magnificent! And as they charged forward your guard stallions were beautiful to watch!"

"It was very brave of you, little foal, to fly into the night and find us so that we could follow you back to where the white herd faced peril. And I see that your wings spread wider than when I last saw you. How does my wonderful bay grandfoal make them grow so fast?"

"Just like me, my wings have an independent nature. When by themselves they decide to grow fast, I cannot stop them." Isabaya looked shyly at her grandsire as she inquired, "How many wolves and warriors did you kill today?"

"My rage against the enemy drew much blood. Still, I can say that I did my best to give wolves and Panther warriors hurt without stopping forever the beating of their hearts. Do you know what? I even think that for all the harm we did, some of the wolves and warriors came to understand that we were not intentioned upon destroying them. That revelation made it easier for some of our foes to turn and flee our advance."

"What will happen next, Grandsire?"

"Having been always honest with your sire, I cannot be dishonest with his foal. The unicorn herd will from three sides face danger. Once the other two enemy armies arrive here, the Panther warriors we battled today will from the east rejoin the fight against us. In the lead of Jaguar warriors and many wolves, comes the giant wolf from the south. And Raven warriors advance from the west. Running away from three warrior armies and many wolves, cannot gain us refuge. From a position of strength we must at the same time confront the three enemy forces. Your sire and his band, and our friend Chief Walking Tree and his warriors, will help the white herd to gain victory. Now, do you know what else?"

"What, Grandsire?"

"My heart tells me that yet this day we will again see Naythorn. You will tell him we are proud of all that he has done."

"Will you tell your colt that you love him?" The winged foal did not wait for her grandsire to answer. "Look, look up there! Do you see the two birds with sparkling necks?"

"Yes, Isabaya, I see them. Their presence tells us that Naythorn draws close."

"Webstir and Featherspark are fun to fly with."

"My little one, can I ask of you a favor?"

"Of course, Grandsire."

"Will you, for me, preserve until tomorrow the strength of your wings? You see, I have the idea that on the morrow there will be some work that only your wings can accomplish."

CHAPTER 25

BEFORE GREAT BATTLE

The column of Raven warriors was by unicorns seen. In the lead of hundreds of weapons bearers trotted more than one hundred wolves.

"Tell me Hoovefort, what is the tactical motivation for the Raven chief's decision to block the westward passage of the white herd?" inquired Cabalblade as he stood quietly with his lieutenant and sergeant.

"Sir, he invites us to break out to the south, and so the chief freely permits us to leave his coveted hunting grounds."

"Do you, Sergeant Haltervor, agree with the lieutenant's reading of the enemy tactic?"

"No Sir, I do not. Possessing good intelligence the Raven chief will know that on our east pursue the Panther warriors, out of the south comes Albarochk and his allied Jaguar warriors, and on our north flows an impassable river. Knowing that we are blocked to the east, south, and north, the obligation of the Raven Chief is to complete the siege by blocking our escape to the west."

"But there is still time! While we can we should break out to the south!" retorted Hoovefort stomping his hooves. "Most unicorns are cowards. Their instinct is to flee danger. I will go order the unicorn guard stallions to lead the breakout."

"Hold, Hoovefort." Well aware that it came natural to the set of his long face, Cabalblade maintained a stern demeanor as he moved hooves to block his lieutenant. "You forget that the captain of the unicorn guards is newly returned."

"You would do well to listen to me!" replied Hoovefort angrily.

"Now I ask my sergeant to again consider the suggestion made by our lieutenant, that the white herd should flee to the south."

"Here is what I think." To help clear his thinking Haltervor shook his mane. "Unicorn flight brings with it a grievous problem. Warriors and wolves will pursue us and slowly but surely kill every laggard mare, foal, and old unicorn that falls behind. On the other hoof, the three reasons to remain on this hill are critically strategic. Height is advantageous in battle, and this hill is the highest place found in these parts. Here we await strong allies, namely Naythorn and his band and the Eagle Feather warriors. And, thirdly, with a river to our rear we will not on this protective height die of thirst."

"Your assessment, Haltervor, is not wrong," responded Cabalblade nodding his head. "While the white herd will be here surrounded, the height of this hill provides important defensive advantage, and at our side will soon be found the Eagle Feather warriors and Naythorn's band. It has become time for us to not flee. This place is where our great battle is to begin."

"But either Albarochk and his Jaguar followers or the Raven warriors will prevent Walking Tree from reaching us," objected Hoovefort.

"No, Lieutenant, you will soon see our western front protected by the arrival of Chief Walking Tree. Until all the enemy armies are well positioned, it is not the purpose of Albarochk to begin this battle. Like you, enemy warriors believe that once we are surrounded they will have the upper hand.

"When arrive Naythorn and his company, many of whom wear armor forged of magic blue gold, they will on our southern front face the great wolf."

"Captain, the battle will surely begin on the morrow," interjected Haltervor. "Whether in one, two, or three days, this field of battle will come to be owned by Walking Tree, Naythorn, and Cabalblade."

"Just as you say... Haltervor," neighed Hoovefort with a smile that given the seriousness of the moment seemed casual and out of place.

Naythorn Rejoined

With no resistance offered by Raven warriors, the column of Chief Walking Tree joined to the white herd. Soon after, the chief sat by a fire with Amaluna.

"I know, Grandfather, that a great battle is upon us, but I am *not* afraid. The reason I do not fear is that I this night see unicorn mares sleep with foals relaxed at their side. The peacefulness of these magic horses inspires confidence in me."

"Good for you," replied the chief smiling at his granddaughter. "Warriors on both sides know the battle will not take place until the arrival of two strong foes, the unicorn with the black mane and the monster wolf. The Raven Tribe will not engage us until their monster wolf commander is here come. Hmph. Just like me, are you excited to meet Naythorn?" With a big smile, the question was answered by the girl.

The night came to be clear and cool with stars crowding one on another, and stacking layer upon layer. Although the band moved quietly, it seemed the entire camp of unicorns heard their arrival before half night. Naythorn and his friends were welcomed with somber unicorn neighs that sounded of hope renewed.

"I have wanted to meet you ever since I first heard the name Naythorn. I am the island girl Alexzana, and I want to join your band. This is my new friend Amaluna." She looked about. "Now, where is Marsand?"

"As you have been told Naythorn, my mother, brother, and I were freed from our Raven enemies by Belfloralex, Lucars, and Buckmight. For that I also pledge myself to fight at your side."

"Amaluna, you and Alexzana are most welcome to join my band."

"I am Marsand!" exclaimed a youth rushing to the side of the island girl. "When Alexzana left behind the Phoenicians to follow after the unicorns, I decided my place was to accompany her. Since I no longer pertain to Phoenicia, I will *also* belong to the band of Naythorn."

Aneilee and Elianor brought the unicorn sage stallions to the southern edge of their encampment where they joined Naythorn, Belfloralex, Buckmight, Taurington, Rainsnow, Lianvil, five pigs, two mountain sheep, two dogs, and the red and yellow wolves. The goose and duck wafted down to land upon Taurington's broad back.

"It was past time that the lost blackmane returned to the white herd!" exclaimed Aneilee in greeting. "I came to truly miss you, and I want you to never again disappear on me."

"The blackmane has grown up," neighed Elianor rubbing her head against his side. "Your strength and size makes you the equal of your sire and Lieutenant Hoovefort."

"The lieutenant absents. I should like to once again see him."

"Hoovefort is right now busy," answered Elianor. "And Naythorn, might I say that you owe Hoovefort no apology for knocking him off his hooves the last time you saw him."

"The white herd is surrounded," interrupted Cabalblade upon joining the matriarchs. "We count on your experience, Naythorn, to help us escape the trap set for us."

"The hearts of the fighters in my platoon beat as true as does mine," responded Naythorn. "It is because of their courage and resourcefulness that I this night regained my herd."

Naythorn turned to Featherspark, "When arrives the giant wolf?" Given the assembled presence of the unicorn leaders and sages, the goose felt compelled to report in a most serious military fashion. He extended high his long neck and with both wings saluted.

"*Hrronkk!* Captain! Sir! At the first light of day the monster wolf, Jaguar warriors, and the wolves that escaped the ambush we laid for them will be approaching. The number of warriors that go with

Albarochk is less than one hundred."

"Less than one hundred?"

"Yes, Sir. I counted them twice."

"But, Featherspark, that is very *strange*. Hundreds of Jaguar warriors were kept in reserve some distance behind the war machine. I counted on them to follow after Albarochk. Nevertheless, that is excellent news. Well done!"

"*Qvackk!* Captain Naythorn! Sir! Err... the wolf acts like he knows exactly where he is going."

"For how long, Aneilee, can the magic unicorn shield called forth by the sage council hold the enemy at bay?"

"Naythorn, in less than two suns the sages will be exhausted. When that happens the magic shield will into thin air vanish.

"*Nyerrrr!* I do need to caution Naythorn about something. As you know, the magic of sage unicorns derives from the purity of the white herd. So the more blood that is shed in battle, the more sullied will be our innocence, and the more daunting will be the path to our new hold. It occurs to me that limiting the blood that is shed, even if it is the blood of evil enemies, will serve to strengthen and preserve the shield."

"In a great battle much blood is shed," interjected Cabalblade.

"High Escort," barked Dansey, "better than anyone here I know well the wolf general. Albarochk is convinced that as long as unicorn magic persists, the evil that possesses him cannot triumph to reign supreme over all beasts. For that, Albarochk's heart commands that your blood be shed, and that all traces of the white herd vanish from the land. Dame Aneilee, you cannot forever run from the monster. Time and again Naythorn has tried to escape Albarochk, but the wolf general always re-finds the blackmane. As you can see, it is now come to Naythorn to forever stop the giant wolf. Not until the monster's heart beats no more will the white herd again know peace and safety."

Naythorn's Destiny

"This is all the fault of the blackmane!" exclaimed a sage unicorn shaking back-and-forth his head. "His *own sire* has neighed that is so! Naythorn's absurd idea to rescue ordinary animals invoked the great wolf's anger and revenge. Since by drinking Naythorn's blood the wolf became a monster, the blackmane must go away from us and take the giant wolf after him."

"By saving me from myself, Naythorn did what was right for his heart," rejoined Buckmight. "Cannot you glimpse in the wings of his foal Isabaya the purity and beauty of my captain's heart? Just as the destiny of the unicorn herd in Wittanor Hold was linked to the destructive fire of the volcano, Albarochk's destiny is to make war upon the magical goodness of unicorns."

"Council sages," continued Taurington. "The evil wolf now turns from hunting Naythorn to hunting the source of all unicorn magic. Unless Naythorn stops him, at dawn the monster wolf will spring upon mares, foals, and stallions. Just consider that only yesterday the great wolf slipped past Naythorn to gain entrance to the unicorn herd. The monster wolf showed that he would willingly allow Naythorn and his band to depart this place, because it would make that much easier the monster's destruction of the white herd."

"Surely Aneilee and the sages know that the past cannot be regained," barked Dansey. "The presentation of the future decrees change. The irreplaceable white herd *must* survive this battle, and also the many new adventures that will follow."

"It is an *unhappy* thing. But I know that the bovines and the yellow wolf are right," declared Aneilee. "Before he was born, the great wolf's evil destiny was set. Our destiny, to learn and grow in a new age and in a new land, was also long ago established. The white herd has no choice but to survive. I only ask that we do not take delight in spilling blood. If from battle waged we learn to lust for the blood of our enemies, our magic will by half diminish. The unicorn peace, the very foundation of our magic, must survive."

"The murmurings against the blackmane must stop," grrrd Lianvil rising to stand on hind legs. "Either the monster wolf dies, or the white herd will be forever destroyed. From the moment the giant wolf's heart beats no more... unicorn lives will be saved."

"Then how, Sir Lion, can the wolf's heart be stopped?" inquired Elianor. With a gesture made by a huge paw, Lianvil handed off the question to Dansey.

"We have formed a plan... that at a moment of climax in the battle... will be carried out by Naythorn. To our captain the plan will mean grave sacrifice."

"Is what the yellow wolf barked, true?" neighed feelingly Aneilee. "Naythorn, you shall suffer? I cannot *lose you!*"

"Know, Dame Aneilee, that my band will carry out a

plan that achieves its rightful end. The attack will begin when Albarochk arrives from the south to lead in battle the warriors allied to him. Have the shield raised strong at the first light of new day."

CHAPTER 26

A SHIELD MADE TACTICAL

"Why is Tristanbear not here?" muttered Naythorn with his head and neck resting between straightened front legs. The sprawled blackmane looked depressed.

"That... is terribly *wrong* of him!" squealed Hamilton intent on lightening the mood of his captain. "It was the bear who began... everything! If Tristan had not gotten himself into a mess, you would not have had to rescue him, and of course then you never would have crossed paths with the giant wolf. Hmph! Everyone else is here! So where is that numbskull Tristan?"

"I have to admit that my boarling brother is right," agreed Timidthy sporting a sly smile. "Since he is not here to finish the fight that he began, this has to be all... Tristan's fault."

The blackmane snorted, shook his mane, and resettled his head between forelegs.

"Just look about you, Naythorn!" admonished Roothyford. "Since the fateful day that Tristanbear joined to you, your band has grown a lot. Five now full-grown wild boars wearing blue gold armor *more than* make up for the absence of the bear."

"Count them, Naythorn!" groinked Practicia as she stood to place front paws onto Hamilton's back.

"Assembled here with you are five wild boars, three men, three women, and three unicorns. And the waterfowl, bovines, sheep, dogs, and wolves number two each. Let me see now, that makes twenty-four. Add to that Rainsnow, Lianvil, and yourself, and that makes the band to number twenty-seven. It is just too bad that Tristanbear has something more important to do than to be right here right now... for I *especially* like the number twenty-eight."

"But of the three unicorns with me," corrected the blackmane, "only Belfloralex and Cabalblade count. Isabaya is too young to take on the responsibility of membership in a military company. Perhaps someday..."

"So your foal is too young to count. So what!" continued Practicia. "It bears mentioning that of the not twenty-seven, but twenty-six band members present, more than half wear the magic armor fashioned by Hammerclaw."

"Precisely sixteen of us wear blue gold armor." Interjected Timidthy.

"Only fifteen!" exclaimed Hamilton objecting to the count of his brother. "I will count them so Timidthy sees that I am right. We are five pigs with armor, plus two men, plus two waterfowl, plus two bovines, plus two sheep, plus two dogs. See, that is *only fifteen!*"

"Hah!" responded Practicia. "Our boarling brother deliberately forgets to include the most important armor of all, that which is worn by our blackmaned captain."

"Well then, we shall have to return to Shining Canyon so that I can forge armor for ten more members of Naythorn's band," observed Hammer.

"Make that eleven more pieces of new armor," neighed Naythorn. "As captain of our band I will insist that Webstir once again find Tristanbear and bring him back to Shining Canyon to be also fitted with the magic blue gold."

"Being myself captain of the unicorn guards, I cannot make myself to be a member of my colt's band," neighed Cabalblade to Naythorn.

"My sire, the guard captain, knows that here with my platoon he is most welcome."

The cheerfulness of the boarlings, no longer piglings but come to be large wild boars, had succeeded in lightening the heavy burden wearing on Naythorn's heart. Not wanting their captain to feel alone at this time of ominous and fateful challenge, the bison and bull moved to sprawl their big bodies one on each side of the blackmane. The rest of the band gathered round.

"Ermm... Captain," declared Thistle. "I have been thinking about the execution of our plan. Before we spring our trap on Albarochk we should put him on edge, make him nervous."

"*Yipe, yripe*, that is smart thinking," reflected Dansey. "More than anything, Albarochk hates any delay of his cruel and brutal violence. We need to taunt him, and so make him to become reckless. So, how do we make Albarochk so angry that he grows careless?"

Timidthy rose, began to pace, and then paused to groink, "Sir Cabalblade, I know that it is impenetrable, but can you please tell us exactly how works the unicorn shield?"

"Well... the unicorn shield that presents like a one-way window has to do with focus, readying, and suddenness. However, it does require some time to establish the full force of the shield."

"How *much* time?" persevered Timidthy.

"It takes five hundred horse breaths of time to call forth the shield," answered again Cabalblade. "In that regard the concentration of the sage unicorns must be absolute and total. Once raised, and so long as Aneilee and the sage unicorns are left unbothered to focus on protective magic, the shield remains at full force."

"And how long, Sir Cabalblade, does it take to undo the shield?" came the boarling's follow-on question.

"When the sage unicorns all together and all at once dismiss their concentration, the shield instantly vanishes from sight, as if it had never been raised."

"If the shield could be suddenly dropped to let us charge at the surprised and startled enemy," continued Timidthy, "it would prove devastating to the morale of Albarochk's forces. Then if after bruising the wolf's warriors and wolves we escaped back behind the protection of the shield... why that would truly *infuriate* Albarochk."

"This lion would not like at all that my enemy charged out from behind nothingness, and then just as suddenly fell back behind an invisible wall of protection."

"That would make Lianvil very angry?" inquired Timidthy.

"That would... *enrage* me."

"I do believe that Timidthy is onto something," neighed Naythorn. "When Albarochk loses his temper he acts rashly. After two or three such false parries, he would become careless and be more likely to leave open his body for me to inflict grave wound.

"Belfloralex can outrun any of us. I will have her to relay instructions to Aneilee so that when the time is right, the sage council drops the shield. For all our allied forces to charge out at once together, we will as well require perfect coordination with Cabalblade on our eastern front and Walking Tree on our western front."

"You do, Naythorn, understand the grave risk of basing battlefield tactics on a disappearing and reappearing protective shield," cautioned Cabalblade. "That maneuver has never before been done by the sage unicorns. What if the sages fail to re-raise the shield in the time allotted?"

"Sire, to unravel the battle plan of the monster wolf... it is our best and perhaps only chance. If the shield does not work in the way we have planned, we shall be forced to continue harsh battle. Great though it be, the risk must be taken."

Webstir and Featherspark flighted down to rejoin the band. Webstir approached strutting, as best could a duck, while saluting the reclined blackmane.

"Captain! Sir! The monster wolf is soon before us!"

"Sir!" honked Featherspark stretching high his neck. "The giant wolf commands seventy wolves and one hundred Jaguar warriors."

"The goose once again tells me that there are no more than one hundred Jaguar warriors ready for battle?"

"Only one hundred, Sir. And we can sight no more

following to join..."

"*Qvackk!* About that Featherspark knows what he honks!"

"That news is helpful," responded Naythorn. "After Albarochk jumped off the war machine, I was sure that all the Jaguar warriors would have followed him here. With our band already badly outnumbered, we can only hope that the remainder of the Jaguar force continues to absent from the battle to come."

The Wolf General

As an impatient edge of the sun began to brighten the sky, Albarochk took his time inspecting his forces. The great grayback wanted every single one of his wolf and warrior soldiers to measure and reflect on the size of his monster frame, and to also notice the teeth protruding savagely from his jowls. While he had mostly recovered his faculty of speech, for Lianvil's treachery it pained the wolf general's tender and still-healing jaws to loudly growl commands.

Before finishing his inspection the wolf general was blinded by a flash of light. After his eyes readjusted, to his astonishment Albarochk found that the unicorns and their allies had vanished behind a wall of blue mist. When the enormous wolf motioned for a platoon of warriors to probe the magic mist, the braves bodily disappeared inside the eerie wall. The still intact platoon re-emerged from the blue mist to report that they wandered in a fog that seemed to have no end. When lookouts confirmed that no unicorn had been seen to depart the white herd, Albarochk understood that the shield was no less than a magical barrier. The pain of his jaws was forgotten as the monster wolf cursed the infernal unicorn magic.

"Tarnation! Behind their shield hide unicorns like cowards! Let them and their poisoned magic... be damned! *Grrarroouu!* Unicorn magicians will soon become exhausted, and when they do, the shield will disappear. When the mist breaks I will have every wolf and warrior to charge forward." After circling his feet about several times, Albarochk sat himself on rear haunches. He could do nothing but wait.

By midday the wolf general had grown very impatient. Things were not as they should be with him in full command of battlefield action. As the sun continued its westward progress Albarochk's mood grew more ugly. The last thing he wanted was to appear helpless in front of the warriors and wolves he commanded.

Through the mist that physically separated them from their enemies, the defensive line of Naythorn's band observed closely the angry faces of Albarochk and his forces. The two mountain sheep stood stiffly with eyes riveted on the enemy. Seated on their rumps next to the ram and ewe, Dansey and Thistle busied themselves imitating the expressions of the monster wolf, of course with suitable exaggeration added to their pliable facial features. The four wild boar siblings engaged in debate about where pig bites could do the most damage to the most imposing wolves and warriors stationed beyond the shield. While maintaining a subtle vigilance Lucars, Marsand, Scarlet Point, Amaluna, and Alexzana quietly sang light-hearted songs with lilting melodies. Holding his sword at the ready in one hand, Hammer did not think it improper to with the other hand have a smoke of rolled tabac.

For their part Webstir and Featherspark continued to scout from the sky and report on the readiness of Cabalblade's guard stallions and Chief Walking Tree's Eagle braves, found respectively on the east and west sides of the white herd. Belfloralex repeatedly updated Naythorn on the status of the sage council. To help pass the time Isabaya made several fast practice flights from Naythorn's location to the position of Cabalblade.

"I cannot believe that the monster wolf so soon recovered his voice," grrrd Lianvil.

"That, was to be expected," observed the yellow wolf. "Perverse and twisted magic continues to flow powerfully through the body of Albarochk, and many suns have come and gone since you broke his mouth."

By late afternoon it was evident to the two traitor wolves that Albarochk and his forces had relaxed their guard. With Belfloralex and the two waterfowl at their sides, the red and yellow wolves reported to the blackmane.

"Naythorn," yipped Thistle, "our enemies now act as if there will be no battle today. Grown tired of the shield, Albarochk has turned himself about to look the other way."

"Your band is prepared," added Dansey. "It is time to test the tactical value of the shield,"

"So the time has come. Tell Buckmight, Taurington, Lianvil, Rainsnow, Hammer, and Lucars that with me they lead our attack. Make sure everyone understands that before reforming anew, the shield will remain for one thousand breaths fallen. If after one thousand breaths of battle we are not set again in our original line of defense, there will be no way to return through the shield. I do not want even one member of my band to become stranded outside the shield." At that instruction the red and yellow wolves turned and trotted away.

"Featherspark and Webstir, fly now to Chief Walking Tree. Tell him that the shield is about to fall, and that it will set again after one thousand horse breaths."

"Isabaya, go quickly and tell Cabalblade to ready his stallions, for the shield is ready to fall, and then raise again. The unicorn guards have only one thousand horse breaths to do battle."

"And I will go tell Aneilee and the sages to let fall now the shield," volunteered Belfloralex.

"Yes, do so. Be sure they know the shield must again stand after the passage of one thousand horse breaths. That means that after five hundred horse breaths, the sages must restart the process of raising the shield."

"Yes, Naythorn. That is because five hundred and five hundred make one thousand."

"Once the high escort confirms that she perfectly understands both halves of my order, have her immediately make the protective shield to vanish."

The Shield Collapses

At the disappearance of the shield the eyes of Albarochk's wolves and warriors filled with disbelief. They could not comprehend that the impenetrable mist, the object of their consternation and anger, had come to be suddenly and mysteriously vanished into thin air. To make matters for them worse, the wolf general's fighters hesitated unsure that the forces charging down from where the shield had been, were not also an illusion.

Hooves, horns, swords, and a great lion wielding two pawed swords cracked hard the center of Albarochk's line of warriors and wolves. A yellow and a red wolf climbed upward the backs of Hammerclaw and Lucars, and from the shoulders of the two Phoenicians launched themselves upon Jaguar warriors.

Five wild boars, two dogs, and two mountain sheep, all wearing blue gold armor, surged forward on one side of those fighting with the blackmane. On Naythorn's other side advanced the swords wielded by Scarlet Point, Marsand, Amaluna, and Alexzana.

The monster wolf watched in stunned disbelief as his line crumbled and his fighters were beaten back. When Albarochk finally sprang into action it quickly became clear that no unicorn, bovine, or lion could stand against the brute strength of the gigantic monster wolf. It also became evident that Naythorn's band was outnumbered several times over. Anchored by Albarochk, the line of his army reformed, fought forward, and began to believe that they could not lose.

After wolves and warriors came to almost reclaim the ground they had lost, Naythorn's band broke fast in retreat only to reset in a defensive line. Unsure what was transpiring, hesitant wolves and Jaguar warriors looked to their leader.

Once again a flash of brilliant light blinded the eyes of Albarochk and his fighters. When their eyes readjusted, warriors and wolves found Naythorn and his allies had again vanished behind the same blue mist that had before hidden them. Scarcely after it had begun, the skirmish had ended.

When no answer came in response to the howls of an incensed Albarochk, his mood darkened. Enemy forces again settled themselves on the line they had formerly held, the same line that had quickly fallen to the charge of Naythorn's allies. New silence came to shroud the battlefield.

Featherspark, Webstir, and Isabaya escorted Chief Walking Tree and Cabalblade to the defensive position of the unicorn's band.

"We knocked the Raven warriors hard enough so that they will unhappily remember it," reported the chief of the Eagle Feather Tribe.

"So far, so good," added Blackmane's sire. "The guard stallions performed admirably. The wounds of many injured Panther warriors will require a moon of time to heal."

"And your losses?"

"Five bloodied unicorn stallions cannot continue the fight," replied Cabalblade to his colt.

"Suffering deep cuts and broken bones, ten of my Eagle braves have to me become lost," answered the chief.

"Aneilee and Elianor will be pleased that our casualties from this foray include none dead," reflected the blackmane. "Since Walking Tree and Cabalblade have found the collapse of the shield for some one thousand breaths to have been a success, at some point during the coming night we will a second time repeat the same tactic. If all again goes well, we will afterward meet to decide if our final charge will come when the sky darkens black before the dawn. For now, let us closely study the composure and morale of our enemies. I myself will be deciphering the body language of the great wolf."

After nodding heads in agreement the two commanders departed so that one could rejoin the corps of Eagle Feather warriors, and the other rejoin the company of unicorn guard stallions.

Buckmight, Taurington, Lianvil, Hammer, Lucars, the wild boars, the sheep, the dogs, and the red and yellow wolves joined their captain. While Hammer rustled up a fire and used an ember to light the tabac that he insisted heightened his ability to think clearly, Naythorn recounted the details of his meeting with Cabalblade and Chief Walking Tree.

A Second Time

"I trust that my loyal friends are as pleased as I am with the first round of our fight."

"Captain," responded the bison, "the tactical use of the shield worked perfectly. Because the monster wolf is indeed swallowing the bait we dangle before him, we have no choice but to again employ the same tactic."

"Sir," spoke next Hammer, "before fell the shield we had watched the faces of our foes and the great wolf to become more and more impatient and confused. At the moment the shield vanished we set upon them in true surprise. I will never forget the fear that showed in warrior eyes as Lucars and I attacked."

"I was certain that we would not all be returned

behind the shield before it rose again," baahed Rambuncture. "But luckily... that was somehow accomplished. However, I warn that the enemy will not a second time be so easily deceived."

"All of us have to prepare ourselves for the action that follows later this night," mrawed Taurington. "I will be ready to do my part. The next charge from behind a fallen shield will set the stage for final victory."

"Just like the big-shouldered Taurington, I too will be ready," answered the blackmane. "When the shield falls again after half night, we will a second time catch Albarochk off guard. I cannot convey how much comfort your courage signifies to me. Since I am certain that the shield for now remains secure, you have well-earned a time of rest."

Members in the band bowed to their leader.

"Naythorn," groinked Timidthy before departing, "your friends never tire of showing you the respect that during our long travel you have so well and completely earned. Thinking about that, I only wish that my bow was as stately as yours."

Naythorn bent his forehead down gracefully, this time to a wild boar that he had seen to become all grown up.

At the arrival of half night soft shafts of purple, pink, green, blue, and silver light came to glow in the sky. The band took comfort from the idea that the light cast down by the Rayalas Borealas represented a good omen for what was to come.

"Look!" exclaimed Roothyford. "The light of Rayalas is making enemy wolves and warriors drowsy." Not long after the wild boarling made her observation, the magic curtain once more dropped.

When from high ground Naythorn's band ran a second time upon Albarochk's forces, warriors and wolves were again made slow to respond. For a second time the braves and wolves loyal to Albarochk were sorely bruised. While this time Albarochk was more quick to marshal his forces in a counter-attack, the great wolf's contentiousness did not avail. Naythorn's band once again retreated too quickly to be punctured by spears, arrows, or sharp wolf incisors.

Upon finding his line of assault to be again battered and broken, and his enemy to be once again disappeared behind the unicorn shield, Albarochk lost self control and his temper turned violent. Biting into the magic mist and howling his anguish, the monster wolf bounded along the shield.

"*Grarrruuurrr!* Your shield cannot last! The weak magic behind this barrier will soon exhaust itself, and then I will by myself destroy every one of the beasts in the white herd! Naythorn is finished and done for! The time of the unicorn is ended! Albarochk will be the only master of this land, and every beast will fear me!"

With eyes flashing crimson the gigantic wolf began to move back-and-forth before where Naythorn stood watching him. Poisoned words came to be more measured.

"I know that the blackmane, the one that I tomorrow will devour, can see and hear me. By the time fades tomorrow's sun your lust to dominate my life will, like your blood, become sprinkled into ground. For you and your miserable servants there will be no escape."

Even though he was to the eyes of Albarochk invisible, the unicorn could not watch the monster wolf spew forth his hatred without feeling his blood to chill, and the beating of his equine heart to quicken. To the blackmaned stallion something felt badly wrong. For the first time ever, as if in a trance the unicorn captain froze where he was standing.

Not knowing what to say to lighten the burden of the blackmane's thoughts, band members stared at their captain. Albarochk's promise of blood revenge upon Naythorn had brought home the enormity of the intentioned dismemberment of his unicorn horn.

"Look at me!" grunted Mama Pig jumping front paws against Naythorn's neck. "Never forget that your destiny is to lead the unicorns! It *will* go well with you tomorrow!"

When the stallion turned to look at Mrs. Razorthwacker she noticed that his eyes shone dull. The matron hog then did what any strong wild mother sow would do. She smacked Blackmane hard with a paw. After shaking his head and mane the stallion came back to himself, and Mama Pig slid down her paws.

"Mrs. Pig, I do not know what just happened. The threats of the monster wolf pounded so dreadfully inside my head that my legs would not move."

"We, each member of your band, will make sure that no great evil befalls you," assured Lucars rubbing vigorously the stallion's mane.

"Never fear my friend," added Buckmight. "Your band will destroy the monster wolf. He will tomorrow be gone, and be from you forever departed."

"It is just that something does not feel... *right*," responded Naythorn relaxing his frame. "I worry that my sire is not wrong, and that I have brought disaster to the herd of unicorns. If this battle were to be lost, I could not live with the consequences of my actions. If by the monster wolf the white herd is ravaged, how will I ever again be able to look my sire in the eye? A voice inside tells me that our plan will not proceed in the way we want." Naythorn abruptly turned away from his friends and walked into a night shining down colorful shafts of heavenly light.

As if to reflect the worries and self-doubt of the blackmane, it was not long before a cold wind started to blow. Clouds presented to hide from sight the moon and stars. With the heavens having seemingly adopted a surly mood, the beautiful colors of the Rayalas Borealas dissipated.

Two mountain sheep and two black dogs watched over Naythorn as he settled to rest. When the head of Rambuncture began to decline in drowsiness, Ewelissas butted her mate awake and ordered, "Pay attention. Your one and only job is to keep watch."

Exhibiting behavior that was completely out of character, neither Blackler nor Trackler scampered about. Eyes glued to the blackmaned unicorn, the two dogs rested motionless with heads set upon forepaws.

The rest of the band tried to lull eyes into a time of short rest. As if nothing weighed on his mind, Dansey was heard to snore.

CHAPTER 27

NAYTHORN'S SHARD

"It is time, Master Smith, to take up your hammer."

"Errrm, yes Dansey, of course." The big-armed Phoenician was quickly on his feet. Hammer nudged his former apprentice awake.

"Lucars, bring a fire torch."

Together Hammer, Lucars, and the yellow wolf went to the side of a wide-awake unicorn whose face they noticed to be deeply drawn.

"My time has come," neighed Naythorn with no emotion sounding in his voice. "Break in two my horn."

"Right over here, Captain," answered the blacksmith. "This rock is as hard as they come. Its further advantage is that its surface lays perfectly flat. All right now, Naythorn, position the flat of your face against the edge of the stone, with your horn set upon its surface. Permit me to do the rest.

"I will first chip a small wedge into the base. The V-cut will be slightly less than half the width of your horn. Even after the length of the shard is cut long, the bottom of the cut shard will yet anchor to the other half of your horn. Until the V-cut at the base of your horn is broken through, and the shard snaps off, magic from the root of your horn will course through both your intact horn and its shard." It was not long before the blacksmith reassured.

"Very good, Naythorn. The base-cut was not so bad now, was it? I will next split your horn down the middle, one little cut at a time. That is what must be done. It will help if while I work with my chisel you employ your willpower to deaden the magic of your horn. I begin."

The Smith worked carefully, expertly. Each and every measured hammer blow struck upon his chisel, hit true. At last, split down the middle as Hammer had promised, the magic horn did not separate one half from the other.

"Naythorn, I take it to be a favorable sign that there is no blood on the shard, or on the half horn still attached firmly to your forehead. Because my hands, as I cut, felt the powerful magic of your horn I am confident that when the shard breaks loose and lodges deep, it will surely deaden the heart of the evil beast."

With big calloused hands that worked with a touch delicate, the smithy slid one at a time slender threads of leather cord around the horn and tied them, but not too tight. At its bottom, center, and top leather strands came to secure the shard to the still undamaged half horn.

"Captain, these three cords that hold together your horn will not break until you make them to tear. Thrust deeply your horn into the chest of the wolf. Twist and jerk your horn from side to side. The quick twisting movement of your horn, against the resistance offered by the sinews of the wolf's heart, will sever the bindings. A few quick jerks will do the trick. The tension of the thrusts will break apart the V-cut at the base of your horn, and the shard will after remain lodged in the heart of Albarochk. While your magic horn will no longer be whole, you will be spared, and with you the precious lives of the white herd.

"Now, get up on your feet Captain Naythorn. Let us make sure that the shard holds stable when you run."

Slowly, and with difficulty, Naythorn rose to stand. Of a sudden his legs buckled and his body slumped down with legs sprawled out.

"My captain," yipped Dansey, "that will not do. You must make your legs to mind you." Naythorn managed to once more gain his legs.

"It is as if my body will not obey my mind. My head feels feverish. It is here become suddenly cold."

"Well, now, Naythorn," soothed Hammer, "with your horn so deeply cleaved your magic cannot feel the same. You just take some time to rest."

Picking his steps carefully, Naythorn walked back to the camp where by an ebbing fire he slumped down.

"I know someone who will comfort our captain," yipped Dansey to Hammer. The yellow wolf soon returned with Belfloralex

The unicorn filly whose half horn still remained lodged in the neck of the colossus of the sea, immediately comprehended what had happened to Naythorn's horn. She settled to the ground and rested her frame against the back of Naythorn. The suffering stallion knew that the filly at his side had once felt the same anguish and pain... that he now felt.

"Naythorn, it did not matter that I broke my horn. My magic is as strong as before. I think that I even command the breeze to blow more violent than I did before I lost part of my horn." Belfloralex jiggled her head and added, "Ha! Well, at that, with only a half horn I am not as pretty as I once was." Naythorn tried, but for that humorous comment could not even a small smile manage.

"But a young and inexperienced filly, you sacrificed your horn. What I do as a veteran war unicorn, counts for less."

"Just rest now," soothed Belfloralex.

Stealing glances at the blackmane's slumped body, Lianvil paced back-and-forth. Of a sudden he stopped and grrrd to the yellow wolf, "Have the high escort come to touch Naythorn with her horn, and so hasten the healing."

"Naythorn is afraid that Aneilee will tell him he was reckless to sever his horn in two. And no matter what she would say, he is convinced the high escort blames him for bringing to happen this terrible war."

The Shield Transforms

Before the magic shield, drums were heard to pound. Warriors rushed forward and stabbed spears into the barrier wall. Howling wolves clawed at the shield.

"It is as if they think to use their own magic to break apart the shield," brayed Buckmight. The howling and yelling grew louder.

"This is terrible to hear," gasped Roothyford as she sprawled on her belly and with front paws covered her ears to muffle the voiced assault of war yells and growled threats.

"Look!" exclaimed Hamilton. "A storm bends toward us; dark clouds funnel down!"

"The clouds go into the shield!" squealed Practicia. The wild boarling noted for her common sense could not believe her squinty eyes, but so it was. Having lost its interior transparency, the shield became a moving wall of clouds.

"The magic of enemy magicians summoned the heavens so that we no longer see Albarochk or his forces," groinked Roothyford.

"Dansey," barked Thistle, "the clouds have taken control of the shield, and it weakens. Can the unicorn sages have become exhausted in their command of magic?"

The noise of unicorns neighing and running about became even louder than the beating of the drums and the shouting and howls of enemy braves and wolves.

"What has happened?" inquired Belfloralex. "Why the sudden tumult?" The filly ran off to find out what had taken place in the unicorn camp.

"Nyeerrrrugugh!" neighed Elianor planting hooves to not collide with Belfloralex. "Three wolves killed a young colt and drank his blood!"

"The blackmane needs the matriarch!"

"I will attend to him, now."

"Elianor, what about us is happening?" neighed Naythorn raising weakly his head.

"When a young colt penetrated his head to touch the clouds that now current the shield, he was by three wolves pulled through. Without giving him a chance to return to our fold, they killed him and drank his blood."

"That is awful!" answered Naythorn. "This is my fault. Feeling sorry for myself, I too long delayed the final showdown with Albarochk."

"You look to be terribly sick," observed Elianor, "and why is your horn tied round?"

It did not matter that Naythorn was unable to answer; the realization of what had happened became quickly evident to Elianor.

"Brave Blackmane. My poor dear." After reaching her head down to nuzzle her nose to Naythorn's eyes, the follow-up touch of Elianor's horn caused Naythorn's fractured horn to glow, albeit dimly.

"I must go to comfort the sire and dam of the slain colt, and counsel calm to all," neighed the matriarch. "Most of all I need to encourage Aneilee and the sages to maintain the magic of the shield. We cannot, we dare not let the shield to fall." After glancing knowingly at Belfloralex, the matriarch looked again at Naythorn. "I know that this incredible thing, your great sacrifice, was done to rescue the white herd."

"Elianor, I felt myself at the edge of death. Your touch just saved my life."

After the departure of Elianor an unexpected screeching sound pierced the ears of Naythorn and his band members. Belfloralex knew immediately what had happened.

"With the horn of the murdered colt gripped in his teeth, Albarochk scratches the shield. Naythorn, the monster wolf will break the concentration of the sage unicorns, and so compromise the magic of our protective wall."

"The screeching is come to be right here made," grrrd Lianvil moving to the wall close to the place where lay Naythorn. Huge claws and the face of the giant wolf impressed further and further into the shield. The point of the colt's severed horn, whose shaft was gripped in Albaroch's jaws, pierced through the shield.

"The monster knows we are found at this spot in front of him," gasped Mama Pig. "The shield weakens, and is going to collapse! Our captain right now needs our help to kill Albarochk!"

"Webstir, Featherspark, Isabaya, lift up on wing to tell Walking Tree and Cabalblade to attack with all they have, now!" neighed Naythorn rising on his hooves. In an instant the waterfowl and winged foal were gone into night sky.

"Look!" squealed Roothyford. "The light of the Borealas breaks through the clouds. In this time of desperation the heavenly grace of Rayalas smiles down upon us!"

"That sign from heaven will seal our victory!" bellowed Buckmight. The bison lowered his head and exploded hooves. When his head blasted into the masked outline of the face of the great wolf, the shield no more protected the herd of unicorns.

Straight at the Monster Wolf

Buckmight knocked backward the giant wolf. Close behind the bison ran the upright Lianvil with a sword grasped in each paw. Taurington, two black dogs, two mountain sheep, and the red and yellow wolves ran next. The monster back-pedaled, turned about, set, and with a tremendous blow from his enormous right forepaw toppled Lianvil. The monster next knocked back Taurington.

Blackler and Trackler sank teeth into the left rear leg of Albarochk, and held on for dear life. The thrown spears of Scarlet Point, Marsand, Amaluna, and Alexzana pricked the right thigh of the great wolf, and there lodged. Dog teeth and spear points impeded the legs of the giant wolf.

Rainsnow began and then stopped his charge; having again witnessed the power of the great wolf, he changed his mind. The uncle horse wheeled about and returned to Naythorn. For the blackmane to play the decisive role in the battle, Naythorn had to first be made to stand upright. The uncle horse joined the efforts of Shawnee, Lucars, and Hammer to make ambulatory the blackmane.

Lianvil shifted to front enemy wolves and warriors entering the fray. Balanced wonderfully on his hind limbs, the sword swings of the powerful lion decimated enemy ranks.

Dansey, Thistle, five wild boars, and the four youth loyal to Blackmane joined the great lion to establish defensive lines on both sides of Naythorn. Gifted speed from the recent touch of Cabalblade's horn, by Jaguar warriors the yellow wolf proved to be both uncatchable and unstoppable.

The bovines charged a second time, but this time side by side. When a paw of the monster wolf threw aside Taurington, bison swerved hooves to butt head and horns into the leg still grasped by the tenacious Blackler and Trackler. The giant wolf was shaken and made to stumble backwards, but he did not crash down. It would at that moment have been opportune for the blackmane to have with his horn pierced the chest of the giant wolf and lodged his shard into the monster's heart. But with Naythorn still absented from the conflict, the second charge of the bovines accomplished one thing only, the delay of the monster's intention to spring upon the neck of the blackmane.

"You *must* do your part, Captain!" pleaded Hammer. "Make good your plan to stop the evil heart of the monster wolf." With Hammer and Lucars offering support on one side, and Rainsnow and Shawnee on the other, Naythorn began to trot toward Albarochk.

Sensing that she was most needed at the side of the blackmane, the observant Alexzana ran to Rainsnow, grabbed his golden mane, and swung herself up onto his back. The girl exclaimed, "Buckmight, Taurington, the time has come!"

"Naythorn, you can and you must do this," encouraged Lucars. "Faster, faster, my friend."

Blackmane accelerated his hooves and neighed, "*Albarochk!*"

Forward of the blackmane, the bison once more sped hooves at the monster.

"*Rarruuugraharr!*" Albarochk's laugh was arrogant. "No mere bison can knock me down!"

With claw clenched, the right forearm of Albarochk delivered a tremendous uppercut that caught the bison's chin and tumbled the bovine head over heels backwards. Buffeted over the charging cattle, Buckmight fell upon the galloping Blackmane. As he collapsed under Buckmight's weight, the head of the stallion hit hard the ground.

His fall cushioned by the body of Naythorn, Buckmight rolled over and in one smooth movement was back up on his hooves. With another devastating uppercut Albarochk pummeled Taurington aside. The bison charged again, and again was thrown back. This time the armored bison fell hard and had his breath knocked out of him.

"Is this *all* the wretched Blackmane has for me?" exulted Albarochk. "Sprawled on the ground Naythorn can do *nothing!* Bison and cattle bones are broken! This battle is finished! The magic blood of the freakish blackmane is now *mine* to drink!"

Lianvil leapt at the monster's neck. Four long incisors punctured into the monster's tough hide. At the same time the mighty lion flailed two swords bloodying the head of the giant wolf. Moving steps backward, Albarochk shook violently his head and repeatedly batted his right paw at the great lion. However, the teeth and swords of Lianvil were not to be dissuaded.

From much experience in conflict Hammer had learned that the time most needed for clear thinking, was when the battle raged its worst. As he ran toward Naythorn the smithy noticed that the split shard of unicorn horn was no longer attached; the hard fall of the blackmane's head had broken the binds that held together the two halves of Naythorn's horn.

"Blast!" yelled Hammer to anyone that would hear. "The shard broke loose! Find the shard!"

Alexzana threw herself off the back of Rainsnow and began to push at the neck of the blackmane. The girl had seen something. Running toward the maiden

Hammer saw it too. From under the blackmane's neck, and out of his thick black mane, poked the point of the horn shard. Hammer wrested free the shard, ran toward Buckmight, and yelled, "Get up! Get up now! Run at the beast!" Struggling to his hooves the bison quickly began to move.

"Quick, Lucars! Join to Buckmight and me!" The fleet apprentice sprang after a bison accelerating in renewed charge at the giant wolf. Hammer's right hand was locked into the shaggy neck hair of Buckmight while his left hand grasped Naythorn's horn shard. Hanging on the right side of the bison Hammer stiffened his body and yelled, "Lucars, climb up me!"

As though his former master were a flight of stairs, the fleet youth ran feet up Hammer's stout body, and wrapped legs around the great neck of Buckmight. Hammer swung upward his left hand and Lucars grabbed the horn shard. The hand-off accomplished, Hammer let go his grasp of Buckmight, and fell away.

The Rayalas Borealas shafted down to brilliantly outline the prostrate blackmane, the monster wolf, and the band members found between the two. The pulsing of the brilliant light momentarily disoriented the heinous wolf. Shaking his head, Albarochk raised his right paw to shield his eyes from the glare. Upon refocusing his eyes the monster saw the bison close upon him. Shocked to see the bison so quickly recovered from the impact of his monstrous blows, Albarochk froze.

An instant later the bison buried his horns into the belly of the giant wolf. Although hard as the limb of an oak tree, the hide of Albarochk could not dismiss the penetration of two sharp bison horns. Hooves thrust forward as the bovine's thrashing horns elongated the rupture of Albarochk's belly flesh. The monster wolf's massive ribs cracked and broke. A current of blood, colored as much silver as red, burst out the belly of the great wolf to drench the mouth, nostrils, head, and hide of the bison.

Shoving his arms into the giant wolf's protruding entrails, Lucars thrust upward. Feeling the pulsing of Albarochk's heart to encompass the shard, the young warrior knew exactly what had been pierced. The horn shard had split the heart of Albarochk. With his fists still grasping the shard, Lucars felt a rush of terrible evil enter into him. Malevolence more perverse than he had before imagined to exist overwhelmed the mind and spirit of the young warrior. With his eyes burning as if fired by hot coals, Lucars found himself come to hate Buckmight, Naythorn, every white unicorn, and even to hate Hammer.

"With this shard I destroy everything!" screamed Lucars at belly darkness as he thrust deeper the shard. "With this beast I will by myself be damned! Death... to... all!" Overwhelmed by the evil coursing through the heart of the monster wolf, the young warrior became powerless to release his hold of the shard.

Hammer was there. The arms of the brawny blacksmith began to wrestle the youth's shoulders from out of the belly of the fiend. Ungrasping a unicorn shard become cemented into the heart of Albarochk, Lucars felt the power of monstrous evil to diminish, and then break off into nothingness. Restored to the reality of a sane mind, Lucars came to understand that the magic of Naythorn's shard had stopped jealousy and the lust for power from commanding the body of the gigantic lupine. The head and shoulders of an exhausted Lucars collapsed onto the chest of his master blacksmith.

Like a dry leaf caught in a wind, Albarochk's body began to shake. Quitted of evil, the monstrous wolf fell to the ground. With a trembling that was almost imperceptible, a riven great-sized wolf heart slowly beat on.

Hammer's Report and Rainsnow's Neighs

The blacksmith bent down on his knees to cradle the youth in his arms.

"I was afraid that my careful chiseling of the blackmane's horn had all been for naught. But, Lucars, you made the imperfect battle plan to achieve perfectly its end." Lucars hit the heel of his hand against his cranium and shook his head to clear his thoughts.

"Uh, Hammer, I never imagined evil so dark... as currented the heart of the monster. When my hands shoved the horn shard into Albarochk's heart I was made to hate everyone, and everything, even to loathe myself. Had you not come to my rescue such hatred would have destroyed me." The eyes of the youth widened as he asked, "And... the bison?"

"Do not worry for Buckmight. After he finishes coughing up the monster's blood that he in much quantity swallowed, which mind you will take some time, the bison will be just fine." Upon hearing that, the youth lost sense to the world.

Carrying an unconscious Lucars in his arms, Hammer walked to where lay Naythorn. The smithy gently laid Lucars down beside the blackmane, and then himself fell upon Naythorn's neck, hard-hugging the unicorn moreso than he might have.

"Captain, I am here to report that Lucars accomplished the needed task. He made your horn shard to quench the evil spewing from the heart of Albarochk. What? Wake up! Do not die on me, Captain!"

Long moments passed as Hammer hugged even harder the neck of the blackmane. As if struck by a lightning bolt, Naythorn's body jolted into movement. Raising slowly his head, Naythorn managed a weak smile.

"I am so glad you moved your head... for an instant I thought you had died on me. Now, as I was saying, the evil that coursed through the heart of the giant wolf overwhelmed the sensitive lad. But Naythorn, do not worry for Lucars. He will shortly come round to resume his old self."

"My captain, you did it!" exclaimed Rainsnow. "Your triumph over the monster avenges the death of both Rayalas and her sire." That neighed, Rainsnow shook himself long as if shedding raindrops from his hide. Then, in a gesture of pure joy the uncle horse with a golden mane and tail, flashed forelegs at the light of new day. Up and down the lines of battle carried the triumphant neighs of Rainsnow.

CHAPTER 28

AFTER THE FALL OF ALBAROCHK

I n every part of the white herd the joy proclaimed by Rainsnow's neighs came to be echoed again and again.

As they watched enemy Panther warriors turn to flight, the unicorn stallions defending the eastern side of the white herd knew at once that the rumor that Albarochk had fallen, was indeed true. Defending the western side of the unicorn herd, many of Walking Tree's braves did not relent, but pursued their Raven enemies taken to flight.

Whether friend or foe, there remained no room for doubt that the great wolf had been vanquished, and that Albarochk's allies were routed. As the sounds of battle quieted, clouds parted and the sun came to crown a morning sky made perfectly blue.

"It was you that gained this victory," neighed Naythorn raising his head to address the members of his band gathered around him. "For my part, I failed. I permitted old and deep memories of insecurity and hurt to cloud and disrupt my thinking. Instead of having confidence in myself, I became fearful that my pride and my recklessness had brought about destruction to all unicorns, and that I would once again disappoint my sire, Elianor, and Aneilee. While still drawing breath, I felt as if my life had ended."

"No... no, Blackmane!" brayed Buckmight shaking briskly his head. "Not you, but I am the one that nearly cost us victory. When you were running at the beast, I was the clumsy one that got thrown backwards and landed broadside on your poor back."

"Naythorn victorious!" baahed the dour Rambuncture. "We *won!* We *won!*" The ram began to bounce up and down in the way of sheep and goats. At the show of her mate's uncharacteristic enthusiasm, Ewelissas began to bounce in step with her mate.

Taking their cue from the ram and ewe, in a display of pure canine joy Blackler and Trackler tore circles around the gathered band yipping and yapping *"Victory! Victory!"*

Even to include the shy Timidthy and the formal Mrs. Pig, five wild hogs fell to rolling about against and over each other, all the while groinking the carefree laughter so long denied them during the long and hard campaign of many battles against the giant wolf.

The cattle and bison decided to bellow loudly at each other and to butt heads, not as they used to do when they pridefully ran against each other for no reason, but this time in celebration. The display of jubilant bovine enthusiasm would be worth any headache to subsequently occur.

Dansey and Thistle took to tumbling, and promptly began to compete for the furthest and fastest feats of rolling head over heels. As she had once requested to do, Isabaya joined at the side of the tumbling Thistle.

Webstir and Featherspark fluttered under the feet

and in the way... *of everyone.* They knew that on this triumphant morning they could get away with unlimited bothersome waterfowl behavior, and to be sure, on this splendid morning no one minded the duck and goose making of themselves perfect annoyances.

The smiles worn by Shawnee, Alexzana, Scarlet Point, Marsand, and Amaluna were radiant. Sporting for perhaps the first time in his life an absolutely enormous smile, the huge lion walked back-and-forth on hind feet nodding approvingly, as if he were charged with the formal inspection of every display of frolic and jollity.

Prophecy Fulfilled

"So, with the enemy in flight all victory is ours!" neighed Cabalblade. *"Nyeaarrrrr!* I will congratulate my colt of whom I am this day so very... but you are badly hurt!"

"Do not worry, Sir Cabalblade," answered Belfloralex. "Just as before happened to me, your colt will again become brand new."

"Relax yourself down on your belly, Captain Cabalblade," requested Buckmight. "We have a long story to tell you." Elianor and Aneilee arrived just in time to hear how Naythorn had courageously sacrificed his horn shard. When Chief Walking Tree joined the band, no one minded that each and every detail of Albarochk's defeat was once more recounted.

"As Cabalblade, Chief Walking Tree, Elianor, and Aneilee have now learned, the real heroes stand before you." That neighed, Naythorn mustered the strength to smile.

"The real hero is Lucars!" exclaimed Webstir. "He

301

was the one that daggered Naythorn's shard through the terrible heart of the beast!"

"Lucars, Hammer, and Buckmight are the three bravest of us all!" interjected Featherspark. At that proffered accolade, Hammer puffed out his chest and shifted back his head to enjoy the compliment. Moved by modesty, the still weak Lucars simply lowered in a polite way, his head.

"Actually," brayed the bison "if the teeth of Lianvil had not grabbed hard the neck of the monster, and so detained him, the charge of my hooves would have been for naught."

"And had not Sir Cabalblade gifted me the ability to walk on hind legs only," continued the mighty lion, "and to fight like a warrior with two swords held in my front paws, I could not have stalled the advance of the monster wolf."

"Haha!" chortled Practicia. "Lianvil fulfilled the prophecy of the mist unicorn which we beheld in Shining Canyon. Remember the apparition that walked across the lake on hind legs, and stood to fight with front hooves as if holding swords?"

At that comment congratulatory animal noises sounded for the benefit of Lianvil. In return gesture, the great lion bowed in acknowledgement to those gathered all around the blackmane.

"But I, for one, cannot imagine the hurt made by chiseling apart a unicorn horn," observed Roothyford bringing the conversation back to her captain. "We can never, ever, forget that it was Naythorn who sacrificed his horn shard to stop the heart of the wolf from promulgating evil. So, my *best* hero is the captain of our band."

It took some time, but the blackmane managed to regain his hooves. Motioning his head to everyone gathered, he neighed, "The resolute line of defense maintained by the remainder of my band permitted Lucars, Hammer, Buckmight, Lianvil, and not failing to mention Alexzana who I was told spied out my hidden shard, to deliver the final blow to Albarochk. So it is clear to me that this long awaited triumph over the evil wolf was achieved by the courage, and fight, of my entire band of friends."

"And let us not forget that at the critical moment the brilliant shafts of the Rayalas Borealas blinded the monster and threw him off balance," added Rainsnow.

About Albarochk

On that day of great victory every unicorn in the white herd, and as well every Eagle Feather warrior, came to look upon the body of the giant wolf. It was repeated that within the still open wound in Albarochk's belly the base of Naythorn's horn shard was there to be seen. Astonishingly, despite his gashed-open belly, Albarochk still breathed. With every quiet beat of his heart the flesh about his open wound, if ever so slightly, could be seen to quiver. It was the next day reported that the cut-open belly of the wolf monster had begun to close and heal itself. Of his wounds and the heart-presence of Naythorn's horn shard, the wolf general was not going to die.

After posting unicorn guard stallions around the body of the great wolf, Cabalblade suggested to Aneilee that Hammer be given license to end the life of the monster. The high escort was assured by Hammer that with a two-fisted swing of his newly sharpened sword, the neck of the giant wolf would be cleanly severed.

Not certain if that was a proper thing for a unicorn high escort to decide, Aneilee intruded upon a resting Naythorn to ask him if he summarily agreed to ending the life of Albarochk. Upon waking the napping blackmane, she thought that she already knew his answer. However, she did not.

"Dame Aneilee, since several animal persons in my band are smarter than I, they will decide this thing. The collective wisdom of my band will provide answer to this compelling question of life and death."

Having gathered his band, Naythorn made the question to be open-ended, "What is to be done about Albarochk?"

While it first seemed that all the members of the band agreed with the idea that Hammer should with one swing of his great arms end once and for all the life of the evil monster wolf, Naythorn noticed that one small voice had not been heard. Timidthy also noticed that Dansey did not look to approve that a sentence of death be fated Albarochk. The smartest boarling was curious as to why.

"Dansey you knew, or know, Albarochk better than any animal person either within or without our band. For that you need to voice your opinion... which is important to us all."

"I could not before bring myself to with full honesty talk to you of my past," barked quietly the yellow hided wolf with a note of gravity sounding in his voice. "Now I will be absolutely honest, for I have a heartfelt confession to make. For the evil brought by this terrible war upon my captain Naythorn, I am as much to blame as my cousin Albarochk."

"That cannot be so!" objected vigorously Mama Pig. "I know you too well! You have made yourself to become a faithful ally of the blackmane!"

Dansey paused to collect himself. He instead began... to sob. Until that moment no one there had ever seen or heard a wolf to cry. Upon observing the tears falling from his eyes, and hearing his plaintive yipes, no one could imagine that the yellow wolf was only acting out a part in his own drama, or playing games with the sympathies of his friends.

"You see... it was I who set Albarochk on his path of evil. I had discovered that with my words, and they were empty words only, I could influence my big cousin. The control of the enormous wolf was... it became... a game to me. Manipulating the mind of a giant wolf gave me vicarious pleasure." The yellow wolf pawed dry his eyes.

"When Naythorn rescued Tristanbear, I made Albarochk to feel terribly humiliated. After Naythorn stepped forward to rescue Mama Pig, her four little ones, and the two waterfowl my words served to heighten Albarochk's rage. I taunted the wolf and made him feel that by allowing a unicorn to defeat him, he had lost face. I was what they call the power behind the throne. Because my ill-advised words made the now-fallen monster to value my mind, a puny yellow wolf was made to feel self-important.

"I wanted Albarochk to declare war on Naythorn and his band so that I could continue to humiliate my great cousin's life. Since Albarochk had for so long browbeat me... I decided to shift his bullying away from me toward you, who I now count as the only friends I have ever had.

"However, the time came when the evil that coursed through Albarochk's body became overpowering, and I him controlled *no longer*. Knowing that on the day of his final victory my miserable life would by the great wolf be given end, I betrayed Albarochk. Against my own creation I committed treason.

"When I found that the rules of my despicable game had changed, it happened that my only means of survival was for Naythorn to triumph. So you see, I changed allegiance to the blackmane only to save my worthless hide.

"About one thing, Mrs. Pig, you are right. When I came to fully grasp the nobleness of Naythorn, I gave my all to his cause. But my change of heart came too late. My instigation of evil madness led to the accomplishment of worse evil, and the white herd was nearly destroyed. You now know why I am as guilty as Albarochk. If his life is now to be taken, then one way or another, my life is also forfeit."

Since no one knew what to say in response to the confession of the yellow wolf, the silence that spread over the band became so heavy that the sensitive Roothyford found it hard for herself to breathe.

Naythorn moved to where stood Dansey, bent down his head, and after long touching his nose to wolf eyes neighed, "Even as my enemy, from the very start you were ever honest with me. I have never loved you more than I do right here, right now."

Naythorn looked to where Hammer and Lucars sat together. "What is to be done to Albarochk is now to me become crystal clear. Since our smithy knows workmanship with metal, I request him... no, this time it is not a request that I make. As captain of this animal person band I order Hammer to build a prison, or to make a cage, to hereafter maintain Albarochk in life. How the smithy will do this is for him to decide." Naythorn looked with gravity at the bison, cattle, wild boars, mountain sheep, dogs, waterfowl, and the newest members of his band.

"You all will come to see the trueness of my decision. While unicorn magic is not perfect, or perfectly right, it signifies goodness, love, and innocence. All, or almost all unicorns recognize that it is better to show mercy than to wreak vengeance. If by Albarochk we now do a good thing, that mercy shown will somehow in some way, be returned to us.

"Had Dansey not found the courage to speak I would surely have ordered the death of my arch enemy. For the words that saved me from committing a great wrong I profoundly thank the lone, yellow, dancer wolf. *Nyeerrrr!* If you do not yet understand what I just ordered to have done, I am confident that when you are shown the prison to be prepared by Hammer, you will not disagree with my clemency. I will have Belfloralex tell the matriarch and high escort that the life of Albarochk is to be spared.

"Now I am going to take a well-earned nap. If you please, my friends, until I again awaken can we suspend the racket... *of victory*. Hmph! A fleeting thought just reminded me of last night's visitation of the Rayalas Borealas. I will dream that the spirit of my winged mare, who was as pure of heart as any unicorn, shall again tonight smile down upon us."

Naythorn turned to a place on the ground that he presumed to be comfortable, set down his long frame, closed his eyes, and fell sound asleep with his head cradled by front legs.

The next morning awoke chilly with frost whitening the ground. No matter. The band members lay quiet in a sweet rest that from big to small, from Buckmight to Webstir, was thought to be completely deserved. Blacksmithing far into the previous night, Hammer and Lucars were the only two band members that did not make up for lost sleep. With Lucars and Dansey at his side, Hammer awoke the late-sleeping unicorn.

"What thinks Naythorn of my finished handiwork?" As would a dog, the unicorn captain rubbed with front limbs his eyes.

"Well, I do not know what to say... what is it... anyway?"

"Hammer made the most exquisite shackle I have ever seen!" exclaimed Lucars.

"The only metal that I had to work with was blue gold. However, I had not enough of the magic metal to build a cage large enough to contain the giant wolf. So I did the next best thing, I fashioned beautiful chain links that will never break. Mind you, I have carefully measured the neck of Albarochk. When clasped tight, this collar will lock the head of the great wolf so that he can never again be free."

"But, why is the other end collared... to Dansey?"

"Instead of anchoring the other end of the chain to a wall in a cave," yipped the yellow wolf, "my body will become the prison made to hold my cousin wolf. I am to share, I might add rightfully so, my cousin wolf's punishment. It will be my responsibility to see that Albarochk is fed, watched over, and comes to no further harm." Band members soon found themselves gathered about Hammer and Dansey.

"Well enough, *I guess,*" brayed Buckmight after smelling and biting the forged links made to imprison Albarochk. "But where exactly will two locked together wolves go in step one with the other?"

"I know precisely to where I will guide the giant wolf," answered Dansey. "We will journey back to where it all started. I will take Albarochk back to the scene of our first crimes against Naythorn. In the shadow of what once was the magic hold of Wittanor we will refind and revisit the arroyo where the great wolf and I beset Tristanbear, the brook to where we chased Mama Pig and her piglets, and the river bank where we killed the ducklings and goslings belonging to Webstir and Featherspark. It will be our pilgrimage of repentance. When he confesses that he is sorry for changing from being a simple wolf to a wolf possessed by great evil, a great weight will be lifted from the heart of Albarochk. Then and there my heart will, likewise, be cleansed of the evil it has committed."

"*Mrrawwaww!* I do not *like* this plan!" exclaimed Taurington. "Before you ever find the side of that distant volcano, Albarochk will have broken Dansey's neck. The giant wolf is through and through odiously bad!"

"I will *not* let that to happen, Sir Cattle," interjected Lianvil. "On this quest I will accompany and protect the yellow wolf. Having not Naythorn's shard embedded in *my* heart makes me twice as strong as Albarochk."

"That is very generous and gracious," responded the yellow wolf. "I most welcome Lianvil's offer to be my bodyguard."

"Embarking on this pilgrimage of escort shows Dansey and Lianvil to be more noble than I can claim to be," grumphed Mrs. Razorthwacker. "I bow to your kindness and courage." She did just that. Following the example of the mama sow, the entire band bent knees and lowered heads to salute the benevolent decision of the yellow wolf, and bowed a second time to salute the helping paws extended by the powerfully built lion.

"You know that I would very much like to see the lands and places the yellow wolf and lion will visit," yipped a smiling Thistle. "For me it would be a journey of... *pure discovery.* But, as sometimes happens with me, more than join your long travel I prefer to hunt rabbits in these hills and valleys that I so well know. The best part of hunting in these nearby places is that it will be ever remindful of the triumph of Naythorn and his band over the monster grayback wolf. Upon your return you will find me to be right here... waiting for both of you.

"And to Dansey and Lianvil I promise one thing. I will save the dodgiest and most wily rabbits for you both to hunt. That will be my personal gift to the dancer wolf and the upright walking lion."

CHAPTER 29

A BISON TRANSFORMED, A BEAR FOUND, AND HOMAGE PAID

After the *Battle of Naythorn's Shard* gave rescue to the white herd, came a time of calm. Tails swished happily as colts played, yearlings raced, and the teeth of mares and stallions tore contentedly at nutritious stems of grass.

One morning the white herd awoke to find the ground covered in hoof-high snow. Because equines find it irritating to have to paw through snow to graze, the white adornment of the ground reminded that it was time to renew search for a protected mountain valley opening to southern sunlight and warming winds. No mare or stallion knew exactly where their new home was to be found, only that it lay somewhere ahead of them. But every unicorn mare and stallion heard and repeated stories of their destination's beauty and peacefulness.

When on the following morning the white herd departed the flint rock hills and set hooves toward the mountains to their west, unicorn hearts brimmed with new hope. After all, war had ended and the neck of the monster grayback wolf had been shackled by a chain made of magic blue gold.

It was said that Albarochk could not speak, that he hardly ate, that under a warm sun his hide remained ice cold to the feel, and that he had become nothing more than a simple and obedient cub doing whatever the yellow wolf told him to do. The fact that on the recently commenced journey to a far southern place, the powerful Lianvil guarded the imbecile monster and as well protected Dansey, made the unicorns on the move to feel completely safe.

From the crest of a hill Cabalblade noticed that Aneilee had begun to walk before the unicorn herd in the company of Naythorn and his band. The guard captain next observed mares pausing intermittently to graze, colts frisking about, and on the flanks of the long column his guard stallions arrayed in position. The captain noticed that the ten young guard stallions that Haltervor had mentored, that no longer wore dirt in their manes, had become serious-minded guard unicorns. Upon sighting the following army of Walking Tree, Cabalblade felt thankful that he could call upon the chief for help were new danger to present. The captain of the unicorn guards relished the high esteem accorded to him by the chief of the Eagle Feather Tribe. With Naythorn's band performing forward patrol, and Walking Tree's braves providing rear escort, what danger could on this day present?

Upon reflecting that the sacrifice of Naythorn's horn shard had negated the blame formerly placed on his colt for bringing the war with Albarochk to the herd of unicorns... Cabalblade relaxed his face into a smile. Finding himself to be no more looked upon as the sire of a blackmaned misfit, the captain of the unicorn guards almost forgot that he had ever criticized his colt for being born different.

Having lost one side of its vertical length, band members had worried that Naythorn's magic would be diminished, and that his strength and power would not fully recover from the mutilation of his horn. About that, the future could only tell. Unfortunately, Naythorn seemed to be convinced that his magic had departed him. Still he did not complain, because he *had won*.

The blackmane even joked that since his mane *was* different, he might just as well wear an odd head that looked different from every other unicorn, except for one. Having suffered much upon the severing of his horn, Naythorn had gained new respect for the courage of the half horned Belfloralex.

Naythorn's first day of travel in the lead of the white herd ended well. While band members went about grazing and foraging for their supper, the blackmane lazed.

"Your horn continues to heal?" inquired Buckmight deciding to accompany the relaxed blackmane.

"At least the pain is lessening. Can I with the bison share something?"

"What are friends for?"

"I find it strange to be so incredibly fortunate. Have you noticed, Buckmight, that after bonding so closely with her grandsire during the first moon of her life, my bay foal has now come to feel comfortable with her sire?"

"I *have* observed that, Naythorn. I cannot help but

think that when on her wings she flits about you, Isabaya makes random moments of your day to be ever interesting."

"Yes, she does do that. But unfortunately, Buckmight, it seems that every time my foal becomes distracted by someone or something and draws away from me, my mind turns again to dwell on the last battle."

"The monster wolf no longer warrants your hatred," brayed the bison. "And let us hope that neither you, nor I, nor anyone in your band ever again experiences a battle so traumatic as the one that ended with your horn shard crippling the heart of the monster grayback. But, it is of course natural that we should long dwell on how we fought, lived through, and survived a great battle involving a legion of wolves, three armies of enemy warriors, our Eagle Feather allies, the unicorn guard stallions, and your band."

"But Buckmight, it is still hard for me to wrap my mind around a complex battle with eagles against ravens, pure white unicorns against insolent black panthers, and me the blackmaned unicorn against black spotted jaguars. And, my mind still cannot reconcile the unfathomable loyalty shown by you and every animal person in my band, each being so different from his or her companions. How can it be that at the end, when everything turned into disastrous confusion, no one faltered and ran away?"

"That loyalty was inspired by your selfless leadership. What amazed me is that whether with teeth, claws, hooves, horns, or swords everyone fought so extraordinarily well... as a team. It is as if we band members were the paws, legs, feet, arms, and shoulders that connected to your spirit. Hmph, that is except for me. I will never forgive my clumsiness for being thrown back to fall so heavily upon you. The weight of my frame crashing down nearly killed you."

"You are never to mention that again. To change the subject, Buckmight, I have a question for you. Had even one member of my band absented from the battle, do you think we could have finally defeated Albarochk?"

"Every single member of your band played a crucial role that mattered to the final outcome of victory. But consider that one member of your band was in fact not present. Of course I refer to Tristanbear. Absent Tristan we still won the *Battle of Naythorn's Shard,* with your band not being at full strength." The bison snorted and jumped his hooves off the ground. "Do you want to hear of what I am most proud?"

"Certainly so, Buckmight."

"I am proud that upon first meeting you, on the morning that Taurington and I endeavored to break each other's skulls, that I immediately recognized you as a true leader."

A Sheltered Place

Walking Tree had told Aneilee and Elianor about a very long lake set amidst high mountains. That lake and its surrounding valley were sacred to every warrior that knew of their existence. Weapons were left beyond its walls, and no warrior entered the valley to hunt or to fight. The lake had deep blue waters that reflected perfectly the images of the mountains and trees bordering its shores. The climate was crisp and cool. But because high canyon walls repelled the biting winds that came down from the north, the winter in that sheltered place was not freezing cold. The grass in the valley's meadows was said to grow as high as a horse's withers, and all through winter maintained a nutritious green color. Regarding the valley described by Walking Tree, members of Naythorn's band were almost as excited to there arrive as were unicorn horses.

Set upon the back of Taurington, with Shawnee holding to his waist, Hammer drew alongside a solitary Blackmane and interrupted the unicorn's grazing, "Captain, there is a matter I would discuss with you."

"Anything at all, Master Hammer."

"Did I ever mention that in the pleasant valleys of Phoenicia we have lords who live in great houses?"

"No, you did not."

"Well, Captain, I think that I will build a sturdy manor at the entrance to the restful valley to where we are headed. You see, I should like to be the lord of... *my own* manor."

"Do you know what else, Naythorn?" added Shawnee smiling shyly at the blackmane, "I would enjoy being the lady of a great manor. That is, if a ladyship were somehow to me made available." With a subtle movement of his head, Naythorn motioned for Hammer to answer Shawnee.

"Well, now that I hear Shawnee say that, a lord really ought to have a great lady to preside over the manor house. And I happen to know where someday there will be a lord with a manor in desperate need of a brave and beautiful lady, exactly like the one that with me rides today." Shawnee, Naythorn, and Taurington smiled, as did at his own words the blacksmith himself. "Ermm... Naythorn, it would be a true gift for me to never again know loneliness."

Camp fire time was that night made talkative.

Lucars and Alexzana, who seemed to like walking or riding in close proximity to each other, listened as Hammer and Shawnee exchanged their views on the import and privilege of lordships and ladyships. Thereupon it occurred to Lucars to also make a request of his captain.

"Naythorn, once we arrive at our new valley home could you also appoint me and Alexzana to be lord and lady of a manor? If you would do that, it would be official, so that everyone would know it to be a right thing. All Alexzana and I would have to do is build our lodge. Then two manor houses could defend opposite ends of the lake."

"Errmm... now just a moment!" responded Hammer. "Lucars is stealing my idea! And by the way I find you two much too young to assume the lofty titles of lord and lady."

"Master Hammer," rejoined Alexzana, "if I were back on my island I would not be too young to marry. And for his part, Lucars has lived through more battles and more travels than has done any young man from my island. Besides, after a journey that has come so far I deserve to be settled with a good man at my..."

"But Alexzana," interrupted Scarlet Point, "you must know that there is someone else that wants to spend much time with you."

"Is that... *so?*" answered slyly the island girl. "And who can that person be?"

"That person is me!" exclaimed Scarlet Point. He forthwith smiled at Alexzana, and then at Lucars to show he harbored no jealousy.

"Until now you have said nothing to me mattering on love. But, during the many suns that it will require to arrive at the beautiful valley with a splendid lake, perhaps Scarlet Point can to me talk more."

"Lucars is *very handsome!*" blurted Amaluna.

As he replied a smiling Lucars nodded at the native maiden, "Although your eyesight obviously weakens, Amaluna, your eyes are very..."

"Errhrrm," interrupted Marsand, "as it so happens I also happen to think that Amaluna is pretty... and not just her eyes. Her heart is also lovely."

"Well, Alexzana. Well, Amaluna," declared Hammer. "I see that our new valley will come to have more than one manor house, and more than one lord and lady. And as for me, I will certainly be proud to visit each and every great manor. The only thing is that apparently along with you two young ladies, I am not exactly sure to which lord or lady I will attend to in the second or third manor house."

"Perhaps some competition for the hands of the island maiden and Amaluna will work to their lasting benefit," commented the blackmane.

"Is it not romantic to hear talk of young love?" baahed Ewelissas nestling closer to her ram.

"Hmph! That valley sounds *too good* to be true! Has

anyone asked Chief Walking Tree if with his own eyes he has seen this supposedly marvelous place to where we now travel? How does this ram know for sure that the story of the wonderful valley... is not just an old and tired myth?"

Buckwhite

At the dawn of a crisp morning born brilliant, Buckmight found that his hide had turned completely and absolutely, *white*.

For the natives of these lands a white bison was the most sacred of all animals. As well befit a sacred bison, Buckmight plodded through the morning with the biggest smile of anyone in the band.

"Naythorn, I was just telling the young blacksmith riding on my back, soon to be a great lord, that I am suddenly come to be a very special bison. Is not my changed hide something worthy to behold?"

"I am glad that the bath of silver-tainted blood given to this noble bovine did no worse than dye white his hide," responded instead Lucars resting both hands on the massive neck of the white bison. "I was afraid that the blood of the great wolf would poison Buckmight's sunny disposition."

"I tell you, Lucars, that I never before coughed so much as I did upon swallowing Albarochk's blood."

Overhearing the conversation while riding close by on Taurington, Hammer added a thought, "Of course Mama Pig will have to now change our bison's name *to Buckwhite.*"

The bison raised as high on four legs as he could, and proceeded to strut a circle around the blackmane.

"You know what, Buckwhite?" offered Naythorn, "I find myself suddenly made envious. From here onward you will be treated with ten times more honor than a blackmaned and broken-horned unicorn." At that comment Naythorn and the now renamed Buckwhite together laughed.

Naythorn found himself to be walking more and more with Belfloralex close beside him. Sometimes their shoulders touched; every once in a while their muzzles lightly feathered against each other.

Since Rayalas had left him to become transformed into a crystal curtain of glorious shafted light that galloped through night skies, Naythorn had felt in his heart to exist a hollow place. However, when Belfloralex walked beside him, the stallion's heart felt to fill the hole made by the loss of the filly that grew wings.

But it was not only the special friendship of Belfloralex that made the blackmane's heart to fill. By some kind gesture or word proffered, the stallion was each day made to think that by others he was valued and loved.

In the middle of morning march Naythorn halted, nuzzled the half horned filly, and with much feeling neighed to her, "Belfloralex, I hope that I am not only remembered among my friends and the white herd as the unicorn that lost half of his horn battling a monster wolf. I repeat what I have before neighed, I want it never to be forgotten... that the blackmane felt loved." Tears moistened the stallion's eyes.

"My dear Naythorn," replied Belfloralex nuzzling her captain's cheek, "no unicorn, bovine, wild boar, sheep, wolf, or dog can love you as deeply as do I."

Upon a Rock Step

When trotting at the side of Naythorn, Aneilee always made a point of neighing a few kind words to the stallion that she now fondly recalled as having been the rebel colt with a black mane. On this day she accompanied Naythorn in silence. That is until she neighed, "Do you see those great rock steps that lie ahead?"

"Yes, Dame Aneilee. Set unforgettably, they are remindful of a place through which our band once traveled. In that before place we saw that three rock steps had been placed for the feet of giants to climb upward a great pillar of stone."

"I am sure that something, perhaps it can be called a great hand, placed them to remind that we all go on a journey of countless steps that climbs skyward."

"That, Aneilee, is a beautiful thought."

"I have an order to give. You will of course obey me?"

"Uh... always, High Escort. But why do you ask me that?"

"It does not bother the triumphant blackmane to be given orders, like an ordinary unicorn?"

"Well, since I have not for a very long time been ordered to do anything, perhaps not since Rayalas insisted I touch my horn to a pool while her wings blew up a magic mist, I will admit that I have grown to be independent minded. But of course I always respect your leadership."

"Perhaps you are not aware, Naythorn, but there is one unicorn in particular that desires to displace me and

Elianor of our authority as High Escort and Matriarch. But enough of that... for the present I command you to mount that first great rock step. That place is more than wide enough to have your band to stand beside you. Go and there wait. I will have you to see something."

"As commands the high escort, I and my band will there wait." Naythorn led to the far side of the great block of granite where a gentle slope permitted his band to scramble up and onto the massive rock shelf.

"What is that enormous black thing over there?" inquired Buckwhite motioning horns as he brayed. "I have never seen a bison large enough to wear such an impressive black hide. Can it be an enormous dead carcass? I go to check it out." Hearing hooves approach, the black form moved and a head raised.

"Bison! Your hide has turned snow white!"

"Over here, Naythorn! You need to see for yourself what I just found!" Not only Naythorn, but the entire band went to join Buckwhite.

"In the middle of the day," neighed the blackmane, "Tristanbear needs to be up and moving about!"

Making himself to stand upright, the enormous bear roared a loud greeting that left no doubt that he was happy to be once again by his friends found.

"What took you so long to rejoin us?" reproached Buckwhite. "Not so long ago we could have much used your help, and the help of your bear friends. So what have you to say for yourself?" Tristanbear shifted his gaze from the blackmane to the bison, and then back to Naythorn.

"Just hold on, Bison," yawled Tristan. "At the

moment you and Naythorn left behind the *Battle of the War Machine* to follow after Albarochk, me and my friends were coming to join you. Since you had departed, but many of your enemies still remained, I decided to set my line of bears to be a barrier. Although they tried time and again, for two days not a single wolf or warrior was permitted to pass through the line defended by my platoon of bears.

"My captain, I will tell you that against many wolves and Jaguar warriors we bears acquitted ourselves well. On the third day of our stand in support of the blackmane, our enemy gave up trying to penetrate the barricade set by my powerful bear platoon, and retreated back down the valley. To make sure that their retreat was not a trick, for two more days we bears there remained on guard."

"I had *not* known that," replied Naythorn. "No one told me what great things you and your bear platoon accomplished. And that at last explains why more wolves and Jaguar warriors did not accompany Albarochk in the final battle."

Like a calf pushes at his mother cow's belly, Taurington playfully pushed his head against a great black bear hide and mrawed, "Friend Tristan, that still does not explain why so many suns have passed since the conclusion of the last, and very great battle, without your return to us."

"I would have found you much sooner," replied the enormous bear rubbing his ponderous belly, "but we bears happened upon a stream flowing everywhere with right-sized fish. We stopped for a day to eat and recover our strength. We remained a second day to recover more our strength. So it continued. In fact, my bear friends are still suppering at that stream."

Band members smiled at the unquestionable logic of Tristanbear's explanation. Considering their great luck to have refound the enormous bear, the mood of the entire band became jovial.

"When you before surmised that it required every single member of our band to defeat Albarochk," brayed Buckwhite quietly to Naythorn, "I disagreed with you. Now it turns out, that about that you were right. Naythorn, it is as I before stated. Each member of your band has become component to your body, and every one of us does our unique part to make your hooves, limbs, shoulders, chest, and neck to triumph."

"The winged foal comes," neighed Belfloralex. "She is grown big enough to run *very fast!*" Shifting from travel on hooves to flight on wings, the filly wafted up the front side of the great rock step upon which stood the band, and landed before Naythorn.

"Sire, I met lots of young unicorns in my time with the matron and the high escort, and from them I have learned a lot. The problem is that my wings need more room to spread themselves wide. So when I asked Aneilee if I could join your advance company, permission was to me given, but on one condition. I need to obtain the captain's approval to become part of his band. I can help Webstir and Featherspark on flights of reconnaissance, and I promise that I will *always* behave myself."

"For you to be at my side requires no permission

given," neighed Naythorn touching his muzzle to the foal's forehead. "And even if you sometimes get into a little trouble, having you near will be just the medicine needed by my half horn."

"Welcome, little one, to Naythorn's band!" grumphed Mama Pig arching her head to rub the underside of the foal's neck. "I am so glad that you have joined us! If any of these unruly animal persons here about you become bothersome, I will thwack them hard!"

Tribute Paid

In the distance something... was happening. Heads turned toward the sound of far away drums beating in perfect time with each other. From their high perch the band glimpsed a long column of Eagle Feather warriors passing through the center of the unicorn herd.

In the lead of his column marched Walking Tree. Behind their chief, warriors began to shout and dance steps to the rhythm of drumbeats. Their feet and voices proclaimed triumph over their dread enemy the Raven Tribe.

When the procession of Eagle Feather braves came before the rock where stood Naythorn, the column split into two parts that moved away from each other, and then moved around and back to become the two ends that joined to connect in a circle. Wearing a leather shirt adorned with sparkling turquoise beads and the finery of eagle feathers, Walking Tree stepped into the circle formed by his warriors.

"I salute Naythorn Blackmane Unicorn!" proclaimed the chief raising his arms. "Fierce eagles today salute

Naythorn and his courageous band!" Brandishing spears over their heads, the dance resumed with each warrior revolving steps in place.

When the emotion of feeling expressed throughout the procession of Eagle Feather warriors gripped the heart of Naythorn, he reared on back legs and whinnied his joy. Following the example of their captain with arms, paws, hooves, and wings every member of Naythorn's band acknowledged the victorious warriors.

The two sides of the circle reformed into a column that in dignified march followed Walking Tree toward foothills skirting the rock steps. The sound, color, and movement of the warrior dance of victory would become a memory often recounted by the members of Naythorn's band.

The unicorn herd began to move. Positioned on each side of Cabalblade, the matriarch and high escort joined to lead the procession of unicorns. Clan by clan the unicorns marched toward the viewing rock. At the rear of the column came the stallion guards led by Hoovefort and Haltervor. When the first clan of unicorns drew before the rock where stood Naythorn and his band, they began to prance. As they in unison raised forelegs, the horned horses held high their heads and tails.

Having not accompanied the Phoenician barges that had carried forth the unicorns from Wittanor, the blackmane had not been present on the occasion when Belfloralex, Alexzana, and Marsand led a unicorn dance dedicated to sailors. On this occasion Naythorn stood transfixed like a child watching his or her first parade of soldiers marching to drumbeats.

Horned horses in the first clan flashed forelegs and whinnied salute to Naythorn and his band. Setting hooves back to earth the clan's mares, stallions, fillies, and colts executed a rightward turn. The prancing of the second unicorn clan was just as remarkable. Band members noted that each clan of unicorns had their own individual style of parade. Their turn finished, while jumping and shaking heads enthusiastically the second clan proceeded to the left. Four clans came to array both to the right and left of the onlooking Naythorn.

Cabalblade had rejoined the stallions he commanded. The prancing of the unicorn guards, with heads shaking vigorously and horns jabbing at invisible enemies, was unique to behold.

"I say that the unicorn guards have learned well how to defend the white herd," mrawed Taurington as he marveled at the athleticism of the guard stallions.

The company of guards and eight clans of unicorns came to stand at rest in a line facing Naythorn and his band. From one end of the column Elianor, and from the other end Aneilee, cantered toward each other. As the hooves of the two leaders progressed each respective clan of unicorns reared in heartfelt salute to the blackmaned stallion and his company of animal person soldiers. It became time for Naythorn to bow in return salute to the white herd. He motioned for every member of his band to join with him.

"Timidthy, I never imagined that an honor like this could come to me, and so I do not know what to neigh."

"My captain does not have to neigh anything,"

answered the shy wild boar. "He is today welcomed as the hero of the white herd, and that is all that he needs to consider."

"Captain," hronkked Featherspark landing on the blackmane's back, "after the processions of the warriors and unicorns, I find myself to be in the best mood a black necked goose can possibly be!"

"Hey, Blackbeak!" qvackked Webstir landing beside the goose, "You and I need to learn to prance and dance like unicorns and Eagle Feather warriors!"

"For the first time in my life a glimpse of absolute beauty made my eyes to well up in tears," confessed Lianvil drawing next to his leader. "Now that I have been made to show emotion, I cannot even guess what my captain's heart feels upon seeing the love and respect this day shown to him."

"Noble lion, the honor given to me this day is a return far greater than the loss of a magic horn shard."

"Sire!" neighed Isabaya excitedly upon rejoining Naythorn. "I was just informed by Aneilee that your band needs to retake the front of the herd. And as for me, I am going to officially perform scouting duty to make sure that no wolves lurk about these hills." After shaking his head yes, Naythorn turned to leave the rock perch with his band following after.

"Naythorn!" yawled Tristan. "All those fish I ate made my belly too much grow. I require another fight... to get my black hide back in condition."

"For my part," grrrd Lianvil, "I would welcome that day. You being the biggest bear I have ever seen, and me being the biggest lion you have ever seen, I say that fighting side by side we two would be a sight to behold."

Made light of heart by all that he had that day seen, and with Belfloralex at his side, Naythorn trotted relaxed. Having witnessed the impressive cohesion of the unicorn herd, he now knew what before he had only half known. The unicorn herd would surely come to find their place of safety.

Naythorn looked back to verify that Tristanbear was keeping up with the rest of his band. The blackmane saw that not the bear, but Amaluna had slowed her steps. Naythorn waited until Amaluna caught up with him.

"I feel like my back should be tested. Jump up and allow me to carry you."

"No, Sire," objected Belfloralex, "well-used to me, Amaluna mounts upon *my* back!" Amaluna smiled big at the prospect of again riding the unicorn filly that commanded the wind.

The next time Naythorn looked back he found that Lucars and Marsand had mounted the strong back of Buckwhite.

When the blackmane again looked behind he noticed Hammer's square body set comfortably upon Taurington, with Shawnee's hands gripping the smithy's waist. And riding on the uncle horse Rainsnow, the arms of the island girl Alexzana clung to Scarlet Point. Soon four big-bodied animal person friends that carried four men and three women galloped in a line with Naythorn.

As he observed Naythorn and his band retake their position as the advance platoon, the captain of the unicorn guards muttered, "I wonder if my colt will ever fully come back to me, or for that matter if I will ever to him give full welcome."

"Do not worry for that," reassured Elianor. "When he finds himself ready to again rejoin our herd, Naythorn will to you return entire. Just like you, I used to be hard on Naythorn. Every day I told him to be polite, to smile more, and to not be grumpy. More than any other colt, my teeth pulled at his ears. I suppose I thought that I was providing discipline in the place of his mother mare that when so young had been to him lost."

"I never dreamt that a colt that was too big and awkward for his age, would grow to become a great war unicorn," added Aneilee joining the conversation. "Now that I think about it, Naythorn has taught me far more than I have taught him. But I now confess a thing of which I am not proud. I used to look down on other animal persons with heads uncrowned by magic horns. But upon seeing the miracle of companionship and teamwork found in Naythorn's band, I have decided that in the suns and moons ahead I will not shun, but rather welcome animal persons different than me."

"Cabalblade," interjected Elianor, "along with Aneilee and myself, you must also sense that the colt with a black mane that in Wittanor Hold was every day teased and bullied, will someday at the head of our herd... *walk alone.*"

Naythorn's Dream

Overwhelmed by the homage that had been paid to him by the Eagle Feather Braves and the white herd, that evening Naythorn wanted to be alone with his thoughts. However, his time of solitude was interrupted by the arrival of the High Escort.

"May I join you," neighed Aneilee. "I want you to tell me about your dream."

"What dream?"

"Your dream with Rayalas, of course."

"How do you know about that?"

"Remember, Naythorn, that my gift is prescience. Your dream was very powerful."

"Walk with me, Elianor." Side by side the blackmane and the High Escort paced steps under a newly starred sky.

"I remember collapsing under the weight of the bison, and my horn shard breaking away. After that I lost consciousness. At that moment, Rayalas was there. When she neighed for me to run with her, my spirit obeyed. I saw myself made to stand outside my body, which I left behind. The next thing I recall is frisking about with Rayalas, as our hooves trod on a meadow with blades of grass that sparkled like stars in the night sky."

"How did Rayalas look to your eyes?"

"She was happy, Aneilee. Her muzzle wore a smile that did not fade."

"The brilliance of her lighted shafts made to freeze the monster wolf, and confuse him. *Nyeerrr!* I am certain that she was proud of the role she played at the instant your fight was won."

"More than her neighs, her eyes spoke to me. They told me that she was so glad that the monster had been overcome, and that she was proud of me... even though I did not deal the crippling blow."

"She wanted you to stay with her?"

"As we galloped together through the stars, she said that from then on we would know only happiness. Aneilee, Rayalas still truly loves me."

"But... you returned to us."

"I wanted so much to stay with the beautiful winged horse, but I found that I could not desert my band. I knew I *had* to return. There remained something more for me to accomplish."

"Yes, Naythorn, your destiny still awaits you. Not only your band, the white herd will also come to require your strength and magic in order to survive."

"Aneilee, there is one thing I do not understand. With Rayalas I galloped far into the night, but when I returned to my body it seemed that I had been unconscious for only some long moments."

"The passage of star time does not abide by our rules down here below, Naythorn. Still, during the passage of those moments of our time, your heart no longer beat in your chest. Had you decided not to come back to us, your earthly body would never have reawakened. I thank the stars that his sense of duty brought the blackmane back to me."

CHAPTER 30

EPILOGUE

Successive moons transformed their orb from full, to half, to a sliver as a strange pair of yellow and grayback wolves traveled with necks bound together by magical links made of blue gold.

Like a subtle moving shadow, Lianvil had every day followed behind the two wolves. At each eventide the great lion brought game he had hunted to nourish two bonded together wolf pilgrims. Then, at a place not far distant from the mound of leaves or brush made to be the nest of the two wolves, the big lion watched into the night.

On the side of a still smoldering volcano a journey of captivity and repentance came at last to end. After traveling so long and so far to finally reach the destined side of the still smoking mountain, Dansey and Lianvil rested with hearts hopeful. Asleep, quiet, and set apart the gaunt monster wolf warmed his grotesque body on rock slabs that deep within still nurtured the sparks of mountain fire.

"Lianvil, my friend," yipped the yellow wolf, "we did what we set out to do. We journeyed far to return to the spot where the war against Naythorn began. And by the way, I take it to be a good sign that the Rayalas Borealas once again this night shines above us, and she is tonight *extraordinarily* bright."

"Dansey, more than journey far, you and I steadfastly petitioned the heavens to pardon the evil we accomplished against a blackmaned unicorn. Did you notice that Albarochk recognized the exact places where he wrote the first chapter of his evil war?"

"The monster wolf that sleeps beside us will soon be freed from the torture of a riven heart. At least that is what I hope is next to happen. In fact, I myself am become tired of wearing a collar and lugging a chain. And, I have wearied of daily scolding the great wolf to move along sharp, and watch where falls his step."

"With our quest now fulfilled, we will well-sleep this night," answered Lianvil. "You and I shall tomorrow awake to a world come to be brand new." A powerful lion, a small yellow wolf, and a giant grayback wolf prisoner come to be only tough hide and bones, slept.

Dream filled sleep did not depart the head of Dansey until the next day had well-warmed in sunlight.

"Lion, wake up!" exclaimed the yellow wolf pawing the shoulder of his friend. "We slept too long. The sun is high overhead. I feel like something, some magical darkness, dulled through the night my mind. In my entire wolf life I have never so soundly slept."

"Dansey, it was not darkness but the Rayalas Borealas that gifted us a night of such deep rest."

"What in tarnation!" barked the yellow wolf jumping all four feet off the ground. "Look! The links that bound me to Albarochk... are severed!" Dansey pulled the loose end of the chain toward himself. "But, Hammer said that he forged these links to be unbreakable!"

"From its burned look, it seems that hot lava flowed over the links binding you to your captive, and melted the chain in two."

Turning to look where had slept Albarochk, Dansey exclaimed, "Can my eyes be true? Where last night rested the great wolf there are now only clumps of steaming rock." The lion and the yellow wolf moved to investigate.

"My big cousin wolf melted... *into rock!*"

"Look here, Dansey," grrrd Lianvil scratching and pulling at something protruding from the rock. "Only this part remains of the gold collar worn by Albarochk."

"Hmm, I see, I see. But I still cannot believe that this tremendous thing could have happened while you and I close by slept. We should have heard Albarochk howl in pain as firey rock made his body to burn and combust."

"Examining closely the melt of the lava, I can see the outline of Albarochk's body. Yellow wolf, a thought just occurred to me. The new lava that formed around the great wolf's chest left this depression. The long shard of Naythorn's horn could have right here sunk into..."

"As you well know, Lion, since powerful unicorn magic protected that horn, burning rock could not have destroyed Naythorn's shard. So, you cannot be mistaken. The horn shard is here covered by the new deposit of lava."

"*That,* has to be so. I would have liked to cradle that magic horn in my big paws."

"As for me, Lianvil, I would have liked even more to have taken the horn shard all the way back to present it to its rightful owner. *Yripehaharr!* I would give anything to see Naythorn's horn put back together, and bound to be whole. Can you imagine the golden spiral Hammer should fashion to reconnect both halves of Naythorn's horn?"

"You are right, Dansey. With two pieces of ivory bound together by lustrous blue gold, it would be a most beautiful unicorn horn." That grrrd, the lion bounded off. Walking upright, as usual, he shortly returned to where Dansey awaited him. In one huge forepaw was held a pointed rock larger than the head of the yellow wolf. Since Dansey was not sure what the lion was up to, he barked as much.

"Just you wait a moment, yellow wolf. You will see that once in a great while, and just by myself, I can come up with an original idea."

Making sure that the tapered point was positioned downward, Lianvil grabbed with both front paws the rock. With his frame balanced on squatted hind limbs, the lion stretched the muscular sinews of his front limbs and back to crash rock point into the center of the depression formed in new lava. When lava rock cracked, Lianvil scraped and batted away fragments of still hot stone. Again and again the lion pounded with the rock held in his large paws. A big piece of lava crust at last broke apart.

"Look there, Dansey! Out of the pieces of broken lava protrudes a point of white. That can only be the tip of Naythorn's horn shard!"

Dansey howled loud, and after began to tumble his body and jump for joy.

When Lianvil next crashed down the pointed stone,

from crusted lava the unicorn shard broke loose.

"Lion, when we bring this shard back to Naythorn, Master Hammer will most assuredly bind it in a gold tie to reform a complete unicorn horn. That done, the blackmane will once again become whole in body."

"When the two halves of his horn are made again one, not only will our Captain Naythorn become whole, his spirit will be remade."

"Yes, lion. And there will no more exist a wolf made of pure evil to haunt the dreams of the blackmaned unicorn."

"Dansey, I just had a disturbing thought. Without the need to defend ourselves in a life and death struggle against the evil wolf, does his band of animal persons fall away from the blackmane?"

"I surely hope not. You know, ever since I was a very small wolf cub I feared the temper of Albarochk. Despite my fear, I could not resist being drawn to him. While I was obedient to Albarochk, at the same time I delighted in tormenting him. And now that he is gone, I never imagined that such a monstrous wolf would so gently leave off this world."

"I have to admit, Dansey, that I too will miss the tyrant wolf. There was something uniquely authentic in the terror that coursed through his life. His black heart remained always loyal to his destiny. Neither you, nor I could have ever imagined that only the magic of a horn shard rivening his heart could so change and transform the grayback."

"The monster wolf is *no more,*" yipped quietly Dansey. "Albarochk will not soon by me be forgotten.

Still, that he so silently and suddenly disappeared strikes me as very strange. Were Rambuncture here and now with us, the pessimistic mountain ram would say that Albarochk is not dead, but only escaped from the horn shard that bound his heart."

"That truly would be something... *incredible.* I tell you that I should not welcome another fight against a reborn monster wolf. Come, Dansey, we begin our return to Naythorn."

Trotting at the side of an upright lion that carried in one immense paw a white shard of unicorn horn, a yellow dancer wolf felt himself to have suddenly become very alone in the world.

Rambuncture Restless

Faraway from where traveled homeward the yellow wolf and the great lion, Rambuncture one night planted hooves in a high rocky place while craning his neck up at the sky. As he expected would happen, his mate came to find him.

"It is the middle of the night. At the side of your ewe you should be fast asleep."

"I know... I know. But a thought, or maybe it was a dream, drew me here. Just look, Ewelissas, at the glorious beauty of the Rayalas Borealas."

"Are you going to tell me what this night disturbed your sleep?"

"Remember when you once before, while we together walked, found me worried because I did not understand the unusual comfort proffered by my blue gold armor?"

"Of course I remember that. My ram baahed that the

trueness of his magic armor felt to clash with his nature."

"Well, dear ewe, I think I finally understand what the spectacular colored lights above are meant to signify."

"Go on. I want to hear your interpretation of the Rayalas Borealas."

"Recall that just a few days after we left Shining Canyon, Buckwhite decided that while *love* had to do with unicorn magic, *trueness* had to do with the magic of blue gold."

"Yes, Ram, I remember that. And when the bison offered that conclusion we all agreed with him."

"I now have come to think that the beautiful display of purple, blue, silver, and crimson light above is meant as a heavenly sign of... *graciousness.*"

"Would you kindly explain to your ewe what you mean by heavenly graciousness?"

"I would like to, but I am not sure that I can. Only... that when I look at the beautiful Rayalas Borealas I feel that some form of beneficence removes from me the dirt and grime of my daily existence. It is as if the display of the shafts of heavenly light washes from my rough coat the envy that I have felt, cleanses my heart of hurtful words unfortunately spoken, and purges my mind of unkind thoughts that I have harbored. If I stand quietly and permit the streams of sky color to wash over and through me, it is as if the heavenly light makes me to be clean and brand new."

"Are you talking about a kind of... rebirth?"

"But I make no sense at all... for how could a beautiful light come from out of the heavens accomplish so much newness?"

"And I do not see how the winged horse that to us is dead and gone, by herself could accomplish so much."

"All I know is that she, the Rayalas Borealas, has something to do with the grace that I am made by the heavens to feel."

"Hmm. I suppose a heavenly graciousness that takes away his selfishness and pride, would for my Rambuncture be a very good thing." With her head the ewe nudged a shoulder of her mate and added, "No, dear Ram. What I just baahed was wrong of me. You may be every day pessimistic, but you are almost never prideful. When as tonight you find yourself to be thoughtful, although I do not precisely comprehend the meaning of your words, for my part I should be respectful of feelings so deeply come to you."

"This is what I think," clarified Rambuncture. "Belonging to the band of Naythorn, by three wonderful things you and I have come to find ourselves favored. We have received the magic of unicorn love, the magic of blue gold veracity, and the magical light of heavenly graciousness."

"Why then, does not the Rayalas Borealas shine grace down to cleanse the badness of mean wolves?"

"To that question, Ewelissas, I have no answer. I can only say that I wish for the heavenly light to someday bring change to wrong-hearted wolves."

"Be that as it may, will my no longer so very pessimistic Ram now come back to camp and by my side go back to sleep?"

"Yes, my sweet ewe, with your wish I will contentedly

comply."

As the two mountain sheep with big curving horns made their way back to the place that for that night they called home, the ewe walked every step touchingly close to her ram.

THE END

ABOUT THE AUTHOR

G. D. Hanson taught at Auburn University and Penn State University. His academic degrees are from Dartmouth College and the University of Minnesota. He and his wife Isabel reside in South Dakota and Costa Rica.